Other Books by Kathleen Eagle

The Sharing Spoon

by

Kathleen Eagle

Bell Bridge Books

Bell Bridge Books
PO BOX 300921
Memphis, TN 38130
Print ISBN: 978-1-61194-366-5

Bell Bridge Books is an Imprint of BelleBooks, Inc.

We at BelleBooks enjoy hearing from readers.
Visit our websites – www.BelleBooks.com and www.BellBridgeBooks.com.

10 9 8 7 6 5 4 3 2 1

Cover design: Debra Dixon
Interior design: Hank Smith
Photo/Art credits:
Horses (manipulated) © Nadiia_Starovoitova | Dreamstime.com
Ornament (manipulated) © Jadehawk | Dreamstime.com

:Lssq:01:

A Letter to My Readers

Dear Reader,

The holiday season is at hand, and you've been preparing. Maybe you're anticipating big doings, or maybe you'll have a simple, quiet celebration this year. Either way, you need a break. It's time to make yourself a cup of your favorite comfort drink, settle down in a cozy place, and lose yourself in a story. Well, my friend, you're holding three of them in your hands, and I know each one will put a smile on your face and a warm glow in your heart.

The holidays can be harried, and we often find ourselves hurrying from one day to the next, counting them down on assorted calendars while we cook up the feasts, tick off the shopping days, and check off the items on various lists. But there's more to it than that. There's more to us, more to our lives, more meaning behind our sundry traditions. No matter who we are or where we live, when we wish each other happy holidays, we embrace those wishes by sharing. We give of ourselves, and we accept others. During the darkest time of the year—the longest nights, the shortest days—we celebrate the best and brightest aspects of our nature. Even when times are difficult or lean or sad, our holiday songs and stories and prayers serve to remind us to open our hearts.

And that's what I've written into these three stories. You'll meet people living in different time periods, different places, and different walks of life who have at least one thing in common: a soul in want of a mate. There are empty places in their hearts that need filling, dark spaces in their lives desperate for light.

This is the time to widen our circle as we join hands in celebration, so bring on the holidays and let's make good memories together!

All my best,

Kathleen Eagle

Dedication

For my girls

Granddaughters Piper and Kraya, who are growing up too quickly before my very eyes; niece Abby, who was five when I dedicated "The Wolf and the Lamb" to her and asked her not to grow up too fast; and dear daughter Elizabeth, who has become a strong, wise, wonderful woman even though I offered to pay her to stay twelve just a little longer.

I love you all at every age, and I'm enormously proud of each of you.

The Sharing Spoon

Prologue

IN HIS MIND, Kyle Bear Soldier turned the brown brick high rise complex into South Dakota buttes. He'd gone back home a thousand times in the twelve months since he'd moved to Minneapolis, but only one of those trips had been physical. In July, when he'd been desperate for South Dakota skies and Lakota Sioux renewal, he'd gone home for the Sun Dance. It was September now, almost time for school to start, and his daily run was a good time to take himself back mentally, over the tops of the tall buildings, beyond the trees and back home.

The city was a good place to find employment. There was plenty of excitement, all kinds of amusement and crowds of people—more people in a few square miles than could be found, living or dead, in the whole expanse of his home state. Most of the time he could live with that. There was a lot of asphalt, tons of concrete, but there were a good number of parks, as well, and ten miles outside the city, a guy could find peace beside a lake or a stretch of open field.

But there wasn't a butte in sight, and there were too many shade trees to suit Kyle. Pine trees were fine, but those big leafy shade trees made it hard to see out, hard to breathe. And winter, which would be coming on soon, might not have been quite as mean as it was in South Dakota, but day after day, month after month, it was one hell of a lot of gray and white.

There was a community of his people here—a community within a community—and Kyle had come to the Twin Cities to be part of it. Not only were there Lakota people from North and South Dakota, but there were East River Sioux—the Dakota people—and there were Minnesota Chippewa, who preferred to be called by their own name, which was Ojibwa. In lesser numbers there were Native Americans from other parts of the country, all come to the city to find a new life. Sometimes, as in Kyle's case, they actually found work. And, like Kyle, they all got homesick. They yearned for the land that had given their ancestors sustenance, places where few manmade structures rose above the ground floor. Their roots were on Indian reservations, places generally known as "God's country."

And God's country it was—God's and what was left of the creatures He'd designated to be the land's native inhabitants. Jobs were scarce in God's country. There was little money there, and the food on the hoof was, for the most part, claimed by somebody other than God these days.

"How's it goin', Kyle?"

He turned and slowed down to offer Tony Plentykill a handshake. "Good."

Tony, a man half a head shorter than Kyle, was wearing a new shirt. He'd forgotten to take the little round inspector's sticker off the pocket, so Kyle did it for him. "Where you headed?"

"Feed." Tony jerked his chin to indicate the direction. "Over to the church. Then there's a doings over at the school gym. Two drums," he said, wielding an imaginary drumbeater in one hand. "Better get something to eat so you can really sing one." He cupped the other hand behind his ear and grimaced, as though he were getting into a song.

"I'll be there. The kids have been bugging me to put on the bear face again. That's what I'm supposed to look like when I dance."

Tony gave a little yelp, punched Kyle's arm, and tapped one tennis shoe against the pavement. For a minute Kyle thought the man was going to start grass dancing right there on the street.

He laughed and returned Tony's punch. "I can feel that drumbeat already. I'll be there."

Chapter One

CYNTHIA BOYER had learned her civic and social responsibilities at her mother's knee. Those who were privileged had their obligations. Of late, Cynthia hadn't felt very privileged, but she thrived on responsibility, and it was about all that made sense anymore.

As a new teacher at All Nations Elementary School in Minneapolis, she had decided to focus her attention on the needs of her students' neighborhood, to serve as she'd always served, twice a month, with her hands as well as her checkbook. It was the "hands" part that always drove her mother's eyebrow into an arch of displeasure, but it was Cynthia's way of going Mother one better.

Her mother didn't understand why she'd taken a teaching position, either, but then, Mother hadn't been childless, had never experienced a frigidly civilized, no-fault divorce, and had undoubtedly never felt hollow inside. Cynthia didn't need a salary, but she desperately needed meaningful work. When school-board member Karen Grasso had mentioned the vacancy at All Nations, Cynthia knew she had found that work. Karen had been her friend forever, and she knew Cynthia better than anyone did.

She hadn't met her students yet. She'd been interviewed by the school principal, two parents, and someone from the central administration. They'd all asked her how she felt about working in the neighborhood. The Phillips neighborhood was a part of Minneapolis she had only driven through, and not often, but now she would be driving *to* it every day. Did that scare her? she'd been asked. Not at all, she'd answered. They'd smiled and nodded and offered her the job.

And so, on the evening before her first staff meeting of her first day as a teacher at All Nations, Cynthia had come to St. Jude's church basement as one of the volunteers who would help serve a free meal to the needy as part of the Loaves and Fishes program.

Linda Kopp ran the kitchen. The church paid her to see that all the serving spoons found their way back into the right drawers, that the health-department codes were followed, and that the teams of volunteers who came from all over the Twin Cities were able to put a meal together on schedule.

"Guests come through the line, but they don't pick up the trays," Linda instructed. The kitchen crew had already done most of their work, but they popped their heads through the serving window to lend an ear while the serving team gathered around the long spread of steaming pans and stacks of trays.

"Trays are handed to the guests after we fill them. If there's enough left for seconds, we have to use clean trays. They can't bring dirty trays back up for refills. Plastic gloves are required for volunteers." She pointed toward the dispenser box, and there was at least one disgruntled groan. "These are all health-department regulations, you know."

"Of course," the woman standing next to Cynthia mumbled, and she took it upon herself to pull out several of the disposable gloves and distribute them. She had introduced herself rather brusquely as Marge Gross. "Aprons are, too. Do you have aprons?"

The aprons, too, were disposable. Cynthia felt as though she were preparing to operate on the green beans. She'd done a lot of volunteer work, but this was her first Loaves and Fishes experience, and she got the feeling everyone around her was gearing up for a race. She wondered who had the starter's gun and where the starting block was. At the very least, she wanted to be in the right place.

"Here they come," someone called from the back of the huge parish basement.

"You can do peaches," Marge said as she edged Cynthia away from the beans. Peaches were fine, she thought absently as she watched the crowd pour in. They came in all shapes, sizes, genders, and colors, but there was a preponderance of Native Americans, and many of them were children. Undoubtedly some of them were those she would spend the next nine months teaching about the visual arts.

The sound of voices rolled over the serving table. Apparently the people were hungry, for the line moved quickly, with each person's eyes following the progress of a tray from hand to hand on the servers' side of the table. Hungry people, Cynthia thought as she strained the juice from a spoonful of canned peaches and plopped them into a corner compartment of a tray. But they didn't look particularly miserable or downtrodden. Mothers were trying to keep their kids in line; friends were chatting, and youngsters were jostling for position. They looked like people attending a potluck supper.

But this wasn't potluck. This was charity, and these were poor people, and Cynthia was performing a service.

The man who faced her across the table looked the part. His bulbous red nose and puffy eyes branded him as readily as his tattered trench coat, which struck Cynthia as odd apparel for such a warm evening. He scanned the table. "Spaghetti, huh?"

"I haven't tried it, but I'm sure it's tasty," Cynthia said as she dished up more peaches.

"If it isn't, I know how to really heat things up."

The remark almost slid past Cynthia, but she stiffened when he slipped his hand inside his coat. It happened so quickly that she didn't have time to get her vocal cords working and warn people to hit the deck.

Louisiana hot sauce. A sly twinkle nearly displaced the weariness in the man's face when he showed it to her.

"Yes, I . . ." Cynthia managed a wan smile as the tension eased from her shoulders. "I guess that would do it."

"Don't hold up the line," Marge warned.

The hot sauce disappeared as the man eyed Cynthia, placing a grubby finger to his lips as a signal that he'd shared a secret with her.

Linda Kopp slid behind Cynthia and touched her shoulder. "We need another beverage-cart handler. George can handle this end of the table," she said, gesturing to the man who was handling trays and utensils.

Cynthia was reassigned to a heavy-duty kitchen cart containing insulated carafes, pitchers, milk cartons, cups, and condiments. She poured as fast as she could, but the requests came faster. Her hands sweated inside the plastic gloves, and hair stuck to her forehead. Two coffees. Five lemonades. Three milks. Four of each. She didn't have enough hands.

"Kyle wants more lemonade."

Cynthia glanced down at a bright-eyed girl who'd just lost her two front teeth. Her pigtails were banded in bows of red yarn, and she offered up a cup and the smile of one who'd been specially chosen for an errand. Cynthia refilled the cup and watched the child carry it toward the end of the table. She expected the child to deliver the glass to the small boy whose chin was barely table level but, instead, she handed it to one of the men.

He thanked the girl, then flashed Cynthia a winning smile before turning back to his conversation with two older men and a teenage boy. The dark-eyed smile stunned her just as effectively as the man in line had, but the shock waves went much deeper. Kyle whoever-he-was was, in a word, a knockout.

The word could not have been her own, Cynthia told herself. It must have been something she'd read recently. There was a blob of sweat in the middle of his blue T-shirt, and he wore a brow band. He'd obviously been running. He was a *jock,* for heaven's sake. Not her type at all.

And able-bodied as all get-out. Why did he expect to be waited on, and why wasn't he out working to pay for his supper?

With a mental "harrumph," Cynthia pulled her thoughts away from the man and continued to fill beverage requests without risking another glance toward the end of his table. But soon the little girl was back.

"Kyle wants coffee."

"The coffee's very hot," Cynthia cautioned as she handed a cup of milk to another small customer. "I don't want you to burn yourself."

"I can carry it. I always get coffee."

"Not for yourself, I hope."

"If I want some, I do." The child waited a few seconds before patiently repeating herself. "Kyle wants coffee."

Cynthia filled the cup and looked his way again. He was studying her, waiting. She smiled pointedly for the helpful child. Not for the man. Did he think he was patronizing a restaurant here? The little girl carried the cup away carefully, and Cynthia went back to her work.

"I forgot. Kyle wants sugar."

Cynthia glanced up from the stream of milk she was pouring for another child. It was the same obliging little girl, same large chocolate-drop eyes. Handsome is as handsome does, Cynthia thought, and Kyle's behavior surely let him out.

"Have you eaten?"

"My mom's in line for us." The little girl cocked her head to one side. "You new?"

"No, I didn't know, but I'm—"

"I mean *new.* A new volunteer. I haven't seen you here."

"Oh. Yes." Cynthia smiled, rejecting the inclination to ask whether she came often. "Where do you go to school?"

"All Nations," the girl said, standing steadfast when an older girl tried to edge her away from the beverage cart. "The *almost* new school."

The older girl's request for lemonade registered with Cynthia, and she set about filling a cup. "I'm going to be a teacher there this year."

"You?" The little girl watched the lemonade change hands. "What grade?"

"Art," Cynthia said.

"Oh, yeah. The last guy quit after somebody sort of doctored up the coffee in his thermos bottle. Can I have the sugar?"

"How about some lemonade? Then I'll just move over that way." She shook a cup loose from the stack as she pushed the cart between the row of chairs. It was time she put an end to this go-fetch routine.

"What can I . . ." She thought better of saying "do for you?" and said, instead, ". . . offer you gentlemen? Someone needed sugar?"

"Kyle did," the little girl insisted. "C'mon, Kyle. My mom's up to the front. I'll let you cut in line."

The man turned and offered the child a smile. "No, that's okay."

He was a guest, Cynthia reminded herself when he lifted his dark eyes to meet hers. She couldn't quite remember why she'd taken up the cool pitcher in one hand and a paper cup in the other. "You should get something to eat," she said to the girl.

"Sugar would be good." He snatched at the tip of one perky pigtail. "Then we'll see if Lee Ann leaves me anything." The little girl giggled and whipped her pigtails with a quick shake of her head. "Go on up there and help your mother, Lee Ann. Hurry up, now."

A tall, gangly young man shoved his empty cup Cynthia's way. "Coffee," he ordered, and when she took the cup, he scowled at her hand. His glasses were held together with adhesive tape at both temples, and he seemed to need to squint to focus. "Do you have a hole in your gloves?"

Cynthia examined her left palm, then turned her hand over, searching as she might for a run in her stocking. "I don't think so."

The tall man peered into her eyes, sober as a judge. "How'd you get your hands in them, then?"

The man named Kyle was laughing along with the rest of the annoying men at his table. Lee Ann had skipped off to join her mother, and Cynthia smiled tightly. She had fallen headfirst for that one. Bristling a little, she moved her beverage cart along and continued to do her job. She knew Kyle was watching her, and so she deliberately ignored him. She had enough to do.

The room was hot, and the crowd kept her pouring in more ways than one. The only way to keep the sweat from dripping off her brow and into the lemonade was to wipe it with her sleeve. Her hands felt so clammy she wished she *did* have holes in her gloves.

A toddler appeared at her elbow with two chocolate cookies. "Milk would be good with those," Cynthia said.

The child put one of the cookies on the corner of her cart, then tipped his head back and waited for a sign of acceptance. Cynthia thanked him, and he shoved the second cookie into his mouth and disappeared under the table.

"Aren't you going to eat your cookie?" Kyle asked as he approached the cart, cup in hand. "The kids are up there clamoring for the last of them, and that little guy gave you one to eat. That's his gift."

Cynthia glanced at Kyle, then at the cookie. No one was clamoring for anything to drink at the moment. She had the feeling this was some sort of test, just like the glove joke. She picked up the cookie with plastic-covered fingers and opened her mouth to take a bite.

"'Course, *I* didn't get any."

She glanced up. "No dinner at all?"

"They ran out."

The hall was clearing out now, and he was right. Cookies were the item most in demand at the serving table. The rest was being cleared away. Spontaneously she offered him the bit of food she held. He put his hand around hers, steadied the cookie and took a bite. "Thanks."

"That's all right. I had supper before I came."

"Figures." He took a swallow of coffee, then shrugged dejectedly. "Guess I'll have to go looking somewhere else."

"There must be something left," she said quickly. "I think there's milk. Green beans, I'm sure."

"I'm like the kids. I hate green beans just naked like that."

He gave her a boyish smile, and she thought, *Picky,* but said, "Naked?"

"I like them better *in* something. Like soup, or a hot dish."

Maybe "picky" wasn't the right word. "But one cookie isn't enough."

"Next time I'll get in line right away." He backed away smiling. "Thanks for sharing a bite with me. Better than nothing, right?"

"I could—"

"Make supper for me?" He obviously enjoyed the look of shock that registered on her face. "Just kidding. See you around." And he left without giving her a backward glance.

Around where?

He looked awfully good in those running shorts.

Make supper for him?

Around where?

Chapter Two

THE ANSWER—around All Nations Elementary School—came the next day when Kyle arrived ten minutes late for the first faculty meeting. He was dressed in blue jeans and a striped summer shirt, which Cynthia would have considered too casual for a day of professional meetings if she hadn't been the only professional in the room who was professionally dressed.

While he was making his way to an empty chair and offering a handshake here, a nod there, Cynthia found herself squirming a little. She was sure he was the same man—the one who'd been sitting at the table with the rest of the guests while she'd been serving, doing her civic duty. She remembered exactly what she'd thought, and she was doing her best to remember anything she said that might embarrass her now. The last thing she wanted to do was offend anyone, and this man, this—

"Kyle Bear Soldier," principal Darlene Toule announced with a teasing flourish. "Still running on Indian time."

Kyle took a seat toward the front of the sixth-grade classroom, where most of the empty seats were. "Left my running shoes at home this morning. That's why I'm late, see. But I got myself all dressed up for the first big meeting of the year."

He hadn't missed much, Cynthia thought. They hadn't gotten down to business yet. So far there'd been just a few introductions and lots of welcome-back greetings. She wanted to be part of this group, and she was anxious for the new-kid-on-the-block feeling to wear off. With Cynthia, it always took time. She had introduced herself to Lily Moore, the elderly Indian woman who was sitting next to her, and their brief conversation had been a start.

"This is Kyle's second year with us," Darlene continued from her place of authority at the head of the class. "We recruited him from South Dakota to teach fifth grade."

"He's one of those West River Sioux," Lily related behind the screen of her hand. "They speak L, and we speak D. I'm East River Sioux." Lily seemed to chuckle, but no sound came. Her ample breasts bounced gently. "The other difference is they're ornery and we're not."

Cynthia nodded solemnly, wondering what river the woman was talking about. She knew nothing about L and D, but since Darlene was moving on with the introductions, this was not the time to ask. She wasn't sure how she should interpret the twinkle in Lily's eye.

Darlene introduced the Indian language teachers. Marty Blue, representing the dominant tribe in Minnesota, taught the Ojibwa language, while his wife, Patty, another South Dakotan "from a little town west of the Missouri River," taught the Lakota language. Lily Moore was not a certified teacher, but she contributed to the language program as a native Dakota speaker. And Cynthia felt somewhat enlightened about the river separating two letters—those living on the west side spoke Lakota, those on the east, Dakota.

The reference to the language program prompted Darlene to mention the experimental nature of the program at All Nations. It was that aspect that most interested Cynthia. She knew a lot about Native American art, but little—with the exception of her artist friends—about the people. She knew all the sad statistics, the dreaded high numbers in illness, infant mortality, alcohol dependency, unemployment, and school dropouts. It was this last statistic that All Nations was attempting to change.

"We've gotten some criticism since we opened last year," Darlene admitted. "This is a public school, and we have to abide by desegregation laws, but we're having a little trouble achieving racial balance."

"The Bureau of Indian Affairs never worried about that," someone in the back of the room commented. "I went to a BIA school. Didn't see the government recruiting anyone for racial balance."

"Well, that's federal, and this is state." Darlene folded her arms across her chest, ostensibly taking a stand. She was a small middle-aged woman of mixed blood for whom taking a stand was clearly not a new experience. "We just have to build such a great program here that non-Indians will flock in and sign up. With this city's magnet school system and open-enrollment policy, we have to be competitive, because parents can shop around."

"We've got Indian kids on the waiting list," Lily reminded her.

"I know, but we can't take any more until we can recruit more non-Indians." There was some grumbling in the ranks, but Darlene lifted a hand to pacify them. "The road isn't always smooth, but I think we have to come together somehow. Our school is called All Nations, and we really want all nations. We have a lot to teach all our students." She looked from one to the other, a gesture that recalled her own teaching days. "We Indian people have good things to share."

"We Lakota end our prayers with *mitakuye oyasin*. All my relatives, which means all nations, all races, all species, even the four-legged ones," Kyle said.

Cynthia was secretly impressed, at once eager and uneasy about coming face-to-face with this man again. He turned in his chair and craned his neck, and she thought, *Oh, dear, not now.* Her pulse fluttered wildly as she escaped his notice. He connected with the Ojibwa language teacher, Marty Blue. "So when Chippewa people come to our sweats, they usually just say, 'All my rabbits.'"

When the chuckles and groans subsided, Marty shot back, "We say, 'All my rabbits got chased away by those damn Sioux puppies.'"

The laughter increased, and Darlene, laughing too, shook her head. "I'd better introduce you to some of our new teachers, who are sitting here laughing just out of politeness and trying to figure out what to make of you guys." She directed her explanation Cynthia's way. "Kyle is Sioux—*Lakota*, pardon me. And Marty is Chippewa—*Ojibwa*, pardon me. Long time ago they used to crack each other over the head with war clubs. Now they just crack sick jokes, mostly about rabbits and puppies."

"Gets 'em in the gut every time," Kyle chimed in. "These guys know a hundred ways to cook rabbit."

"But they've only got one recipe for puppy soup. No imagination, those Sioux."

"You guys just gave me a great fund-raising idea," Darlene said. "The All Nations Elementary School Recipe Book, compiled by—" she presented each with a flourish of the hand "—Kyle Bear Soldier and Marty Blue."

"What's that recipe for Chippewa-chip cookies, Marty?" Kyle's taunt brought out a few more groans, but the uninitiated were not to hear the punch line this day.

"I don't want my new teachers skipping the coffee break just because we're serving cookies, you guys, so let's get on with the introductions," Darlene said. "Cynthia Boyer is our new art teacher, and she's a personal friend of more Native American artists than she could shake a stick at, if she were into shaking sticks at Indians."

"Which I'm not," Cynthia said quickly. Several heads turned, and she could feel her face flushing as she told herself, *It was a joke, Cynthia.* "I mean, I'm not . . . I mean, I *am* a connoisseur of Native American art, and I do know . . . because I have studied . . ."

Darlene smiled. "You know a lot about art, and you're going to be good for our kids. We're glad to have you."

"Thank you. It's very exciting for me to be here."

The meeting continued in the same low-key vein, information mixed with humor. Cynthia took notes whenever schedules or procedures came up. She gave herself permission to be comfortable with the casual atmosphere, and she knew she'd actually be able to do that once she'd dealt with the moment that was bound to come when the meeting was over.

When it came, he kept it light.

"Got any cookies on you?" Most of the staff had left the room, and Kyle had obviously hung back, waiting to deliver this line. "I missed breakfast."

"I guess I'm a little unprepared," she confessed as she tucked her notebook under her arm, squared her shoulders and returned his smile.

"I think you're a lot surprised to find I'm gainfully employed, as they say. Welcome to All Nations, Cynthia." He offered his hand.

"Thank you."

"Hey, listen." The handshake ended abruptly as he shoved his hands into the pockets of his jeans. "'Nothing's good or bad, but thinking makes it so.' That's one of my favorite lines from ol' Will Shakespeare, and you don't have to be worried about whatever you were thinking last night. You'll get over it. All Nations will help you get over it."

"Really?" Together they headed for the classroom door. "What was I thinking, other than that you were there for the meal?"

"That I was there for a *free* meal, and you felt sorry for me." She looked up, and his knowing smile surprised her. "All Nations can help you get over that, too, if you stick around long enough. But you'll have to pay some dues first."

"I don't mind paying dues. In fact, I expect to."

"Trouble is, you can't pay them with U.S. coin."

"What'll it take, then?"

"I s'pose puppies are out of the question." He stopped in the doorway and turned, blocking her exit, waiting. She wasn't sure whether to laugh or be appalled. It was a strange sense of humor these people had. Puppies, indeed. He offered that infectious smile. "Cookies, maybe. We like sugar."

"I noticed."

"Then you'll do fine. Where do you live?"

"I just moved. I grew up in Wayzata, but I just bought a condo in the Lake District. I thought it would be good to become part of the city now that I'm working." He raised an eyebrow. "*Here.* I mean, now that I have a job in the city, I want to be involved with city life. *Personally* involved. You know what I mean."

"Sure." He seemed to be looking through her eyes and into her head. "I live on Portland Avenue, just a few blocks from here."

"That's convenient. In good weather, you don't even have to bother about taking your car out of the garage."

He laughed. "I don't have to worry about it in bad weather, either."

"Ah, so you're one of those die-hard joggers. I admire that."

"I admire someone who's willing to venture out of the suburbs and put her life on the line in the Lake District." The Lake District was definitely high-rent, and his sarcasm, however gentle, came as a surprise after all his good-natured teasing. "And to park her car here in the lot."

"They told me the parking lot had security." Again he raised an eyebrow. "It does, doesn't it?"

"It does." He leaned against the door frame, studying her. "Do you? You look secure enough not to need this job, which isn't going to be easy. You know that."

"I know." Needing pay and needing work were two different things in Cynthia's book. "But I *want* this job. And I want to do well. Even though I'm not First Nation, I've always admired your art."

"First Nation?" He chuckled. "Is that the latest? I think I was Native American last year."

"Is that preferable? I mean, I know you don't like—"

"I prefer Lakota over 'them damn dog-eatin' Sioux,' but you guys keep on changing your politically correct terms on me. I can't keep up. As for my art, I can't even draw a decent stick figure. Some of these kids are really good at it, and some of them are like me."

"But you have a heritage in the visual arts that's admired the world over. I'm . . ." Not an expert, she told herself. Don't claim that. And she certainly wouldn't admit to being an avid collector, because that would only underline the high-rent label. ". . . quite knowledgeable in that area."

"Good. Make up for what Andy Rooney once said on TV—that there's no such thing as Indian art, that our religion is superstition, and whatever the hell else he thought might amuse the public." He wandered over to the chalkboard and picked up a first-day, first-assignment piece of chalk. As he talked, he sketched a stick man. "It takes another white person to dispel the white lies. Tell the kids that people like you realize there's great Indian art. And that theirs isn't half-bad, either."

"Hmm," Cynthia said, considering his drawing. "Speaking of half-bad . . ." She took a step closer and experimented with a teaching strategy. "What would you think about adding a face? Would you do that for me?"

He played along. "In a million years you couldn't get me to draw a face. I can't draw."

"But you just drew," she coaxed. "How about a face that shows you how you feel right now?"

He wagged the chalk at her and grinned. "Nice try, teacher, but you ain't gettin' nothin' out of me *that* easy. You've gotta work a lot harder for that one."

"Well, then, draw my face." She responded to his wary scoff by touching his arm. "Go ahead, draw what you see. Just the expression."

"You're really stickin' your neck out now." His eyes narrowed. "That's an open invitation, right? You'll take what you get?"

"Anything."

"Brave lady," he said. He studied her for a moment, then touched the chalk to the board again.

"Those are very big eyes," she said after a moment.

"They're wide open. A little bit scared." He was getting into it now. "This is a nice mouth. Not mean."

"I can see that. You're doing very well."

"It's a mouth that would say kind things. And it would taste good." He glanced up, challenging her with a mischievous male look. "You're not married, right?"

"How did you know?"

"Because you said *you* bought the condo. Not *we*." He added another feature to his drawing. "This is an ear that listens closely, even to the smallest voice, or maybe especially to the smaller ones. The ones who get pushed aside in the lemonade line. You'll need this ear." The chalk squeaked as he drew. "And here's the other one. It's a little bit lower than the one on the other side."

"Hmm," Cynthia said, evaluating again. "You have a keen eye."

"I like what I see, too. I just can't draw it very well." He tapped the tip of the chalk against the ear he'd just drawn. "See, this is the one I think might be just a little bit more sensitive to touch. Like warm air, or maybe a moist, um—" his voice took on a quiet mellifluous tone, and he lifted one shoulder "—puppy's nose or something. You know, if one jumped in your lap and started licking your ear. Then these eyes would close," he said, putting in a series of crescent shapes, "and this mouth would turn up at the corners and smile." He turned to her. "Just like that."

"My eyes are still wide open."

"Nobody's licking your ear, though. I'd give it a shot, just to prove my point, but it's not a good time." He offered her the chalk. "Now you draw me. Whatever you see."

Their fingers brushed as she took the chalk in hand. It was as though static electricity had caused a crackle, and they exchanged wary glances. She shook off the wobbly feeling as she set to work.

"Ve-ry good," he drawled. Too easily, she thought. Far too glib, this man. "Do I have that much hair? Aw, c'mon, you're making me look a little too cocky with that—"

"You *are* a little too cocky. You've got a certain look in your eyes, but I can't capture it with this chalk."

"Here, I'll show you what it is."

Kyle took the chalk from her and had his say, making spring-loaded cartoon eyes pop out of his cartoon head and bounce toward his own drawing of Cynthia.

"That's it!" she exclaimed, delighted. "That's it. You should be an animator."

"I am." He smiled, delighted, too. "You should see your face now."

"You're a very good teacher, aren't you?"

He set the chalk down and brushed the dust from his fingers. "I have my good days."

"I'm a little scared," she confessed with a sigh. "I'm long on content and theory, but a little short on classroom experience."

"Your theory worked on me. First time a woman ever got me to draw her a picture." She decided not to ask how many had tried, and he smiled knowingly. "I don't want you to think I'm always this easy. The kids here aren't, either. But we're not impossible."

NOT IMPOSSIBLE. During the first week of school Cynthia reminded herself of those words over and over again. It was not impossible to hold a third grader's attention longer than three minutes at a time. She simply hadn't figured out a way to do it yet. It was not impossible to keep the fourth-grade boys from making projectiles out of modeling clay and bombarding each other from across the room. It was not impossible to get through a whole class without having half the paint spilled on the carpet and half the art paper turned into airplanes. But maybe she wasn't up to the challenge.

Each class was scheduled for the art room twice a week. Teachers dropped off their kids and reported back at the end of the period to escort the students back to their regular classrooms. But changing classes, like everything else, wasn't running smoothly for Cynthia. She was standing outside her door, thinking the kids' noise was no worse with her outside than it had been when she was standing over them, when Kyle came down the hall with his students, more or less in single file.

"What's wrong?"

"Miss Tetley hasn't come for her class yet, so I have no place to put *your* class, and I need a few minutes to clean up the mess and—" she sighed as she waved her hand over her head "—collect my thoughts."

"What we do is we get Miss Tetley's class to clean up after themselves."

"Yes, I've—" she was trying not to sound as totally defeated as she felt "—tried that."

"You people take a seat on the floor here and keep your hands to yourselves," he told his kids. One by one, they slid their backs down the wall and settled on the floor. "Because if you don't, I might not feel like playing basketball at recess like we planned. Cynthia's going to tell you something about some famous artists—"

"Ms. Boyer," Cynthia insisted wearily.

"About *Ms.* Boyer, plus some other famous artists, while I show some fourth graders how to clean up in a hurry."

"Way to go, Kyle," one of his bunch cheered.

"James, we don't call our teachers by their first names," Cynthia said.

"You're Ms. Boyer," came the correction. "I'm Kyle. I like to keep it simple."

She stood guard in the hallway with his comparatively well-behaved class. All she heard him say after he entered her room was, "If you guys don't want to see me get angry, you'll get this mess picked up. *Now!*"

She had tried words to that effect, but the "now" part hadn't sounded quite so forceful. Jennifer Tetley came scurrying around the corner as though she'd heard it, too, and she waved one hand excitedly, patting her chest with the other to prove how she'd worn herself out hurrying. She gasped out bits of excuses and apologies for being late.

"Paper jammed in the copier . . . phone call . . . ran into Marty on my way down to—"

"Mr. Bear Soldier's class is waiting for their—"

"*Kyle's* class," four of the children sitting on the floor chimed in unison.

"And I'm cutting into their time, I know," said Jennifer, "and I'm sor—" Kyle stepped back into the hallway. The room was quiet, and the two women exchanged looks of surprise. "What did you do to them?" Jennifer asked.

"Intimidated them nicely. You owe me, Jennifer."

"I realize that." She smiled sweetly. "And I will definitely make it up to you."

"You bet you will. Three minutes for every one, that's what I charge." Her students poured out, and his filed in under his supervision. "Hey, keep your shirt on, Tom. You know where to sit. Remember that basketball game."

"Yeah, bean brain," one of the boys chided. "Don't get him mad."

"What happens when you get mad?" asked Cynthia.

"It's not pleasant," Kyle assured her. "Just plain not pleasant."

"I see." He gave her a sly wink, then turned and headed down the hall, leaving her feeling a little bereft as she closed the door. "You wouldn't want to get me mad, either," she said as she turned to the class. Most of them were seated, and there were a few quiet titters. Tom Gorneau snatched a ruler off the table and playfully slapped the top of Shelley White Lightning's head with it. Shelley yelped as Cynthia moved to her desk with a sigh. So much for her power of intimidation. She wondered who she could get to trade her just one minute of tranquility for every three of the kind of chaos she'd endured in the first five days of school.

On the bright side, she had only 165 to go.

Chapter Three

AFTER THE SECOND week of school, Cynthia was ready to quit. She didn't need the paycheck, and she certainly didn't need the headache she took home with her every night. The students had wonderful potential and she had wonderful ideas, but she couldn't seem to get those two pluses to add up right. She had posted her list of rules, and she referred to them often. No one paid much attention. She wanted to spend more time teaching and less time handling crises, but her classroom was in crisis much of the time.

At the end of the second Friday, there was another mess to clean up. Cynthia peeled a blob of rubber glue off one of the tables and looked to her bulletin board for encouragement. Five finished pencil sketches out of a class of eighteen. She had taken the sixth graders outside to use the intersection and the buildings around the school for a lesson in perspective. She'd lost two girls, who had crossed the street and kept on walking in defiance of Cynthia's vehement protests. Meanwhile, one of the boys had scribbled on another one's paper, and two others had decided to play hackey-sack. Cynthia supposed she was lucky to have gotten five drawings out of the deal.

"Got some time on your hands?"

"More like glue," Cynthia replied as she scraped the remnants into the trash can. Kyle had taken to checking in on her at the end of each day, and the sound of his voice had become a balm, as well as a signal that the day was over and she'd survived.

"Things getting pretty sticky, are they?"

She started to nod, but his calm smile annoyed her. Instead, while he perused her bulletin board, she went on with her cleaning, carrying on as if this were just another day at the end of just another week.

"Some of us are getting together at Big Jim's for the TGIF blue-plate special. Care to join us?"

"I can't." The abrupt refusal sounded ungracious to her own ears, and she hastened to soften it. "Thank you, but I really can't."

"Somebody waiting for you?"

"No." He looked skeptical. "No, there's no one waiting. I have this mess to clean up, and I have lessons to prepare, and I have . . ." She was floundering now, partly because she wanted to go with him and be part of the group. She gestured vaguely. "I have tropical fish. You know, they have to be fed."

"Tropical fish, huh?" He smiled. "That's a good one."

She turned and moved toward the window, where she could get a look at the courtyard below. A chipmunk scampered the length of a stone retaining wall and disappeared into a clump of spent daylilies. "And I think I have a letter of resignation to write."

"After two weeks?"

"I'm no good at this. They need someone who can . . ." She'd expelled too many disconsolate sighs of late, regretted too many outbursts, lost too much ground. She wanted to get with the program, say the right words, tell the right jokes, but she couldn't seem to think fast enough. "They need someone else."

"They'll have a hard time finding someone else now." She lifted her hand to her temple as he closed in behind her. "Headache?"

"Every day. And I'm not usually prone to headaches."

He put his hand on her shoulder. "Take some aspirin and then come with me."

"That sounds ominous." But alluring, like the warmth of his hand.

"Maybe it is. I want you to meet some people. I've got a couple of ideas I want to bounce off you," he said, taking both her shoulders in his hands and turning her to face him. "I've got a problem and I need your advice." She shook her head slowly, inviting him to try again. "Okay. I need a ride, how's that? I don't have a car. But the rest was all true," he added quickly.

"Everyone else has left?"

"Blew out of here with the last bell."

"Okay," she said, secretly glad he'd come up with a compelling inducement. "One blue-plate special with a side of aspirin. I've never been to Big Jim's, but I've heard it's a very interesting place."

"Almost as interesting as All Nations," he assured her. With a look, she questioned the likelihood. "*Almost.*"

BIG JIM'S WAS an old-fashioned downtown diner that specialized in hearty American meat-and-potato meals. The owner, Mavis Chin, had left Southeast Asia and come to the States in the hope of locating her

American father. Instead, she located the perfect site for the business that would make the best use of her skills. Shrewd businesswoman that she was, she resolved to serve American-style meals at recession-style prices, and the place was always packed. Diners conversed in the multitude of tongues that reflected the diversity of inner city America, but when they ordered, it was in the language of chicken-fried steak with home-style potatoes.

For many of the teachers from All Nations—mostly those who were single—the Friday-night special was a regular weekly break from quick-stop fast food and microwaved diet entrées from the freezer. They occupied their usual territory—three booths and two tables toward the back. Whenever anyone had a date, it was an unspoken rule that they got the corner booth. Rumor had it that it was only a matter of time before Kyle Bear Soldier would occupy that booth with Cynthia Boyer.

When the two walked in together, the high fives from Marty Blue and Pete Stoker acknowledged Kyle's quick work. He knew they'd been betting on him, and the shy side of a month would have been commendable in their eyes. But the lady was the serious type. She was trying too hard. Another two weeks and she would be gone. Maybe she didn't really belong here. Maybe she wasn't a survivor, in which case she would leave sooner or later. But Kyle had decided to do what he could to make it later, and for that he'd been rewarded with those "nice goin'" gestures from his male colleagues.

As for the women, Jennifer Tetley gave Cynthia the once-over, and Patty Blue warned her to "stay away from the combination plate if you're wearing a girdle."

Kyle glanced at Cynthia. There was a hint of added pink in her cheeks, but her delicate laugh covered for her nicely. Sober shoptalk came fairly easily to her. When people started joking around, she listened, bright-eyed and pretty as a princess in a child's picture book. She would join in eventually, he told himself. He had to give her time.

"Hard week, Cynthia?" Pete asked.

"About as hard as it was for the rest of us this time last year, when we were all new," Kyle supplied as he directed Cynthia toward the corner booth. "Remember?"

"Things are going a hell of a lot better than they were this time last year," someone else muttered.

Marty added, "It took a year for you Sioux to get with the Ojibwa program."

Kyle laughed as he handed Cynthia one of the menus from the slot behind the napkin box. "It took a year for you Chippewa to let us have something besides rabbit for school lunch."

"I was kinda gettin' to like that cottontail stew," Pete put in. "You ought to put it on the menu, Mama Chin."

"Home-style American cooking." Mavis herself delivered the water to the tables, keeping her customary high profile. "That's my specialty."

"You've got spaghetti on here." Kyle perused the laminated menu.

"Minneapolis spaghetti only. Chunky style."

"Patty'll show you how to make chunky rabbit stew, Minneapolis-style." He winked at Cynthia over the top of the menu, just to let her know they were teammates in this game. "Well, Minnesota-style, anyway. Those Chippewa wives, they know how to keep a guy's weight up. Right, Marty?"

Marty patted his bowling-ball belly and grinned at his wife. "Damn right."

When the iced tea and hot coffee came, Pete Stoker raised his glass. "Here's to a year of survival."

"Here's to four hundred years of survival, and to us finally getting to be part of the public-school system," Kyle said. Cynthia touched her water glass to his coffee mug, and he appreciated her willingness to get into the spirit of things. "I don't know if you remember, but this time last year we were taking a lot of heat—in the press and elsewhere."

"I remember. That's what first caught my interest about the school."

"We were just starting out," Marty put in. He leaned across and offered a sample of the deep-fried battered onion rings he'd ordered as an appetizer. Cynthia took one as he elaborated. "New school, new concept, and half the educational community hoping we'd fall on our faces."

"Yeah, but the other half wanted to see us make it." Kyle shook off the onion-ring offer. "And we are making it. Hell, if I'm making it here, it should be easy for you natives."

"You've lasted one whole year in the city, cowboy," Patty said. "Congratulations."

When the food was served, people settled into quieter conversations at their own tables, along with serious eating.

"Do you miss South Dakota?" Cynthia asked. She watched Kyle sprinkle his baked potato generously with black pepper.

"I miss it so damn bad sometimes I feel like packing up in the middle of the night and hitching a ride on a westbound rig." He offered the shaker. She shook her head. "I generally get over the urge by sunup."

"What do you miss most?"

"The big sky." He studied the crust on the hot breast of fried chicken he balanced gingerly over his plate. "The buttes. The scraggly ol' buffalo grass. The sound of the wind. It doesn't sound the same here, you know."

"I guess I thought wind was wind."

"Just like mashed potatoes are mashed potatoes?" He eyed the white mound on her plate and wondered how much of that she would eat. So far she was just playing with it. Hadn't even spiced it up. "Urban cowboys aren't anything like real cowboys, and urban Indians . . . well, the two words just don't go together naturally."

"I remember once when I was a little girl, downtown shopping with my mother, we saw a group of, um—" She seemed intent upon drawing furrows in the potatoes with her fork, but he could almost hear her flipping through her mental file of correct terms "—Native Americans. I mean, I don't know what tribe they were affiliated with, but I saw that two of the men wore braids, and I asked my mother if they were *real* Indians."

"What did she say?"

"I believe she said, 'Not the kind in the movies. They're not savage.'"

Kyle laughed. He sank his teeth into his chicken, taking pleasure in its juiciness and her honesty.

"But, you know, that confused me," she said. "It left me wondering what a 'real Indian' was."

"So you took this job to find out?"

"I know a number of Native American artists. I know lots of people who are . . . you know." She shrugged. "Lots of people."

"Lots of real Indians?" He figured he could push her a little now without losing his advantage. He lowered his voice. "How well would you like to get to know me?"

"Better than I do now," she told him. The look she gave him added that getting to know him would be a prerequisite to *knowing* him.

"Fair enough." He set the chicken back on his plate and leaned a little closer. "I'm going to tell you a secret." Her eyes said she was ready. "Since I left home, I get to wondering sometimes whether I'm still real."

"A real Indian, you mean?"

"I'm going to a sweat this weekend just to make sure."

"What kind of sweating are you into, besides jogging to work?"

"I don't jog to work." He sat back, smiling. Those big blue childlike eyes of hers were so much fun to talk to. "If I did, I'd be sweaty for the rest of the day. And, while our job isn't exactly what you'd call 'no sweat,' you don't want to start the day out that way." She nodded in guileless agreement. "I'd rather sweat at night. Wouldn't you?"

"Strictly speaking, I'm not much of a sweater."

"I caught you at it today. After school was out, when the world was coming down pretty hard on you, and you were ready to quit. Instead, you came with me." She refused to meet his eyes, and he knew she was embarrassed to think she'd tipped her hand his way, or anybody's way, in a moment of frustration. She would have preferred to keep all her frustration to herself. "This is better, isn't it?"

"I know two weeks isn't much, but I'm not accomplishing anything in the classroom," she confided almost in a whisper. "Not a thing."

"I saw five good drawings on your bulletin board. If you stay, next week there'll be more. If you leave, there won't."

"How many more will there be?"

"In a week, maybe ten. Maybe just one. But you've got five right now. Five good pieces."

"Don't say 'easy,'" she warned. "They weren't five easy pieces."

"Nobody said it would be easy."

She nodded again, and he felt a little guilty about minimizing her difficulties. He'd had his share, too, and he would have gladly taken on hers if there had been a way to do so, simply because those eyes were so big and needy. He was sure she didn't realize what clear windows they were to her soul. Looking in on her each afternoon had been his way of offering support. In the end, he knew it was up to her. She didn't need this job the way he did. But she damn sure needed something, or some*one*.

"A sweat is a purification experience. The Lakota call it *inipi*. One of the teachers who lives out of town has a sweat lodge on his property. You get about six, eight guys, and go into this dark little wigwam type thing," he explained, making the shape with his hands. "You heat a bunch of rocks in a fire outside. Now, the Lakota bring those rocks in a few at a time, but the Chippewa, they just wanna get things steamed up in a hurry, so they put the whole pile in at once."

"Ojibwa," Cynthia corrected with a smile.

"Ojibwa," he confirmed. She was adding to her file of proper terms, and he didn't mind helping out. "Anyway, you sprinkle water on the rocks, make steam, make sweat . . ." He smiled playfully. "Lots and lots of sweat. Good for the soul. And you share some thoughts, some hopes, some concerns. You pray together, basically."

"Pray while you're doing all this sweating?"

"Sometimes you're just praying for a little cool air." Her soft smile drew out his confidences. "Sometimes you're just praying for the strength to stick it out a little longer. To stand the heat a little longer." He paused, studying those pretty eyes. "What made you come to All Nations to teach, Cynthia?"

"I thought I could do some good."

"And you've decided you can't?"

"I could if the kids would settle down and pay attention." She sampled her meat loaf. "Obviously they do that for you."

"Sometimes they do, sometimes they don't. I'm doing better than I was a year ago. And I've done a lot of praying for the strength to stand the heat a little longer." She looked at him skeptically. "I lose them, too," he assured her. "I lose their attention. Sometimes a kid just ups and walks out."

"That's happened to me."

He nodded. The news of such incidents always got around. "They come back. Some of these kids have it rough. You know that, don't you? That school is a safe haven for many of our kids. There's not a lot of money in this neighborhood. A lot of unemployment, too much alcohol, drugs anywhere you care to look."

"I know." She toyed with another bit of meat loaf, spearing it, dipping it in gravy that had to be cold by now. "It made me sad to see all those people coming to the church just to find a decent meal. I haven't been back since."

"Why not?"

"I don't want to embarrass anyone."

"I wasn't embarrassed. Were you embarrassed?" She was still playing with that meat loaf and avoiding his eyes. "You were, weren't you? Cynthia, people coming together to share a meal is not a sad thing."

"At least they're getting something to eat. I know. But to be obliged to accept that kind of charity simply because our society—"

"Ours?"

"Mine, then," she amended.

"Society girl." He shook his head, chuckling. She stared at him, letting him know she was serious. "You *don't* know, Cynthia," he said indulgently. He knew she would have objected to being patronized if she'd thought he was in a position to patronize her. In her world, an

Indian man could hardly be a patron, which might have angered him if he could think of one good reason he might ever aspire to such a stupid role. Given time, she would come to realize these things. Given time, she might even come to value them.

"If people without money embarrass you, you've come to the wrong place," he instructed patiently.

"It's not that poverty em—"

"Well, poverty's another issue. There's more than one kind of poverty." He slid his hand over hers. "Stick with us a while longer. Let us show you the difference between charity and sharing." She started to object again, but he persisted. "I know you came to teach. All Nations needs good teachers *from* all nations, and I sure think you've got the makings. But if you learn nothing else from us while you're teaching, learn what 'Indian giving' really means."

AFTER THEY LEFT Big Jim's, Kyle directed Cynthia to an address not far from the school, but it wasn't his home address. Despite the fact that she knew the neighborhood, somehow he wasn't quite ready to show her where he lived. He took her, instead, to a small strip mall, where shops that had fallen into disrepair were now being renovated by community crews, people who had elbow grease to invest rather than dollars. He was pleased to see the spotlight over the new sign above the shop in the middle, which read, "Expressions of the Four Winds."

"There's someone I want you to meet," he told Cynthia.

She peered through the windshield. "Is it open?"

"Doesn't matter. She's always here at least an hour after closing time." He couldn't see Cynthia's face clearly in the shadows, but he thought he detected a bit of neck stiffening over in the driver's seat. "My sister-in-law. She's working real hard to get this place back on its feet."

Delia Bear Soldier was working very hard indeed, and Kyle was proud of his brother's wife. Because of her experience in a South Dakota gift shop, she'd been hired to work for the neighborhood arts and crafts co-op, and she'd been putting in long hours. The shop was intended to provide a marketplace for Native American jewelry and art. There were many such shops in Phoenix and Denver. The people of the Phillips neighborhood had decided they ought to have one, too.

After the two women shook hands, Cynthia perused the glass cases containing turquoise and silver jewelry, wondering whether she was expected to make some comment, since she'd been an art buyer, too.

Comment, she reminded herself. She was learning to reserve judgment, and she got the feeling it was too soon to make any recommendations that might occur to her. Delia was watching, waiting to see what Cynthia would do. She wanted to say the right thing—if she could just figure out what that was.

An exquisite squash-blossom necklace caught her eye. "Are these made by local people?" Cynthia asked.

"That's Navaho," Delia replied as she lifted a whimpering toddler into her arms. "We're taking some things on consignment from New Mexico and Arizona. Directly from the artists. No middle man. Trying to open up the market in this part of the country."

"It's a wonderful idea. You have some beautiful pieces here." She glanced up from the display case and found that Delia, bouncing the baby to quiet him, had taken a step closer. "I used to buy Indian-made jewelry for several galleries," Cynthia said. Then she turned to Kyle, who offered no hint as to whether she was taking the right tack. Elbows on the counter, chin in hands, he was studying a display of beaded cigarette lighters that Cynthia would have said did not belong in a shop with fine jewelry. But she reminded herself that she had not been asked.

"They were located in a different kind of neighborhood, right?" Delia asked pointedly. "Our prices are reasonable here, and the artists will get a better return for their work. If we can get the word out, we think people will come to our shop, located in *our* neighborhood." She pointed to the quill and bead earrings. "These were made by local crafters," she said. "And the quilts."

"They're beautiful. And the baskets." Cynthia admired a large duck woven from split willow. "I'm more familiar with Papago and Apache basketry, but this is Cree, isn't it?"

"She passes the basket test," Delia told Kyle, and he chuckled.

Cynthia wasn't sure what was funny about it, since she figured it might have been the first test she'd passed in weeks.

"How do you like teaching at All Nations?" Delia asked.

"I think I may become a basket *case,*" Cynthia admitted readily. "I've been out of the classroom for a long time. I'm trying to get a handle on the discipline end of it, but I'm afraid I'm not doing very well."

"These kids can be a handful for any of us," Kyle offered. "Cynthia has some great ideas. She's gonna do fine."

"If you have trouble with any Bear Soldier kids, you tell me about it," Delia said.

Cynthia started to thank her, but the baby in Delia's arms was reaching for Kyle, and it surprised her to see him take the little boy into his arms with practiced ease. The men who had been part of her life so far—her father and her former husband—had scrupulously ignored small children.

It surprised her, too, when Delia complained to Kyle of another child. "Carla didn't come home from school, and I don't know where your brother is."

"I'll find Carla," he told her. "As for Jamie, you've gotta stop worrying. He's doing good now. He passed all his summer courses, didn't he?" Delia nodded, and Cynthia caught herself smiling along with Kyle, as though she somehow had a stake in all this. "See there? He'll be finished with school and working before you know it."

Cynthia left the store smiling. She felt as though he'd included her in some family business, and the feeling was good. She realized it was probably silly, but in a way she felt privileged. She knew his niece, Carla, from school, and now Delia, and next she would meet his brother Jamie, because Kyle had obviously taken it upon himself to include her in—

"I'll walk from here," he told her when they reached the car. It was the last thing she'd expected him to say, and he surely saw that in her face. "Got my jogging shoes on, and I haven't had my workout yet today," he explained casually.

Cynthia felt as though someone had pulled the plug on her swelling heart. "It's no trouble to drop you off. Besides, I'd like to help you look for Carla."

"Delia's laid down the law to those kids about going home after school, but that Carla . . ." He shook his head as he braced one hand on the hood of the car. "She probably went to a friend's house, so it'll be easier if I just make the rounds on foot."

He cut off further objections by changing the subject. "I see you're going to help chaperone my field trip next week. Did you volunteer?"

"I offered to help out," Cynthia answered, still feeling a little shell-shocked. "After all, you'll be taking the students that I would have had in class on a normal day."

He grinned, looking boyishly pleased with himself. "Then you can't quit yet. You'd leave me high and dry."

"Someone else would take my place."

"That might be hard to do. Take your place, I mean. Not too many people would give up a slack day. That was nice of you."

"I like to stay busy." Warming to his praise, she felt like a schoolgirl lingering under the porch light when it was clearly time for her to get in her car and leave. She'd made her offer. He'd turned her down.

"Are you busy Saturday night?"

It was her turn. "Actually, I do have plans."

"How about a week from Saturday? I'd like to see a play."

"A play? Which one?"

"Any one. You choose. They want me to put on a play for parents' night, and I don't know a damn thing about plays. Thought I'd go see one, if I could find myself a date."

"Actually, the Children's Playhouse would be—"

"'Actually' makes it sound like you're taking exception." He stepped closer, blanketing her with his shadow. "But I don't think you are. How well do you want to get to know me, Cynthia?" She gripped the handle on the car door, but she'd completely forgotten how the thing worked. His smile faded as his fingertips grazed her cheek. "After hours I'm not looking for any children's playhouse. If I want to play house, it's going to be on an adult level."

"I've played house before," she recalled regretfully. "With a man who neglected to mention that he didn't play for keeps. 'Getting to know you' means one thing to a man and something altogether different for a woman."

"My definition might surprise you, Cynthia." He slid his thumb beneath her chin, tilting it up. "Here's something else that might surprise you."

He lowered his head, blocking the light completely, but then he tipped his head to the side, and the light struck her eyes again. She closed them against the rude street lamp, heard the soft intake of his breath and felt the warm dewy impression of his lips on hers. The sweetness of his mouth was no surprise, but she would never have guessed how delicious his brand of sweetness was.

Chapter Four

FIRST STOP ON the fifth- and sixth-grade field trip was a wildlife sanctuary in a wood north of the Twin Cities, where two canvas-draped sweat lodges of the type Kyle had described were already set up, and an old man was waiting to lead the boys in *inipi*. Lily Moore, who was officially on staff at All Nations as a classroom aide, was truly the school's on-site elder. She was prepared to lead the girls, as was traditional, in a separate sweat.

Few of the children had ever participated in such a ceremony, and they were all given the option of declining. The fire tenders, who were part of the ceremonial team, stood ready to roll in the first rocks. A dozen boys, dressed in shorts or swimming suits, went in, challenging each other as to who could stay in the longest. Without expending many words, Kyle, dressed in gym shorts, imposed one hand between two boys who were sparring while he stripped off his T-shirt with the other. "You guys might make me angry if you ruin my concentration in there," he warned before saluting Cynthia with a quick wave and disappearing inside.

Cynthia had worn shorts and a T-shirt as instructed, and she was about to heed Lily's hurry-up gesture when Carla Bear Soldier put the skids on the proceedings. "I'm not going in there."

Cynthia glanced at the men's lodge and realized that Carla had carefully calculated her timing. "That's fine. It's your choice." She smiled pleasantly. "I'll stay out here with you."

At twelve, Carla was already as tall as Cynthia. She had sturdier shoulders, more bust, and at least as much resolve. "Chicken?"

"No. I think it would be very interesting to participate." She signaled Lily to go ahead without her. Lily nodded and ducked into the cave-like door on what had been designated the women's lodge. "Well, maybe a little chicken," Cynthia confided then. "I passed out in a sauna once, and it would be awfully embarrassing if you girls had to drag me out of there."

"I can't imagine *you* passed out." Carla wandered across the clearing, away from the two young men who were busy separating rocks from the hot coals in the fire pit. "You're too neat and clean to be passed out."

Cynthia followed. "Well, it happened. I was clean, but I don't know about neat." Cynthia tossed a doubtful glance over her shoulder. "Can you be neat and naked at the same time?"

"I think *you* could." The girl took a seat on the ground, hiked her knees up and leaned back against a tree trunk. "Listen, you don't have to watch me. I can't go anywhere." She indicated the woods with a nod of her chin. "There's no place to go."

"I'm not worried that you'll skip out on us, Carla. I just thought I'd keep you company. I suppose you've done lots of sweats, huh?"

The girl shook her head. "My uncle Kyle is the one who's into it most, and he's just dying to get us kids to try it. But I'm not gonna." Glaring at the men's lodge, she snatched a twig off the ground and snapped it in half. "He was mad at me for going to Rhonda's house after school on Friday, and I told him it was no big deal."

Cynthia sat down on the ground opposite Carla. The late-summer grass crackled as she crossed her legs and settled in. "Your mother didn't know where you were. She was worried."

"They think I can't take care of myself. I'm twelve years old, you know."

"I know. I'm thirty-two years old, but people worry about me when they can't find me." Carla gave her that skeptical look again. "After a few days, anyway. If I don't talk to my mother every few days, she gets worried. But, then, I live alone, so . . ."

"So you don't have to explain every move you make, right?"

"It can be a comfort to know you're accountable to someone if that someone cares what happens to you. Your uncle Kyle was worried, too."

"Well, he's not my dad, and sometimes I wish he'd mind his own business." She scowled at her right knee, which bore the remnants of a week-old scrape. "But sometimes I don't. Sometimes he gets my parents to lighten up."

"You must be a very close family," Cynthia said, suddenly wishing she could say the same about hers. What little she had.

"Well, yeah, we have to be close. We're—" Carla straightened abruptly. Her eyes brightened as she cocked her head in the direction of the activity she'd stubbornly denied herself moments ago. "Listen to those boys messin' around in there. Uncle's only gonna let them go so far, and then he's gonna—"

"You guys need more steam?" they could hear Kyle say. "Add a little water, Earl."

"No more steam," a younger voice croaked. "We'll behave. We'll behave."

"I don't know. Sometimes it takes more steam to get the songs going."

"We'll sing."

"Give us a break, Kyle."

Carla and Cynthia shared secret smiles.

"Hey, I said we'll sing!"

And sing they did.

LATER, AFTER A quick dip in the YMCA pool, the group was joined by the Ojibwa language teacher, Marty Blue, for a trip to the local science museum. The steam had sapped some of the mischief out of the boys, but the swim revived them. Many of the displays invited visitors to take part somehow, which meant, as far as the kids were concerned, touching everything in sight.

Mr. Drayton, the white-haired volunteer host who introduced himself as a retired teacher, was eager to educate. "The artifacts belong to all of us," he explained, clearly proud of his part-ownership. "This is a safe place to keep them, a place where we can all see them, but we realize that the Native American collection is a very special . . ."

Cynthia hung back, herding the stragglers along. She decided her most valuable contribution to keeping order was to lend a watchful eye. It was a skill she'd learned from her mother. There was a time for touching and a time for just looking, and when a young face was pressed against a glass window, it was time to say, "Tom, don't put your mouth on that."

Tom Gorneau leaned back to admire his lip print, surrounded by the steam from his breath. "It'll wash off."

"But it's not clean," Cynthia reminded him, just as her mother, or *any* mother, might have done. "Other hands have—"

"Looks clean enough." He glanced up at her, grinning with pride. "I left my mark."

"His big flapping lips," James Red Leaf taunted. James licked his thumb and pressed it next to Tom's lip print. "Good as fingerprints. Cops can track you down now. Get you for abusing our artifacts with those big flapping smackers of yours."

"You're an *artifact*," Tom accused, as if it were the worst insult he could come up with. Actually, Cynthia admired Tom's choice of words. "You're just lucky you're bigger than me."

"Shh. Boys, you're making people—" she glanced around, noting they were drawing a few cool adult stares "—nervous." The boys giggled. "You mustn't be so loud," she pleaded.

"This ain't no library."

"Yeah, this ain't no church, neither."

"Oh, dear." Cynthia sighed, wishing she could go back to square one and let Tom kiss the glass to his heart's content.

"C'mon over here, you guys," Kyle said, motioning to them. "Watch this demonstration."

Mr. Drayton showed the group an old Ojibwa drill, and then he took out a reproduction and demonstrated how the machine was used. He was clearly enamored of its simple efficiency and his own practiced proficiency.

"Pretty clever of us Ojibwa to come up with a thing like that," Marty observed. "Wonder how the Sioux drilled out their pipe stems." While Mr. Drayton beetled his brow and racked his brain for the answer, Marty eyed Kyle. "Bet it took them weeks to finish a pipe."

"Hey, while you guys were fooling around with that little toy, we were using the method told to us by Iktome, the trickster, which we don't reveal to too many people." He turned to Mr. Drayton, who was all ears. "But today, just for the sake of comparison . . ."

He picked up a piece of white ash that had been partially whittled for demonstration. "Every Lakota pipe stem was bored straight and true. We were known for this. We would build a small fire first. Then we would carve a notch in the end of the pipe stem," he explained, making the motion over the butt of the unfinished piece to demonstrate.

Cynthia watched the gathering of faces, dark-skinned and light, brown-eyed and blue. The students were curious. Marty looked skeptical, but Mr. Drayton was thoroughly absorbed.

"Then we would put a termite headfirst into the notch, tamp in some clay and suspend the whole thing over the fire. When that termite's rear end heated up, he'd *really* drill that hole in a hurry."

Marty was the first to respond. "Ayyy."

James Red Leaf gave Kyle a thumbs-up.

Mr. Drayton laughed so hard Cynthia thought the man might have to be carried out on a stretcher.

The children were still full of energy when they returned to school that afternoon. Their second wind always seemed to outstrip Cynthia's first. After they were dismissed for the day, several of them dashed into the art room to check on the progress of projects still in the drying stage, or to ask what they were going to do tomorrow, or to see if a cap somebody had swiped had been stashed there. She was too tired to arbitrate the running battle between the last holdouts—James and Paula Red Leaf—so for once she went about her business organizing student portfolios and ignored the whole thing.

Kyle stuck his head in the door. "You guys get going before you miss your bus. Paula, you left your saxophone in my room."

"I know," she said on her way out the door. "I don't want my older brother to hock it again. I almost didn't get it back."

Cynthia motioned Kyle into the room and closed the door, scowling. "Her brother *pawned* her saxophone?"

"The school's saxophone," Kyle corrected. "And if that shocks you, I'm afraid you've led a very sheltered life, my friend. Or maybe I shouldn't say I'm afraid. Maybe some people are supposed to lead sheltered lives." He shoved his hands into his pockets and looked her in the eye, adding, "When they're children."

"These *are* children."

Kyle shrugged. "Money's hard to come by around here, and the kid might have figured that hocking the instrument was better than selling drugs. Then again, he might have used the money to buy drugs."

"I hope not." She would not apologize for being shocked by unfairness, nor for hoping for change, and if that made her sound unrealistic, so be it.

"I hope not, too. I hope he used it to buy his mom a birthday present. The good news is Paula got her saxophone back."

"It must be quite a challenge to put a band concert together here."

"We're all here because we just *love* the challenges," Kyle teased, which brought a reluctant smile to Cynthia's face.

"Actually, I *did* enjoy the field trip today."

"Really? I thought you were going to lose it at the museum. It's a hands-on museum, Cynthia."

"I know that, but hands-on has its limits."

"Does it, now?" With a twinkle in his eye, he took a step closer and lowered his voice. "Suppose you enlighten me in advance, because I've always been pretty hands-on myself."

"In advance of what?"

"In advance of further advances," he said lightly.

She folded her arms and glanced away. "Hands-on has its limits."

"You said that." They stood in silence for a moment and then he asked, "What kind of limits do you put on your heart, Cynthia?"

She glanced up at the intercom speaker, thinking this was not the place to discuss such things. She answered quietly, "I'm cautious."

"Fair enough." He touched her arm, easing away a tension she hadn't realized was there. "When you care, you care deeply, don't you? You care about these kids."

"I care," she admitted as she released her arms slowly and let them relax at her sides. She avoided his eyes as she moved past him. "You were right. I was ready to give up before I'd really gotten started. But now . . ." She directed his attention to a long table. This time she had fourteen projects sitting out in various stages of completion. *Fourteen.*

"We started making papier-mâché faces yesterday, and the kids have come up with some animal masks that would scare—" she looked at his handsome face and broke into a broad smile "—the most stalwart of us."

"This ain't no mask, lady," he drawled in protest. "This is the real thing, scary or not."

"And it was inspirational, I must say. You were the model for the bear mask," she explained. He quirked one thick eyebrow, clearly amused by the idea. "I said, 'Imagine Mr. Bear Soldier's face when he's angry,' and that sparked all kinds of creativity."

"Believe it or not, I don't have to get angry much. I just keep telling them they wouldn't want to see me get angry, and they believe me." He touched the pointed nose on one of the newsprint masks. It bent beneath his finger, and she reached for his hand, gently pulling him back from doing any damage.

He turned his palm to hers. "I used to get angry a lot when I was younger. Didn't do anybody a damn bit of good. Especially not me." He smiled as he hooked his long fingers around her wrist and caressed the hollow of her palm with the heel of his hand. "I have to be cautious, too."

"Are you apt to be dangerous?"

"I'm apt to withdraw, just the way the kids do sometimes. I guess that's dangerous in a way, especially when you start gnawing at your own insides."

Flustered, she drew her hand away and began rearranging masks that needed no rearranging.

"What about you?" he asked. "Do you get angry?"

"Sometimes." To prove her point, she snatched up one of the

projects. "Look what they did to this. These aren't dry yet." It was Tom Gorneau's mask, and someone had stuck a wad of pink bubble gum on the lips.

"But you stay cool, basically," Kyle observed.

"I try to, yes." She peeled the gum away. Some of the paper came with it. "I think I can fix this."

"I'd like to see you heat up a little. Maybe I'll try on that bear mask and see if it gets *your* creative juices flowing."

"Actually, it already did," she said, brightening. "I have an idea that might solve your production problems."

He offered a champion-male smile. "What am I supposed to be producing?"

"A play."

"Oh, that." He sounded disappointed. "You've got some ideas?"

"I think we might make it a joint effort, using my masks and your knack for storytelling. You might have to write the lines yourself, but I have a feeling you're never at a loss for lines."

"You question my sincerity?" He clapped his hand over his heart. "Ms. Boyer, you wound me deeply."

"I happen to have tickets for tonight's performance at the Ordway. Will you recover from your wounds by seven o'clock?"

"I don't know," he said, eyeing her suspiciously. "Is this one of those fancy theater deals?"

"Haven't you been to the Ordway?"

"I suppose I haven't *lived* unless I've been to the Ordway."

Cynthia welcomed the excuse to link arms with him and lead him to the door. "Deliver me from my sheltered existence, and I'll deliver you to the theater."

"Such a deal," he conceded, but he needed more coaxing. "Ordinarily I'd take you up on it, but my tux is at the dry cleaner's."

"Dress comfortably." She wanted to tell him to wear his hair just as he always did, sometimes with a little queue in the back, and not to forget his boots and the Western-cut jeans that always rode nice and low at the base of his long back.

"And how will you be dressed?"

She wondered whether he could read her mind. "Comfortably."

HER HAND-PAINTED jeans nearly knocked his socks off. He didn't get the full effect until they'd parked the car, he'd opened the door for her, and she'd stepped out onto the pavement. When she'd come to pick him up, he'd been waiting on the porch for her. Behind a pillar. Fortunately Jamie had a night class and Delia was at the store, so his nephew, Markie, was the only one who'd followed him out the door with a ten-year-old's version of a wolf whistle. Hell, his outfit had seemed like a good idea until he'd put the damn thing on.

But Cynthia's outfit . . . Now *there* was an outfit, and it fit her classic female shape just fine. Her hair, the color of a shiny chestnut, was done up on top of her head, and her jacket collar stood up fashionably at the back of her neck. A silky red scoop-necked blouse hinted at the presence of cleavage. He gave a low whistle, thirty-five-year-old-style, and motioned for her to do a quick turn for him. Denim made a very classy canvas, he decided as he admired the abstract artwork, punctuated with glitter and flashy fake jewels. Especially draped over a nice curvy . . . easel.

"You look great. That's a real work of art. One of a kind, I'd say."

"I'd say so, too. I painted both the pants and jacket myself."

"They look just—" he shook his head, clucking to himself "—great, which sounds like a puny word, but I'm a little tongue-tied. I thought you'd be wearing some real fancy dress, so I . . ." He looked down at his black dinner jacket, white shirt and tie, and shrugged uneasily. His shoulders felt a little cramped.

Those big blue eyes widened innocently. "Are you disappointed?"

"Hell, no," he assured her, giving her an appreciative once-over. "Are you?"

She motioned for him to give her a spin. He had tied his hair back, and he'd polished his black cowboy boots. When he completed his turn, she smiled and reported, "I'm dazzled."

"Good." He offered his arm. "I feel like the flip side of Cinderella. Tomorrow this thing has to be back in the dry cleaner's window, so I've only got a few hours to be dazzling. I plan to make the most of them."

The play was a musical, featuring some toe-tapping country-and-western tunes. Kyle had a good time holding Cynthia's hand and patting it against his thigh. He liked the way her head bobbed and her shoulders swayed just a little when she got into the swing. She'd chosen the play because she thought it would please him. And it did. He wondered if it surprised her that it pleased her, too.

She invited him to her home, explaining that she had prepared some food and that she wanted to show off a little. "Since I missed my chance to show off my fancy clothes, maybe I can impress you with my interior decorating. It's the first time I've lived in a place that's all mine."

"You haven't missed your chance with anything so far," he assured her as he took the key and unlocked the door.

Cynthia's condo was one of several that had recently been offered for sale in a converted late-nineteenth-century fire station. The architect had added wood and glass to the rich hues of old brick and had achieved dramatic high ceilings, clean lines, and an airy open feeling. It was a complete departure from any place she'd lived in before, and she loved it. It was the perfect home for her Navaho rugs—the teal-and-russet Crystal pattern that graced the polished floor beneath the glass coffee table, and the highly prized Two Gray Hills she'd hung against the old brick. She had some exquisite Pueblo pottery—a white Acoma seed pot painted with fine black lines, a startlingly beautiful black Santa Clara pot, and the more colorful Jemez pieces. There were three large paintings by up-and-coming Native American artists—bold lines and bright colors exploring timeless earthy themes.

He took it all in, and she waited for his reaction. He couldn't help but like what he saw, she thought. Even the big cylindrical aquarium blended with the decor.

"So this is where you live?" Kyle's boot heels echoed against the hardwood floor. He shoved his hands into his pockets and ambled toward the huge window overlooking the lake. City lights twinkled beyond the glass like jewels in a shop window. "Pretty nice." He touched the white leather sofa and eyed the freestanding fireplace. "Kind of a lot of room for just one person and a couple of fish."

"I'm used to a house, so I've had to make some adjustments. But after the divorce, I couldn't stay in 'the house that Jack built.'"

She went to the kitchen, wondering whether the tray of cold cuts she'd carefully arranged and stashed in the refrigerator was such a good idea. She listened to the sound of his footsteps as he moved about the living room, presumably taking a closer look.

"I have an assortment of beverages here," she called out as she slipped out of her jacket and hung it on a hook. "Name your heart's desire, and I'll tell you if I've got it."

His first answer wasn't quite intelligible, but the request for "just coffee" came loud and clear. She flipped the switch on the coffeemaker, which was ready to go. She resisted the urge to peek out, see what he was inspecting and try to read his thoughts. Did "pretty nice" mean he liked the place? One of the paintings was done by a Sioux artist, and she wondered whether he recognized the name. She wondered whether he liked her color scheme, whether he was tempted to relax on her sofa, or whether he thought this was all too pretentious for relaxing.

Mostly she wondered whether surroundings like these would prevent him from kissing her again.

She turned, shutting the refrigerator door behind her, and found him standing there, leaning against the door frame, hands still in his pockets. "Who's Jack?" he wondered.

"My former husband was an architect. I decided that I didn't need a big house. I didn't need rooms full of perfectly coordinated furniture and office-suite artwork." She set the snack tray on the tiled counter and gestured toward the tall stools. "I loved this place the moment I saw it. It's something old made new again."

"Made new and neat and . . ."

"My taste in art was never to his liking. He used to criticize me for, as he put it, bringing my work home with me. For my new home, I bought new things to suit my new life."

He helped himself to a block of white cheese and a black olive on a toothpick. "Sounds like the old life was a real downer."

"I married the kind of man I thought I was supposed to marry. He came from the right family, and he had all the right credentials." It was good to keep busy while she related all this. She took two mugs from the cupboard and made sure she put out the sugar. "We had no common interests, no children, and no real life together. He went his way with another woman, and I—" she tried to dismiss seven years of her life with a wave of two blue paper napkins "—eventually went mine. To All Nations."

"You got left with a broken heart," he concluded for her. He rested his hip on the stool, hooking his heel on the crossbar.

"That sounds like a line from a country song," Cynthia said with a smile.

"It's probably in at least half of them. Deep down I'm just another cowboy poet."

"I don't know any other cowboy poets. You make me sound sweetly tragic, and I'm not." He didn't seem to notice when she served his coffee. He was watching her face, and it made her a little nervous. "It was a very civilized parting. Nothing as moving as you describe."

"You weren't hurt at all?" She pushed the sugar across the counter toward him, but he ignored that, too. "I know more about you than you think I do, Cynthia. No matter how classy the ironwork, I know a wall when I see one. And now you've got it in your head that you're gonna do your charity work with me while you keep your valuables locked up."

"What valuables?"

"Your heart." He captured one of her busy hands and drew her over to his side of the counter. "Your soft and tender little heart."

"Oh, Kyle," she groaned, shaking her head and smiling at him indulgently. "I wouldn't have taken you for such an incurable romantic."

"You wouldn't have taken me, period. Not the first time you saw me, anyway. You wanna talk about my heart's desire?" He slipped his arms around her waist and laid his cheek against her chest. For a moment, she didn't know where her next breath was coming from. "Your heart's beating pretty fast, Cynthia. You'd better use some sophisticated trick to make it slow down."

"I don't—" her hands fluttered uselessly, then found his shoulders "—know any tricks."

"You know how to walk away. You could walk away and take this little problem with you." He raised his head slowly, coming up smiling. "It feels like it's trying to break out of this beautiful fortress, where you keep it locked up."

"I knew you'd have no trouble with lines." Tentatively she touched the silky hair that swept over his right ear. "Dreamers have all the best lines."

"Dreamers are dangerous, and this heart of yours is scared to death of me. But it's still knocking on those iron bars." She closed her eyes and he whispered, "Hear it?" And then he kissed her there. She felt the dampness of his kiss through her thin silk blouse, and her blood pounded in her ears. "You hear it now, don't you?"

"Yes, I hear it."

"I won't take it from you, Cynthia," he promised as he rose from the stool and took her in his arms. "Poor little society girl, that's all you really have to give."

"I can give my time . . ." He was nuzzling her neck, and she found herself rising on tiptoe to give him better access as her point, whatever it was, drifted. "My time and my—"

"Your sweet time?" he whispered close to her ear. "I'll take that, honey. I'll take your sweet, sweet . . ."

She put her arms around his neck, and the last words she heard were ". . . Indian time."

Chapter Five

DEEP INTO THE month of October, rehearsals were still too loosely structured by Cynthia's standards. There were some fun times and some frustrating times. She wanted more *productive* times, and she couldn't understand where Kyle got the idea that everything was "going great."

Gopher, Badger, and Bear were stirring imaginary soup in the wastepaper basket with a yardstick. Kyle had explained that the yardstick represented the sharing spoon, and they were supposed to take turns tasting the brew, which made for one antic after another. The battle over who would actually hold the yardstick had been won by Tom Gorneau, who was Bear. Gopher was in charge of salt, and Badger added the pepper.

"Fly was coming along," Kyle narrated, "and he smelled the soup."

Enter Bertram Yellow, the biggest ham in the class.

"Okay, buzz around them like a fly, Bertram," Cynthia coached. "Pester them, just like a fly."

"You know how to be a pest, Bertram."

"Yeah, just be yourself."

Bzzzz. Bzzzzzzz.

Mischief burned in Tom's brown eyes as he took a batter's stance with the yardstick. "Should I kill it?"

"That's not in the script, Tom," Cynthia said with a sigh, but the whole crew had already cracked up. "One more time, *seriously* now."

She didn't know why she kept using that word when she was the only one who understood its meaning. Kyle was worse than the kids. He couldn't keep a straight face when Bertram stuck his foot in the trash can and Tom yelled, "There's a fly in my soup!"

It was straight downhill from there. Nobody seemed to mind when she scheduled yet another after-school rehearsal "after you've all had time to pull yourselves together." Kyle smiled innocently when she gave him a look he couldn't possibly misinterpret.

"Want to grab a bite to eat?" he asked after the children were gone.

"No, thanks, I have a prior commitment." Besides that, she was a little put out with him. She took her light wool jacket off the back of her chair and gathered up her papers, her purse, and her plan book. When she finally looked up at him, it was still there. That irresistible, infuriatingly innocent look. "I'm back on the volunteer schedule for Loaves and Fishes," she told him.

"Great. That's where I was headed if you turned me down."

"For coffee?"

"Depends on what else you're serving."

She shrugged off his answer, his plans, his attitude. The program was for the have-nots, and he knew what that meant. Yet he chuckled, as if *she* was the one who didn't understand.

"It's a feed, Cynthia. I grew up on church-basement feeds, powwow feeds, marriage and funeral feeds. It's part of our . . ." He rubbed the back of his neck as though his efforts to get through to her produced pain there. "When there's food, everybody eats," he said simply.

"I think that's wonderful." Primly, she completed the buttoning of her jacket. "But this program is meant to feed the hungry."

"Well, then, I sure can qualify." Slinging his jacket over his shoulder, he made an after-you gesture toward the door. "And I belong with the rest of the people who'll be in that line. I'm not too good to sit down and share their meal."

The gauntlet was down, and she wasn't going anywhere. "Kyle, I'm not sitting in judgment, but what if everybody in town decided to—"

"Then you take what you have and make it stretch. Isn't that the way it works with loaves and fishes?" He smiled and touched her hair. "You're a nice lady, Ms. Boyer, but you're such a stickler."

"I like to stay on track. Or nearly on track." He brushed her chin with the backs of his fingers. "I like to be within shouting distance of the track, how's that?"

"Close enough." His hand went to her shoulder, which he kneaded, loosening the muscle. "We like it that you're such good hosts. But just remember, when there's food, everybody shares it together. Where we come from, it's supposed to be that way."

"It takes a lot of work." His touch made her soften her tone. "Lots of working hands to feed so many—" at the word, he took her hand in his "—people."

"Don't get me wrong," he said quietly. He brought her fingertips to his lips, kissed them, then smiled into her astonished eyes. "These hands do good things. Fine things. Come a little closer."

"You said close enough," she reminded him.

"So close, but still so far away. Go all the way with us, Cynthia."

"You *know* how that sounds, Mr. Bear Soldier."

"Of course, I do." Still holding her hand, he led her toward the door, urging, "Fill your belly with us, Cynthia."

"This is a little heavy for cowboy poetry."

"It's Indian philosophy."

"Or humor."

"One and the same." He gave her hand a quick squeeze as they headed down the school corridor. "Suit yourself. Put the food on the table and watch us eat if that's what amuses you. What you see and what *is* are not necessarily the same thing."

LINDA KOPP PUT Cynthia to work on the serving line. Since Kyle was not one of the volunteers, they had parted company at the door, and he waited outside with the guests. She was learning to dish up the food fast and furiously, but she kept glancing up, eager to see him in the line. *Eager* for the man she'd come to care for to show up for a charity-sponsored meal.

Eager to see his face, she realized, anytime, anywhere.

Finally he appeared, standing in line behind the tall man she remembered from the last time. The line moved quickly. Kyle was greeted by several of his students. He shared a laugh with the woman behind him, and Cynthia found herself wondering what *that* was about.

"Hey." The tall man gave her a deadpan stare from behind his taped glasses. "Do your gloves have holes in them?"

Cynthia glanced at Kyle, then smiled as she dished up the coleslaw. "Two great big ones."

"Good. Smart woman."

"It takes a smart woman to put on a feed like this," Kyle said. The remark surprised her, and she wasn't sure how to take it. She was a volunteer, yes, but not a benefactor.

"Hey, you're my teacher," a small voice said. One of the second graders peeked out from behind her mother and waved at Cynthia.

"Hi, Jenny."

"Is there seconds on the lasagna *without* the coleslaw?" Jenny asked.

Cynthia nodded as she watched Kyle accept a tray from the server at the end. *When there's food, everybody eats.* And there was plenty of food. Volunteers and guests were just people, and people needed to eat.

Cynthia started to fill a tray for herself, but then thought better of it.

Instead, she stripped off her gloves and let the last two people behind the table fill it for her. She thanked them and took the tray from their gloved hands with her bare ones.

"May I join you?" It pleased Cynthia to see that she'd taken Kyle and his friends by surprise. "Or are we seated by gender here?"

Kyle laughed as he pushed the empty chair away from the table. "First they quit walking five paces behind us, then they want to sit on the men's side and eat their food. We're losing our traditional place, you guys."

"Earlier this evening Mr. Bear Soldier treated me to a bit of 'Indian philosophy,' which included an invitation to 'fill my belly.'" She ignored the appreciative glances and sly chuckles exchanged among the five men at the table. "I believe those were the words. He didn't tell me about any seating rules."

"You have to watch yourself around Kyle," the heftiest man warned. "He has a smooth way with words."

"This is Tony Left Hand," Kyle said. "He's from my reservation. And this is Paul and Jim—"

"This guy's such a smooth talker," Tony told Cynthia, cutting in on the introductions. "He got them to name a town after him. Kyle, South Dakota."

"*I* was named for the *town*. That's where the car broke down just before my mom went into labor." Kyle joined in the laughter, and then gave Tony a nod. "You should've been there, man. We might've made it to the clinic."

"Or you could've broke down again in Porcupine," Paul chimed in.

Merry men, Cynthia thought. There was surely merriment in their dark eyes.

"Or Wounded Knee. They could've called you Wounded for short," Tony said, and they all nodded, chortling.

"He did mention something about being wounded." Cynthia had come this far, and she wanted in on the fun. "Was that for sympathy or for short?"

Kyle clapped his hand over his chest and managed a pained expression. "Whoa, she got me again." His act over, he gave his old friend a nod. "Tony's a damn good mechanic. He came here looking for work."

"Looking for someplace off the reservation where they pay in U.S. dollars, instead of trying to trade me their junk cars. I've got a yard full of junk cars and no cash income."

"Anybody who can get a rez-runner back on the road is a master mechanic," Kyle told him. "You ought to be in high demand here."

"Or get yourself some training in bodywork, man," came the suggestion from Jim, sitting across the table. "These Minnesota cars rust out in a hurry."

"I feel right at home," Kyle said. "More junk cars on the road in this city than in all the yards in Pine Ridge Reservation."

"You advertise your South Dakota cars here, you can make money. No rust on a South Dakota car. Doesn't matter about the engine." Tony turned to Cynthia. "You got a car, ma'am?"

"Yes, I do. It's true about the rust here, but good mechanics are hard to find, too. I have a tough time finding a full-service gas station anymore." She let pass the arched-brow looks the men exchanged. "Either way, I'm sure you'll find work, Tony."

Tony nodded. "This is good food. Did you make it?"

"No, I—"

"Hope you were wearing your gloves," Paul said. "Wouldn't want you to be spreading germs among the guests."

With a chuckle, Kyle touched her shoulder and leaned closer. "You oughta carry those gloves in your car, for times when you have to pump your own gas."

"Rugged guy," Tony scowled. "They get inspected by the Health Department here. They gotta use gloves." He turned to Cynthia, kindly assuring her, "A lady shouldn't have to pump her own gas."

Cynthia liked Tony.

But she liked Kyle, too, impossible as he was when he got into his ribbing routine. Just to prove it, she caught up to him before he made his exit with his friends. "Can I give you a ride home this time?"

He considered the idea. "Why don't you drop me off at the co-op? Delia wants me to help her move some furniture."

Cynthia went into the store with him to say hello and ended up helping to rearrange display cases. The remodeling was taking place bit by bit, as funds allowed, but the place was shaping up nicely, as the smell of fresh paint attested. Kyle took direction from Delia, contributing his muscle to each task. Between orders he played with Ronald, Delia's little boy.

"He's good with kids, isn't he?" Delia said, noting Cynthia's interest when Kyle was out of earshot.

"I know he has a way with the older ones. It's fun to watch him with one that age."

"Kyle's looked after my husband, Jamie, off and on ever since I can remember. He's been after Jamie to go to school for a long time, got him into a program here, and now—" Delia gave a quick nod as she added more men's rings to the tray she'd been arranging "—I think Jamie might just stick it out this time. Kyle didn't have much help when he went back to school. Just the G.I. Bill. Started out at Oglala Community College back on Pine Ridge and stuck with it until he became a teacher."

"He's surely the right man for the job."

"We need a lot more like him." She set the tray in the front of the display case. "Reservation life is hard on the men. There's not much for them to do. The land is poor. There's no jobs."

"What about the women?"

Delia shrugged. "For most of us, we put the first baby to breast and there's a purpose for us, pure and simple. We know we're needed then." She slid the glass door closed.

Cynthia folded her arms across her chest almost defensively as Delia moved along to the next display case. She handed Cynthia a box of silver bracelets, along with a velvet-covered stand upon which to arrange them.

"The old way, everybody played a part in raising every child," Delia continued. "The whole village was the family. But all that was taken away back when they started the reservations and put the children in boarding schools. The mission schools, the BIA schools . . ." She shook her head. "I went to boarding school. So did Jamie and Kyle. Our grandparents and our parents, they had no say in it, and we were taught nothing but white culture."

Pausing, Delia looked up at Cynthia, not for sympathy, but for understanding. "Our generation is trying to get back some of what was lost. Even here, in a city that's about as far from Pine Ridge, South Dakota, as you can get. It's hard to leave home, but there's work here, and maybe a market for some of the things we make."

"And there's a good school here," Cynthia added, hoping she might someday feel she'd contributed. "One that's part of the community."

"It's getting there. It's not easy, starting a new kind of school, and you can't build community pride overnight." Delia eyed Cynthia critically. "You can't wait for somebody else to do it for you, either. Somebody else isn't likely to see it through."

Cynthia studied the rows of silver rings in the case beneath her elbows. Some were excellent pieces, others less so. This was her field of expertise. In the classroom she had a lot to learn, but here she could easily take over and run the show. A few months ago, her first suggestion would have been to move the shop to another part of town. But no one had asked her, which was a good thing. She was finding easy answers harder to come by these days.

"Did Kyle tell you that I talked about quitting?"

"He said everybody's talked about quitting at one time or another."

"Sometimes I think I'm more of a liability than an asset."

"Are you gonna quit?" Delia challenged.

"Not this week." Cynthia lifted her chin and smiled. "Wait till you see the play, Delia. I think it's going to be wonderful."

"LET ME DRIVE you home, Kyle," Cynthia tried again when he walked her to her car.

"Let me drive *you*," he said. He would let her get close, but he wasn't ready to let her get *that* close. Not inside his front door . . . "Let me get behind the wheel and drive. I miss it," he claimed as he opened the passenger door for her. "I know a real nice spot I'd like to take you to."

Indian summer had warmed the last days of October, and although the night air was crisp and sometimes frosty, there hadn't yet been a hard freeze. The harvest moon rose over the small tranquil lake that Kyle had discovered on an excursion in the country months ago. He'd returned by bus, borrowed car, and on foot. Often when he'd needed time alone, he'd come here. Now he needed time with Cynthia, and he needed a place where no excuses or explanations were necessary.

"I sure like these ten thousand lakes," he told her cheerily as he parked the car at the end of a narrow, tree-lined dirt road. "Back home, we've got buttes. You take your girl up on top of a butte and show her the stars." He put his arm around her shoulders and drew her closer. "But there's something fundamentally sexy about water."

She slid easily across the leather seat, but not altogether willingly. Through her thin wool jacket he could feel the tension in her shoulders. "We could go to my place and have . . . coffee," she suggested with young-girl shyness.

He brushed her hair back from her temple and smiled. "Or we could stay right here and have . . . each other."

"Don't you like my place?"

"What's not to like?" He began kissing her softly, nuzzling her ear, nibbling her cheek. "I like your clothes. I like your place. I like your car." He thought "admired" would have been a better word, but he wanted her to relax while he moved deftly to the more personal. "I like your hair," he ventured as he took her face in his hands. "I *really* like your eyes."

But her lips became the object of his attention. He took several leisurely nibbles before fitting his mouth over hers, offering a gentle promise even as he hinted at the hotter demands he had in mind.

"I like your kiss," she acknowledged in a soft whisper.

"Plenty more where that came from." He slipped one button from its mooring on her jacket, and she hesitated on the verge of an objection, then slid her arms around his neck. He dispatched the second and final button. Just to make her more comfortable, he told himself as he kissed her once again.

Neither of them wanted to rush. They had found a quiet place where there was only the night sky and the moon's reflection in the lake. The time was theirs.

"I wasn't expecting anything like this when I came to All Nations," she said.

"Neither was I—" he kissed her forehead "—when I came to the city."

It was a toss-up as to who was really the visitor in whose world. He wanted her to take off her neat little jacket. She wanted him to stay longer than just a while. "I needed a change in my life," she told him honestly, "but I don't know about—"

"Shh. Nothing's going to happen. Nothing bad," he amended. "Nothing you don't want."

"I don't always want what's good for me."

The comment rankled. He fully intended to be good for her. He drew a deep breath and opened the car door. "Let's take a walk."

"Autumn chill," she said as she emerged from the car and folded her arms tightly beneath her breasts. The jacket that matched her slacks had been all she'd needed that morning. "I didn't come prepared."

"I did. I came prepared to walk home, if it comes to that." He took off his own jacket and draped it over her shoulders. "I'm prepared, Cynthia. Whenever you're ready."

They walked beneath a shadowy canopy of trees in transition. The night breeze rustled in the leaves still holding out overhead, while those that had fallen swished and crackled underfoot. Kyle had in mind a special copse of droopy willows, a particular view of the lake, an absolutely private spot. He would take the chill away, and he would do it in a natural, neutral place, a place where he owned as much of the world as she did.

He drew her by the hand, and he could feel the struggle between her hard-earned skepticism and her heartfelt willingness. "I want to be with you here in the grass." He swept the willow curtain aside and took her down with him onto a bed of leaves. "Before all the green is gone," he told her. "Before winter comes."

Wrapped in his jacket, she gave herself over to the cradle he made for her in his arms. "Oh, Kyle, this is crazy. We're out here in the middle of—"

"One lake in ten thousand. There's nothing separating us here, no . . ." He heard the catch in her breath when he slipped his hand inside her open jacket. "Just let me touch you, Cynthia."

His hand sneaked into her blouse. He made her shiver when he touched cold fingers to her warm breast. It took no more than that to bead her nipples. He smiled against her lips. "I'll keep the cold away from your body, but you have to warm my fingers."

"Oh, Kyle, that feels . . . absolutely . . . crazy."

He thought of her as a fragile stringed instrument, and he played upon her until she rewarded him with a soft musical moan. "Let yourself go, and I'll make it crazier."

"You'll make *me* crazy," she whispered.

"I promise."

And he kept his word. Her pleasure grew at the touch of his lips and his hand. He kept their clothing close about them even as he moved it aside for intimate touching and kissing and pressing together, flesh upon flesh. They kept their backs to the cold as they made their own heat and kept it trapped between them, cherishing it as they cherished the feel of one another. He pleasured her, and when it came time, he protected her. It was a simple gesture, performed without discussion, executed out of care and respect, and it made her heart soar. She welcomed him deep inside her, as though she were taking him home. She gave him pleasure.

LATER THEY CUDDLED together, his back braced against the trunk of the tree, hers against him. She sat between his thighs. He was wearing his jacket now, with her tucked snugly into the front of it. The lake was as smooth as glass, and Cynthia felt so lighthearted and light-headed that she was sure she could skip across to the other side without getting wet. But she would have to stir from her comfortable spot, which she was not the least bit inclined to do.

Such buoyance freed her to say whatever was on her mind, whatever popped into her head. And because he had taken such care with her, she trusted him with one of her formerly weighty thoughts, now simply a wistful wondering.

"Do you think I'm getting too old to have a baby?"

He laid his cheek against her hair. "I didn't catch the numbers."

"I'm thirty-two."

"If you're getting too old, then it's way too late for me." His lips brushed her temple. "I did right by you, honey. I said there'd be nothing separating us, but I didn't mean . . ."

"I know. That statement is covered under your cowboy poet's license." She turned her face toward his pleasant nuzzling. "You did right by me in more ways than one." He smiled and kissed her. "Now it's your turn to reveal numbers."

"I'm an old man. Thirty-five."

"And you don't have any children, old man?"

"No wife," he said matter-of-factly. "No kids. At least, none that anybody's told me about. I can't say I didn't sow a few wild oats, and I can't say I've always done right." His voice sounded hushed, as though in the quiet of the night their leafy bower had become a confessional. "All I can say is that I'm doing better. Almost got married once, but it didn't work out. She got a better offer."

"That's hard to believe. Like Kevin Costner saying he couldn't get a date when he was in high school."

"Whoa, that's a pretty lofty comparison. Question is, would I be a good catch for somebody like Cynthia Boyer?"

"Cynthia Boyer learned a lesson about getting caught in her own net. I don't want any more 'good catches.'"

"Damn," he said, chuckling. "You should've met me ten years ago. I was a bad catch then. Hell on wheels."

"I don't think I want a bad catch, either. I want the freedom to do something with my own life. Something that might make a difference."

It pleased her to be able to say these things to someone who actually cared to listen. That the *someone* was a man seemed a rarity too precious for any woman to reject. "What did you offer this woman?" she wondered aloud. "Was it hell on wheels?"

"I was in college by then, and I'd pretty much quit raisin' hell. I wanted something else, too." He moved his arms a bit higher around her shoulders, drawing her closer. "I offered her what I had. Myself in the raw-material stage and a few possibilities."

"I like what you've done with the raw material." And what he'd done with the neatly finished fabric that was Cynthia. "You're a person who makes a difference, Kyle."

"Have I made a difference to you?"

"Oh, yes. A memorable difference."

"There are a few differences I'd like to forget." She turned, and he cupped her cheek in his strong hand. "Differences between us, besides you being a woman and me being a man."

"Right now I can't think of any others that matter."

He stroked her tapered eyebrow with his thumb and smiled. "Right now neither can I."

Chapter Six

THE PLAY WAS postponed twice. On parents' night, Cynthia deemed the troupe and their masks "not ready for prime time," which was just as well, since only a handful of parents showed up. On the alternate night, four key players had strep throat. A second parents' night was scheduled by a hastily formed "All Nations Alliance." Members, including parents, teachers and students, handed out flyers door-to-door, inviting people to attend the school function.

The words "Celebration and Feed" at the top of the paper helped to bring out the crowd on the Wednesday before Thanksgiving. Despite the gray clouds that filled the skies and the quarter-size snowflakes that had been falling since late afternoon, the people came. The early comers pleased Cynthia. She was glad when more came. But when they kept coming, she began to worry.

They filled all the seats in the gym. They filled the extra folding chairs that were rounded up to accommodate the overflow. She was afraid there would not be enough room, that some would be without a place to sit and would have to stand. Then they might leave. Or they might stay and keep milling around, and then what? She had to seat the older people. No, she had to seat the small children, whose pre-show antics in the middle of the gym floor threatened to ruin everything.

When show time came and went and still neither the audience nor the players were in place, she fretted over that, too. But Kyle assured her the show would go on when the people were ready. "That's Indian time," he reminded her with a cavalier wink. "Indian time" made Cynthia all the more nervous.

She needn't have been. Kyle had assigned the narrator's role to Marvin Gates, a small boy with a big voice. When Marvin stepped up to the microphone to announce the players' names, they all appeared on cue. The colorful masks with their pointed ears, massive muzzles, and brightly shining human eyes drew murmurs of approval as each was introduced.

It was all out of her hands now. Bertram, the effusive fly, was overacting to beat the band, and if Tom Gorneau decided to upstage him with an unscripted swat, there was not a thing Cynthia could do to prevent it. She didn't have to look away from the action to know it was Kyle's shoulder touching hers, his hand enveloping hers, and his smile mirroring the one she wore.

"Your hand's cold." He put it between both of his and gave it a brisk rub. "Nervous?"

"I'm a wreck." She smiled brightly. "But aren't they wonderful?"

"This is definitely one of their finer moments," he agreed, returning her smile. An onlooker might have mistaken them for the proud parents of the entire fifth grade. Recalling Delia's comment about having a purpose, it occurred to her that without putting these children to breast, she had done some nurturing. And there was plenty more where that came from, she decided.

Cake and sandwiches were served in the windowless gym. The children were wound up over the success of their performance and the excitement of the season's first snowfall. As people began to leave, word drifted back that "it was really piling up out there." Kyle offered to take care of the costumes and cleanup if Cynthia wanted to get on the road, but now that they'd finally pulled off the event, she wasn't about to miss any part of the fun.

After the last of the cake had been served and the masks had been placed in the hallway display case, both Cynthia and Kyle were surprised to find at least eight inches of snow on the ground. There was a holiday atmosphere in the parking lot and the street beyond, where streetlights cast an opalescent glow over blanketed cars and stoplights and porch railings. Eight inches wasn't *that* much snow for Minnesota. The sound of spinning tires was nearly drowned out by the shrieks of children getting pelted with the season's first snowballs.

Kyle turned his collar up to his ears as they stood together on the doorstep. Somebody had shoveled a path to the street, but that was filling up fast. He shook his head. "You shouldn't try it."

"Everyone else is headed home."

"Everyone else *is* home, or close to it."

"It can't be too bad once you get going. It hasn't been snowing that long." She buttoned her long white coat and smiled up at him. "I really think we do good work together, Mr. Bear Soldier."

She was wearing low-heeled shoes, and it occurred to him that he'd never seen her without an umbrella when it rained or without sunglasses on a bright day. She always seemed to pull out the proper accessory at the proper time. "So where're your boots?"

"Where's your cap with the earflaps?" she countered with a laugh.

But Kyle wasn't laughing. "I could drive you home."

"I'm as good a driver as you are," she claimed brightly as she slipped her hand into an unlined leather glove.

"But are you as good at shoveling?"

Cynthia's smile dimmed. They stood there staring at one another while the snow sifted down around them. I'm good at many things, she thought. Just ask me. She knew if she accepted his offer, it would be a one-way trip. And he knew it, too. The thought of being snowed in with him for the holiday was delicious.

But his place was more accessible, and he had never invited her there. For some reason the idea of taking her home with him made him uncomfortable. His offer was gallant, but he had reservations about opening his own doors, reservations that might be a prelude to second thoughts. And experience had taught her that second thoughts in a man's brain had a way of cutting off the blood flow to his big feet.

"Independence becomes me, I think." She smiled bravely as she began picking her way down the shoveled path. "These days I can pump gas and shovel snow with the best of them."

"I guess you're on your own, then." He caught up to her in time to lend a hand when she started to slip. "Do you have a shovel along?"

"I'll be fine. I'm a native Minnesotan, you know. Tough as—"

"You could stay . . ." She slowed her steps, and he did, too. His voice trailed off, and again they searched each other's eyes. Snowflakes salted his black hair. One settled on her right eyelash.

She blinked it away. "My mother's coming for dinner tomorrow. I have those fish to feed, and I have . . ." Her car was only two steps away, whereas his unfinished suggestion had drifted well into the distance. "I have to get back. My car's really good on snow, so I'll be just—"

"Better get going, then."

He stood there stubbornly while she started the car, turned on the heat, the defroster, the defogger and emerged with scraper in hand.

He relieved her of the tool and brusquely ordered her back into the car. He cleared the back window, then moved around the car, reaching her side last. She rolled the window down to thank him.

"I don't think your mother's gonna make it tomorrow," he said gruffly.

"Oh, you'd be amazed. She does what she sets her mind to."

"Yeah, well, good luck following in her footsteps. Or tire tracks, or whatever." He shook the snow off her scraper and handed it back to her. "You'll need this."

He stood in the parking lot and watched her make the turn into the street. She waved, letting him know everything was fine. He didn't wave back.

She got stuck before she reached the first intersection. The school janitor, who was on his way home, stopped to help her. One good push and she was on her way again, but the second rut she plowed into had her socked in tight. The windshield wipers were losing the battle for visibility, and she resigned herself to the fact that she would have to open the door and plant her sensible shoes in excessive snow.

Suddenly the door handle was torn from her hand. She gasped as she made a useless grab for it, but it swung out of reach. Kyle's angry face appeared in its place, his head bare, his ears red and his shoulders hunched against the wind.

"Move over."

"Kyle, you can't—"

"I won't be in the way when Mother comes for dinner," he barked as he took the seat she quickly vacated. "*If* she shows up. I'll find a way to get back."

"You don't really think that would bother me, do you? For her to—"

He ignored her anxious tone. "I don't really think I can drive this crate any better than you can, but I don't want you getting stuck by yourself."

"Thank you for the concern. I'm just wondering why—"

"About the other—" he put the car in reverse and glanced in the rearview mirror "—I don't really give a damn what bothers you."

"I see." Which was more than he could say, since, like the windshield wipers, the defogger was losing ground.

He tried a forward-reverse rocking maneuver, buried the car to the top of its wheel housings, pounded a fist on the steering wheel and muttered a colorful expletive. Still muttering, he got out and dug the front wheels out. With a couple of shouted instructions and a lot more muttering, he pushed while she manned the controls.

"We'll be doing this all night," he called finally. "You're coming home with me."

"All right."

They eyed one another for a moment. Her face was a study in artlessness, which deep down he couldn't quite buy. She knew where he lived, and damn his hide, he *would* care if it bothered her.

By white society's standards, his two-bedroom walkup housed too many people, and he'd already had some trouble with his landlord over it. But his brother's family needed a place to stay. It was as simple as that. Jamie and Delia slept in one room with the baby. The three girls shared the other bedroom. Kyle had the sofa, and the two boys camped out on the living-room floor. The arrangements were only temporary—at least, that was the plan—but when Kyle led Cynthia in the front door he wished he'd at least moved the bed pillows out of the living room that morning.

For announcing guests, the kids were as good as having a doorman.

"Kyle brought somebody over!"

"Ms. Boyer!"

"Mom, my art teacher's here!"

"Your art teacher? Cynthia?" Delia emerged from the bedroom carrying little Ronald on her hip. "Can't get your car going?"

"She got it going, then got it stuck." Kyle handed their coats to Carla, who stared as though Cynthia had just been beamed down from the starship *Enterprise*.

"I should have left earlier, but *I* didn't want to miss out on anything." Cynthia took off her wet shoes and set them near the door. "Now I guess you're stuck with me until this lets up."

"According to the revised forecast—revised from 'chance of flurries' to 'no chance of travel'—nobody's going anywhere tonight," reported thirteen-year-old Arlin, whose eyes were glued to the little television set in the corner of the room.

"Did everybody make it home?" Kyle asked as he took a quick survey of all the faces. "Let's see, Tanya, Markie, Susie . . ."

Brother Jamie appeared behind Delia in the bedroom doorway. "We're all here, Sergeant." The resemblance between brothers was especially evident in the teasing grin that brightened Jamie's eyes. "No need to send out a search party. I got all the way across town to find my class had been canceled, so I had to hike all the way back. The buses quit running."

He turned his smile on Cynthia. "Is this the pretty blue-eyed one I've been hearing about?" Cynthia looked at Kyle, who raised a warning finger at his brother. "From the kids, I mean," Jamie clarified, palms raised in ready defense. "The new teacher, right? To hear everybody tell it, there's only one."

Cynthia introduced herself, extending her hand to Kyle's smirking brother.

"Well, I don't know about you guys, but all I got to eat tonight was one little piece of cake," Kyle said as he headed for the kitchen. "I'm making soup surprise. That means, whatever's in the cupboard added to what's left in the refrigerator."

"I've already started some," Delia said.

Since the TV was blaring and all available seating in the living room was full of kids, Cynthia followed. She remembered being snowed in at her grandmother's at Christmastime one year. She had been the only child there, besides her cousin Alex, who was always a brat. He took away anything she found to amuse herself with, be it pencil or book, claiming he'd "had it first." Grandmother's house, big as it was, had not been big enough for the two of them.

Kyle's kitchen, small as it was, accommodated all cooks. The old saying about too many cooks spoiling the broth—which was as far as Delia had gotten—didn't apply as people came and went to "see how things were coming."

Jamie peeled the potatoes, but when he was handed an onion, he relinquished the knife. "You'll have me cry, cry, cryyyyin' all night long," he crooned.

Cynthia saw the chance to make some points, and she moved in on the onion, even though Kyle assured her that she was a guest tonight and not a volunteer.

"Can't I be both?"

He'd been angry with her a little while ago. Since they'd walked into the apartment, even though his anger had dissipated, his eyes had glanced past hers more than once. Now, with her hands full of onion and his resting on the shoulders of one of the little girls, their eyes met.

She smiled, "I want to be both."

He nodded, and as he smiled the tension drained visibly from his shoulders. He gave the child a quick pat. "Can you find enough bowls for us, Tanya?"

Six-year-old Tanya deftly negotiated the jungle of adult legs, while Kyle took over in front of the simmering kettle. "Let me test it out here. Where's the spoon?"

"I can add another can of tomatoes," Delia said.

"Pepper," Kyle judged. "Come taste this, Cynthia."

Cynthia cocked her hip to one side to allow Tanya's older sister, Susie, access to the utensil drawer. A handful of spoons clanked on the counter next to Cynthia's pile of chopped onions as Susie rummaged around for more. Cynthia picked one up and took it with her to the stove, where Kyle was waiting with her taste already dipped out.

"This is the sharing spoon." He blew into the big serving spoon to cool the soup before he fed it to her. "Everybody gets a taste and everybody has a say." He didn't give her much time to consider. "Pepper, right?"

She pressed her lips together, assessing the flavor from start to finish. "I always add vinegar, too."

"Vinegar!" he called out to Delia, whose head was buried in another cupboard.

"And sugar."

"Sugar?"

"Just a little." Cynthia showed him a half inch of space between finger and thumb. "It brings out the flavor."

"I've got nothing against sugar," he said, reaching for a plastic bowl. He added a pinch and gave her a wink. "You know that."

"Now taste." It was her turn to dip, blow and hold the spoon while he sipped. He licked his lips, then smiled as he took the spoon from her hand and fed her another sample. She nodded. "It's getting there."

Custom dictated that the children be fed in the kitchen, while the adults would take their soup to the living room. While Delia and Jamie added a leaf to the table, pushing the edges close to the walls, the boys moved two chairs in from the living room. Cynthia joined Kyle in the living room for a brief moment of semi-privacy.

"Are you sure there's room for me tonight?" she asked as she stretched her shoulders and used both hands to iron the day's kinks out of her lower back.

He gave her a guarded look. "What kind of room do you need?"

"Just a chair, or a little—" she measured a square foot of air with her hands "—place to put my head down."

"Next to mine would be good," he whispered, and she feigned shock. "A guy can dream, can't he?" Smiling softly, he slipped one hand behind her and gave her a soothing back rub. "We have plenty of room for you. I just hope you're not too fussy about . . ."

"I thought you didn't care what bothered me."

"I do." He glanced at the rest of his family, still jockeying for space at the kitchen table. "They'll be able to get a place of their own soon, but right now they need a place to stay, and it's kinda crowded, but . . ."

Cynthia put her arms around his waist and gave him a hard squeeze. Then she surprised herself by kissing his cheek, right there in front of everyone. "Thanks for taking me in tonight."

He ignored the giggling and shushing that was going on in the kitchen. "Any time."

"I won't take up much space."

"Take all you want. What's mine is yours." He was still rubbing her back, running his fingertips up and down her spine as though they'd been together a long time and he knew exactly what she needed just now. "I'll move the kids around, and you can bunk in with the girls."

As the snow piled up outside, Kyle's family regaled her with stories that had clearly been part of the entertainment on other nights, since even the young ones had an occasional punch line. Kyle was the star of many of the family tales, and everyone seemed to enjoy telling on him for Cynthia's benefit. She heard about the time the sorrel horse flopped him in the manure pile and the time the ghost his brothers had seen in the yard turned out to be Kyle draped in the bedsheets he'd just taken off the clothesline.

Following each story he gave her a secret look that said, *Don't take it too seriously.*

She returned a merry smile that said, *I believe every word.*

The laughter was part of the storytelling rhythm, and the storyteller's hands animated each incident. Meanwhile, the television droned in the background, and children crawled from one lap to another. During a lull, Kyle stepped over one wrestling match and one sleeping child on his way to the kitchen, where he made popcorn in the iron skillet. It was like a big slumber party, Cynthia thought, and nobody spoiled it by announcing bedtime.

But there was a winding-down as quiet settled in over contentment. Those who had fallen asleep were either moved to another spot or just covered up with a blanket. The girls' room had twin beds, and Carla insisted that Cynthia get one all to herself. She accepted little Tanya's offer of her special pink blanket, turned off the lamp, moved close to the wall and waited. Springs creaked in the dark. She lifted the edge of the blanket, and Tanya scrambled in next to her.

Then came Carla's harsh whisper, a little-mother warning. "Tan-yaa . . ."

"It's okay," Cynthia said, smiling happily in the dark. "This is the sharing blanket."

SHE AWOKE THE next morning to the smell of coffee. Eager for the taste of morning and for a daylight look at what the skies had delivered overnight, she slid down to the foot of the bed, slipped into her clothes, and followed the aroma. Toes and cowlicks peeked out from under the blankets on the living-room floor. The two boys were still asleep, but the pillow on the sofa had been abandoned.

Cynthia put in a call to her mother, wished her a happy snow-bound Thanksgiving, and promised to celebrate with her over the weekend. Then she helped herself to a cup of coffee and took it outside to the porch, where she had a hunch she would find Kyle.

He'd draped his shoulders with a striped blanket and stood holding his own steaming mug of coffee, looking in amazement at the way the snow had filled up the small fenced-in box that was the front yard. Turning at the sound of her footsteps, he shook his head in mock disapproval. "Where's your coat, young lady?"

"Your niece let me share *her* blanket last night."

"And I lay awake half the night wishing you were sharing mine." He opened it now, and she stepped inside, fitting her shoulders into the shelter of his arm. "I've never seen this street so still," he said. "So quiet. It's almost like back home."

"It'll take some time to get things moving again." She sipped her coffee, savoring the rich flavor and the warmth of the rising steam. "How much did we get?"

"Almost two feet."

"How much did they get in South Dakota?"

His smile acknowledged his habit of taking note of the weather report for his home state. "The storm went around them, as usual."

"Ah, we're talking Camelot, then."

He chuckled. "When I first moved here, I met a guy—a white guy I used to know when I was in the army. Told him I'd gone back to school and become a teacher. He introduced me around as someone who'd 'come a long way.'" He glanced up at the snow-laden branches of the big sugar maple that stood in the front yard. "To him that meant I'd come up in the world. To me it meant I had traveled over a long distance. That was my first thought. It's a long way back to Pine Ridge."

"You've done both, haven't you?"

It took him a moment to answer. "We see things a little differently, your people and mine. Ordinarily I'm inclined to shrug it off, but with you . . ."

He studied the coffee that was left in his mug. Half a cup. "I know what your place is like. It's like *up* in the world," he said quietly. "And I wasn't anxious to bring you here because I didn't want you to think—" their eyes met over the coffee he'd made and the doubts he'd been unable to dismiss "—less of me, I guess."

"Less than what?"

"I don't know." There was a teasing glimmer in his eyes. "Less than you thought the first time we met?"

"I wasn't the same person then that I am now. I hadn't tasted from the sharing spoon."

"What? You mean if you were making a pot of soup in your house, you'd all taste from different spoons?" He laughed and squeezed her shoulder. "You must like to wash dishes."

"You know what I thought the first time I saw you at the church feed?" He had a ready answer, but she hugged him around the middle and cut him off.

"No, you don't, because I've never told you. The first thought that came to my mind—" she gave him a sober look "—automatically, before it occurred to me that you had some nerve putting in all those orders for coffee and sugar, what I thought might roughly translate into—" ah, she could tell by his eyes, she had him cold "—this man could probably charm an Ojibwa rabbit into a Lakota kettle."

Kyle's eyes lit up like fireflies. Then he grinned naughtily. "Easy."

Chapter Seven

"THERE'S A BUNCH of turkeys in the kitchen at the church," Kyle reported to the snowbound cardplayers as he hung up the phone. The game of hearts had gotten started over morning coffee, and now it continued through the parade of children marching back and forth between the kitchen and living room, cereal bowls in hand.

"A new street gang raiding the cupboards?" Jamie drew a few chuckles as he trumped the trick on the kitchen table. "Or are we talking real turkey here?"

"I'm talking edible turkeys, the kind we've just been talking about and wishing we had in the refrigerator."

"I was going to buy one yesterday," Delia said for the third time, "after I checked in the Phillips Village newsletter and said to myself, What? No turkey bingo here?"

"That can be your next project," her husband told her, then grimaced when she played a card. "Eee, this one. We're supposed to be partners, and she's thumping her trump over *my* trump."

"Sometimes your trump needs thumping." Kyle tapped his brother's shoulder with a playful fist while he took a peek at Cynthia's hand. He'd turned his seat over to Carla, whom he'd trained as a hearts partner. He didn't know how Delia and Jamie had managed to make so many babies when they couldn't get it together on a game of cards.

"It's not snowing in New York," Susie announced as she passed by in search of more cereal. "But the wind is picking up, and it looked like the gigantic Miss Piggy balloon *almost* took off."

"You'll thump my trump when pigs fly, brother," Jamie said with a laugh as he swept the cards off the table. "And 'almosts' don't count."

"We have a turkey crisis to consider," Kyle reminded the foursome. "It's Thanksgiving, and we've got no turkey, and the church has a whole flock of birds, all thawed out and waiting to be cooked. But they've got no cooks." Cynthia looked up at him, then Delia. "The cooks can't get over here. The teams that were scheduled are from way out in the suburbs."

"Will there be people showing up for dinner in this weather?" Cynthia asked.

"Will the people show up for dinner?" Kyle repeated slowly as he moved behind her, resting his hands on her shoulders. "We have here a woman who has seen but does not yet believe."

"If you cook it, they will come," Delia said solemnly. Carla giggled. Cynthia shrugged. "Then we'll cook it."

As he spoke, Kyle massaged. "I like your spirit, Pilgrim. Trouble is, the padre says we'll have to round up the mashed potatoes and corn and pumpkin pie." Cynthia was getting into the massage, and Jamie was getting a peek at her hand. "The volunteers were bringing that stuff, so all there is now is turkey."

"We'll go to the store." She tipped her head back against his stomach and smiled up at him.

Carla groaned and threw in her hand in utter adolescent disgust as Kyle returned the smile, along with a question. "You got a team of sled dogs handy?"

"Mary White Eagle has a four-wheel drive," Delia said as she added her cards to Carla's. "We'll do it the way we do at home. We'll round up donations."

"How far away is the church?" Cynthia asked.

"About six blocks," Kyle told her. "We'll have to hoof it."

Cynthia shifted in her chair, stuck her legs out to her side and looked at her feet. She was wearing a thick pair of Kyle's socks.

"I've got boots you can wear, Ms. Boyer. I can wear my high-tops," Carla said.

It pleased Cynthia to realize that the children had gotten the hang of calling her "Ms.," even though it probably sounded funny to them. It was beginning to sound funny to her, too. "Call me Cynthia."

Carla gave her uncle a knowing look. "Probably be callin' you 'Auntie' pretty soon."

THE FIRST CHALLENGE came in breaking a trail through the city snow. In the course of six blocks much of the sidewalk was still covered with snow, although many people were working their shovels in that direction. Lola Johnson, one of the neighborhood's black elders, agreed to watch baby Ronald in return for some help with the chore. Arlin and Markie stayed behind in trade.

At the church, an anxious young curate, Father Preston, greeted them gratefully. He said that while the word of the need for local effort was getting out, only a few helping hands had made their way to the massive old brick landmark that was St. Jude's.

"No one expected all this snow." Father Preston gestured dramatically as he bustled ahead of the small group on the way to the kitchen. "So, of course, the turkeys were thawed out. It would be a *sin* to waste all that food." He chuckled. "So to speak."

An elderly nun and three of the church's closest neighbors were visibly relieved when they saw that help had arrived. "We're tired after just unloading the coolers," one woman said. "But if we don't get them started, these things won't be done before Sunday."

"Cynthia is on the official volunteer schedule," Kyle announced. "She knows just what to do."

Cynthia failed to take the bait. She was too busy taking account of the birds, still in their packages. "I've never seen such big turkeys." She took a slow turn around a steam table that was piled high. "I've also never seen this *many* turkeys—" a plastic-covered breast yielded beneath the pressure of her forefinger "—thawed out, all at once."

"Next she's gonna tell us she's never *cooked* a turkey," Delia predicted with a smile.

Kyle laid a hand on Cynthia's shoulder and recited with mock solemnity, "But when the guests arrive, she'll be happy to pour."

"In your ear, Mr. B.S." Cynthia's comeback gained her several appreciative snickers, along with Jamie's unrestrained hoot. "I certainly know how to cook *a* turkey."

"All you have to do is cook *a* turkey." Kyle gave her a conciliatory pat on the back. "Times twenty."

But there were plenty of hands to help with the preparations, and they were hands of all races. They were the face of all nations, too. They came by twos and threes, bringing sacks of potatoes and flour, cans of fruits and vegetables. Up to her elbows in giblets, Cynthia was awed by the increasing stockpile. She decided not to worry about what kind of a mixture all these foods would make. It would be a neighborly blend.

Carla and two of her pals took charge of the ever-present little ones in the dining hall. In the kitchen, few of the helpers needed directions, other than where to find the right pot or spoon. Since it would have taken too long to cook stuffed turkeys, the bread stuffing—which was a recipe never to be duplicated, since no one was measuring—was prepared on the side. And since pumpkin pie was out of the question, a team of women set about making traditional Indian frybread, while another group improvised a fruit compote.

Mary White Eagle was a large woman with an imposing voice, and when she appeared at the top of the steps and announced that she had rounded up several four-wheel drive vehicles, all heads turned. Mary was dressed like a cossack. She was used to giving orders.

"I've got three four-by-fours outside and two more stuck somewhere between here and Franklin Avenue. This was your idea, Kyle Bear Soldier." She tossed him a ring of keys. "Blue Suburban. Start hauling the old folks in."

And so the feast was prepared, and the people came. As always, they came in all age groups, all shapes, sizes, and colors. The elders and the children were fed first. Some of the people came to be served. Others took their meal, then spelled those who had been working in the kitchen.

Cynthia was happily exhausted by the time Kyle made her sit down with her own tray. He said it was time she met some people, and he introduced her to the editor of the neighborhood newsletter, the chairman of the neighborhood safety committee, and the head of the neighborhood-renewal task force.

These were people Cynthia had read about or had seen in television interviews. But she never would have met them, really met them, had she not come to work at All Nations. These were the community leaders who had led the fight to close down a liquor store near the school, who had objected to the plan for locating a city garbage-transfer station in their neighborhood, and who organized property cleanups and street patrols. They were the people who were making a difference. They welcomed her to their table simply because she was willing to come. She was willing to share. She wanted to be part of it all.

And from people she had once presumed to be stoic, she was learning a lot about the nature of humor and the benefits of laughter.

"Did you hear the one about the boy whose mother was Chippewa and his dad was Sioux?" Anna Martinez, the newsletter editor, asked. "Went out hunting, took along a dog. Out on the flat he saw a rabbit." She pointed toward the far wall. "Dog took after it. Boy didn't know which one to shoot."

Everyone laughed—except Cynthia. Wide-eyed and perfectly innocent, she said, "What did he decide?" Kyle groaned as she lifted a hand for truce. "No, wait, I can figure this out. Just tell me, was his mother cooking that night, or his dad?"

Now *everyone* laughed.

"Okay, time out," Cynthia pleaded. "Now, explain to me why you guys give each other such a hard time over rabbits and dogs."

"The Chippewa like to take credit for chasing the Sioux out of the woods and pushing them onto the prairie," Anna explained. Cynthia wondered which side Anna might be on, then decided it didn't matter.

"But the way the Sioux remember it," Kyle said, "it was a much more powerful tribe that had us on the run." He paused for effect. "It was the north-woods mosquito people," he said, garnering a round of chuckles. "Anyway, they were rabbit-chokers, according to us, and we were dog-eaters, according to them."

"So you're traditional enemies," Cynthia concluded. "And you're able to laugh about it. Meanwhile, you can probably find ancient enemies still killing each other at any given time somewhere in the world for reasons that probably don't matter anymore."

"Maybe it started out when somebody served up the wrong kind of meat to his guests." Kyle pushed his empty tray back a little. "And while they were fighting over it, maybe somebody else came along and pulled the rug out from under them both."

"Maybe," Cynthia allowed.

"Sooner or later, you have to pull together," Kyle said. "Can't say we don't get into it sometimes, even now. You oughta go to an intertribal basketball tournament if you wanna see traditional enemies battle it out." Murmurs of agreement drifted around the table. With a nod, Kyle raised an admonishing finger. "You Pilgrims were lucky you met up with our relations on the East Coast, instead of any of us. Otherwise the traditional Thanksgiving spread would have looked a lot different."

"When the Pilgrim shall come to dinner, the rabbit shall lie down with the dog." Cynthia smiled, making a mental note to submit her new saying to a greeting-card company. She speared a piece of dark meat, studied it, then giggled. "And the turkey shall wish he had long ears and a wagging tail."

"Ow-owww," came the response from one of the men, and the laughter flowed freely.

IT WAS WELL PAST nightfall by the time everything was cleaned up and put away. The rest of the family had gone home, but Kyle and Cynthia waited to stroll back at their leisure—alone. The streets were snow-bright, and the traffic, both automotive and pedestrian, was sparse. The dominant sound was that of a backup beeper on a snowplow that was probably a block away.

"That was the best Thanksgiving meal I've ever had," Cynthia declared. "I've never worked or laughed so hard."

"That reminds me—" Kyle put his arm around her shoulders and gave several playful squeezes as they shambled along the narrowly shoveled path "—where do you get off, calling me Mr. B.S.?"

"I couldn't help it." She glanced up, offering her sweetest smile. "It just came to me. Sprang to my lips and I couldn't hold it back."

"I like to hear you laugh," he said.

"I like your crazy sense of humor." She slid her arm around his waist. "And I enjoyed meeting people tonight. Some very well-known local people, people I've read about."

"Whether they're famous or notorious depends upon your point of view."

"I was glad to meet them. It was a good time, and a good place. And I thought about something Delia said." Their eyes met, and his were expectant. "Something I'm only beginning to understand. That it takes a whole community to raise a child."

"It used to work that way." He shrugged as they came to a stop at a quiet street corner. "I don't know. The community's getting to be a pretty big place."

"And you've let a lot of pilgrims in."

"They just sorta showed up, and you know how it is." He took both her hands in his, and she looked into his eyes, waiting to be told how it was. "When there's food, everybody eats."

"From the sharing spoon."

"You guys have a sharing cup, don't you?" The light turned red as she nodded. "That works, too," he said.

There was no traffic. There was no reason not to cross the street, except that they were mutually stunned by each other's eyes.

"The main arteries are open now."

"I really need to get home," she said softly.

"After all, you've got those tropical fish," he reminded her. "I wouldn't mind digging your car out and driving you home. 'Course, then you'd have to drive me back, and then I'd be worried about you going in the ditch, so I'd have to drive you back again . . ." He tipped his head from side to side, suggesting a perpetual motion.

"Let's just do it once."

He grinned slowly. "Just once?"

"One trip." The light turned green and she hopped off the curb, towing him along. "Then I'll make us a cup of coffee—"

"Just *one?*"

"—and we'll share." She tossed her hair as she turned, smiling, feeling light-hearted as a child. "We'll keep the cup brim-full. Bottomless. Runneth-ing over. And we'll keep on sharing."

The Wolf and the Lamb

Prologue

ON THE THIRTEENTH of June in 1879, the day she reached the matronly age of thirty, Miss Emily Lambert received a wondrous birthday gift. The widower Charles Tanninger, who owned house, land, and livestock in the far West and with whom she had corresponded briefly after answering his advertisement in the Boston Herald, had proposed marriage.

"I suggest that we be wed forthwith by proxy, my dear Miss Emily," his letter said, "and that you hasten to join me and my two motherless daughters on my estate in this beautiful Montana territory, for I fear that some other beau might snatch you away from me if we wait to tie the Blessed Knot after you arrive."

"The Blessed Knot" struck her as a charming phrase, almost as charming as the face in the photograph accompanying the proposal. Charles Tanniger was clearly a distinguished gentleman, "neither callow youth, nor dotard," with a well-groomed mustache, gentle eyes, hair graying at the temples.

And he was a Westerner. Emily had never been farther west than the Berkshires, but she had read a great deal about the people who lived in the Territories and the adventurous lives they led. Mountains whose peaks disappeared into the clouds, and meadows so vast that their carpets of wildflowers rolled beyond the horizon . . . such vistas challenged the limits of her considerable imagination. Before another birthday rolled around, she vowed she would see them.

Granted, she was taking a gamble in this venture, possibly the first real risk she had willingly undertaken in the entire predictable course of her thirty rather sheltered years. While her sister, Susan, had accepted the first proposal of marriage that had come her way, Emily had chosen to study classical literature, Romance languages, and the viola at Wellesley. When her father could no longer afford her tuition, Emily had accepted employment as a governess, much to her father's dismay. She liked children. She had held comfortable positions within the households of two well-respected Boston families, and she had enjoyed a certain sense of independence. Her third position had been less satisfying for her. The time had come for a change.

She wanted a home, a husband, and children of her own, and, despite the fact that she was still a "handsome" woman, as her present employer had recently noted—much to her discomfort—she realized that she was past prime marriageable age. No matter. Out West the opportunities were plentiful. There, surely, a clever woman might be appreciated for her resourcefulness. And there, her fundamentally timid heart buoyed by the spirit of adventure, Emily would make her mark. Vowing to reach her new home in time to make this Christmas a very special time for two young girls in need of a mother rather than simply a governess, Emily took deliciously secret satisfaction in giving her notice.

Chapter One

"PARDON ME, SIR, but I think you ought to wake up now."

Had the voice been an octave lower or a decibel louder, Wolf Morsette might have pulled his pistol and shot someone. But since it was barely strong enough to tickle his ear, he only growled. That should have been warning enough.

"Pardon me, but, you see, we've stopped at a roadhouse, and I believe we might have something to eat if we go inside. The driver said . . ."

Wolf opened one eye as he shifted his shoulders into the corner of the stage's unpadded and wholly austere interior.

The fine-featured woman bunched her fingertips together and brought her hand toward her mouth, eyeing him eagerly. "Food," she said. "Inside."

Condescending as the gesture was, it was almost pretty. He'd seen only one other hand as smooth and as pale as this woman's was, and it had belonged to a high-priced whore in St. Paul. The whore had also shown some concern for his hunger—the kind that earned her a living. This woman didn't stand to earn a penny for her trouble. Had he been in a better mood, he might have spared a smile.

She raised her voice enough to compensate for any hearing impairment he might have had. "Do you speak any English?"

Wolf grimaced and shut his eye again. Noise and food were equally unwelcome at the moment. "Some," he grunted.

"Very well, sir, in light of your self-inflicted infirmity, which one can easily detect in such close quarters as these, I should think it would behoove you to eat some—"

"Not *that* kind of English." He folded his arms over his chest and settled deeper into the corner, muttering, "In plain, simple, *quiet* English, I ain't hungry."

"I see."

He felt a tugging beneath his boot heels.

"Then release my skirt, please."

Wolf opened his eyes and glanced down the considerable length of his legs, which stretched to the opposite corner of the coach.

"You are stepping on my skirt, sir."

"Pardon." Unconsciously he allowed the accent of his upbringing to soften the word, for he remembered his parlor manners only in the Canadian French his parents had spoken.

"Certainement," the woman quipped, her tone brightening considerably. "You speak French, sir?"

"Only in bed." Wolf raised his heels a couple of inches off the floor of the coach and offered a menacing smile. "Better hightail it into the roadhouse before, in my self-inflicted state of weakness, I take a notion that's where we are right now."

"I beg your pardon, sir." With a deft flick of her wrist she jerked the bottom of her black skirt out from under his heels. "I am a married woman."

"Minor detail. I can overlook it if you can." He nodded toward the open window and the soddy that stood beyond it. "You'd better get in there and grab a plate before your man eats your share."

"That man is certainly *not* my husband." Her indignation was directed toward the soddy first and the passenger who had already gone inside, then at Wolf. "Despite your rudeness, sir, and since this might well be the only opportunity I shall have, I feel it my Christian duty to inform you that—" Again she glanced toward the windowless hut that sprouted buffalo grass and thistles from its roof. "I believe our traveling companion may have picked your pocket."

Wolf arched an eyebrow her way. The information interested him less than the fact that she had seen fit to share it with him. Another surprising show of courtesy from a woman whose people rarely saw fit to show his kind much of any consideration.

She lifted her slight shoulders as her slender fingers fluttered about the pink and white cameo pinned to her tucked white blouse, just at the base of her throat. Her blue eyes failed to meet his as she spoke, barely above a whisper. "I have seen pickpockets at work before, on the streets of Boston. When this abominable conveyance lurched to a stop, our companion—Mr. Johnston, I believe—jostled you, and I am quite certain he slipped his hand inside your coat."

The shared confidence earned her half a smile. "It's a rare woman whose eyes are as sharp as her tongue."

Briskly she adjusted her gray wool jacket as she lifted her small, pointed chin. "And a foolish man who succumbs to stuporous sleep in the presence of strangers."

Wolf laughed and shook his head as he straightened. "You're no stranger, Miss Emily Lambert." He flashed a knowing look. "*Married* woman."

"How did you know my name? My *maiden* name."

"Heard you tell the stationmaster back in Deadwood."

"Old habit." She dismissed it with a wave of her left hand, flashing the thin gold band on her third finger. "Less than two months married, and I'm still unaccustomed to my new name. Mrs. Charles Tanninger."

"Miss Emily Lambert sounds nicer." Wolf eyed her appreciatively. He figured her for a proxy bride, in which case *Mr.* Charles Tanninger was in for a pleasant surprise. She had a little age on her, and she was pretty high-headed, but she was easy on the eyes.

He jerked his chin toward the coach window. "Go on in and get yourself something to eat, Miss Emily. You need to be puttin' some meat on those bones before winter."

"I'm from New England, sir. I'm well acquainted with cold winters."

"You might know snow, but you've got no acquaintance with wind, Miss Emily. Out here, the wind'll cut right through a wispy frame like yours. You need to tie on the feed bag." He reached out and pushed the door open for her, enjoying the look of indignation on her prim face. "Johnston came up empty-handed, but thanks for the tip, Miss Emily."

He watched her through the window, admiring the smooth way she walked, shoulders back, head held high. He liked the way her skirt swished in the grass and the way the ends of the bonnet ribbon tied in a bow to the left of her chin fluttered over her shoulder.

Boston. Long ways away, probably a whole different world. Gave a man pause to wonder whether a woman from Boston would even recognize him as a mixed blood.

EMILY HAD NOT anticipated such a long and bumpy ride on the stagecoach. She had traveled as far as she could by train, then connected with the Deadwood Stage Line in Dakota Territory. As she had anticipated from her sundry readings, the farther west she had traveled, the rowdier the communities she had encountered. It was rather exciting.

Deadwood, a rickety gold miners' settlement tucked into a crevasse in the pine-covered Black Hills, had been the rowdiest so far. The residents consumed more whiskey than water, discharged their firearms simply to make noise, bet anything they owned on any challenge anyone cared to offer, and took it for granted that every woman had her price. Emily's short stay had proven to be quite interesting. She had never received so many improper advances from such a plentiful variety of scoundrels. And now she could have added her fellow traveler to the list, except that he had not mentioned his name.

It surprised her that he'd bothered to take note of hers. She'd thought he might be related to the Red Indians somehow, but if that were the case, his remark about speaking French in bed was a bit confusing. She had never met anyone quite like him—not that she had actually *met* him. Dressed in buckskin pants and a wool coat with fringe at the shoulders that looked as though it had been fashioned from a blanket, he had purchased his ticket in silence and boarded the stage the same way. It was Emily's sensitive nose rather than the man's behavior that told her he was either drunk or suffering from the aftermath.

But it was the third passenger in the coach who truly made Emily feel uncomfortable. He was a fast talker with little to say, and his attention shifted constantly, as though he'd lost something and thought it might reappear anywhere at any moment. As the afternoon light dimmed and the evening shadows lengthened across the low-lying hills, Mr. Johnston's evasive eyes became more and more disconcerting. The passengers spoke less, bounced around more, and the interior of the coach gradually darkened as the enigmatic man dressed in buckskins slept on.

Suddenly the coach hit a deep rut, first the front wheel, then the rear. Emily bumped her head on the ceiling and then fell back to her seat with a teeth-gnashing thud. The driver whistled and popped his whip, and the coach lurched, surged forth, and dumped Johnston onto Emily's lap. He shouted. She yelped. During the chaos his hands were all over her, everywhere at once. His sheer weight knocked the breath from her lungs, and she couldn't get it back, not even a little. She hadn't the voice to order him off, hadn't the strength to push him away.

But the weight was finally lifted. A glint of metal flashed in the shadows, and a cold, steely click arrested all motion.

"You know what, Johnston? You've overstayed your welcome."

Johnston stiffened as he slid away from Emily. "What're you talking about? I can't help it if this road's got more holes than—"

Gasping for air, Emily shrank back as she groped for the edge of the seat.

"You were gettin' off anyway, weren't you? Assuming you found something on one of us worth makin' off with." The man Emily had thought to be sound asleep jerked Mr. Johnston close beside him on the seat opposite hers and menaced his ear with the barrel of a pistol. "You want to make your apologies to the lady before you take your leave?"

Emily gasped. "You can't—"

"You're damn right, Miss Emily, a man sure can't get much sleep when there's a snake in his bedroll. Now you can either jump out, or I can hold this gun right where it is until the next stop." He paused, looked Johnston in the eye and slowly grinned. "'Course, we hit another good rut, it just might go off." The grin vanished. "If it doesn't, we'll see what the Deadwood Line does with weasels who—" he reached into Johnston's coat pocket and pulled out a gold watch and chain "—steal from its passengers."

"That was pinned inside my jacket," Emily exclaimed as her hands flew from the pocket in the lining of her wool jacket to the one in her skirt. "My purse is still . . ." She pulled against the drawstrings and shoved her fingers inside the small satin pouch. "You managed to take the money out and leave the purse? How remarkable, Mr. Johnston."

"You can't prove nothin'."

"Whatever you've got on you must be hers." The gun barrel touched Johnston's temple. "You got nothin' off me."

"But I *had*—"

"Empty your pockets."

With unsteady hands, the man complied. Emily claimed her small roll of paper money and the six twenty-dollar gold pieces she'd had when she left Boston. "The rest is not mine," she said quietly.

"You sure you're not missin' anything else?"

"No, I—" Peace of mind, perhaps. Dignity. In a matter of moments Johnston had managed to assail her person, her private self, with his quick, invasive hands. Her fingers trembled as she touched the brooch at the base of her throat. "Yes, I'm sure."

"What'll it be, Johnston? Take your chances with the coyotes, or deal with the wolf?"

"Wolf?" Johnston turned his head toward his captor. "Wolf Morsette?"

"Forget the formalities," Morsette said. "I've got my hands full, and yours are shakin' pretty good already."

"So . . . you just gonna let me go?"

"You're going to make him jump out—" Emily looked out the

window, into the desolate, deepening dusk "—here?"

"*Here* keeps changin'," Morsette blithely pointed out. "It's gettin' pretty dark out, Johnston. Pick your spot before I change my mind."

They were slowing down for a hill. "Looks good here." Johnston opened the door and paused long enough to tip his bowler hat. "Sorry for any inconvenience, ma'am, but a man's gotta use whatever talent he's got. Morsette's got his, I've got mine."

"Mr. Morsette, you must let the law handle this," Emily pleaded.

"This is the law out here, right here in my hand." And the barrel was pointed at the man who was already on his way out the small door. "It says, 'Thou shalt not steal a lady's dowry.' It's gettin' drafty in here, Johnston."

"Damn your soul to hell, Morsette."

"Reckon I'll see you there."

"Remember to roll when you hit bottom," Johnston muttered to himself as he balanced the balls of his feet on the threshold and prepared to spring. "Pleasant jour—"

One boot heel kicked the flapping door.

"Oh, my—"

"Nice jump." Uncocking his pistol, Morsette grabbed the door and pulled it shut, thwarting Emily's attempt to see what kind of a landing the man had achieved. "That fella's had himself some practice."

"I know he's a thief and—" She sat back, staring at her remaining traveling companion in disbelief. "And a scoundrel, but what about the Indians?"

"Indians?" Morsette tucked his pistol under his coat. "The thieves and the scoundrels have cleaned them out already. They've got nothing left for a pickpocket to steal. Don't have to worry about them."

"Are there no wild Indians close by for *him* to worry about?"

"A few, yes."

"How close?"

"Quite close." He leaned forward. "Close enough to make out the color of your eyes, Miss Emily."

"Then—" she gestured toward the window, sputtering dramatically "—putting that man out on the road was an unconscionable thing to do. They might—"

"They won't bother. They don't give the slightest damn about the color of *his* eyes. But yours . . ."

"It's too dark to see my eyes."

"Wild Indians see very well at night." He sat back with a

self-satisfied smile. "You have pretty eyes, Miss Emily."

There was a pleasant lilt in his voice, a cadence unlike the drawl she'd heard in Deadwood. But she thought surely his English was too good to be that of a Red Indian. "I am *Mrs.* Charles Tanninger, sir. It would behoove you to bear that in mind."

"My name is not 'sir.' It's Wolf." He cocked an admonishing finger her way. "And you'll want to bear in mind that my name fits me well."

BILLINGS, MONTANA was a ramshackle town surrounded by rim rock and scrub pine. The November wind had driven everyone indoors. No one came to meet the stage. There was no husband with a fresh shave and polished boots, no little girls dressed in their Sunday best waiting on the landing at the depot.

Emily's inquiries at the mercantile and the land office were met with cold stares. "The Tanninger place is out in the hills west of town," the telegraph operator told her. "Ol' Tanninger keeps to himself. He ain't picked up his mail in a month or more."

She decided to rent some manner of transportation at the livery, even though she was uneasy with the thought of trying to find her own way in the wilderness. From what she had seen, what passed for a road in this country was little more than a cow path over rugged terrain.

"A buggy will do nicely," she told the white-haired man with the tobacco-stained beard.

"Ain't got a buggy for rent." The man folded his arms over his chest, turned his head to the side and spat into the dirt, barely missing the spotted dog that was curled up just outside the doorway.

"A buckboard, then."

The man shook his head.

Emily glanced pointedly at the wagon that was clearly visible through the back door of the big, dilapidated barn. "This is a matter of some urgency. I would be willing to pay—"

"Is the bride running out on the honeymoon?"

Familiar though it was, the deep voice startled Emily. When she turned, dark, smiling eyes unnerved her. The spotted dog scurried out of the way of the black horse at the end of Wolf Morsette's lead. "I'll give you twenty-five, Harding."

The bearded man stuck out his hand for Morsette's money. "Don't matter what you'll pay, missy. If you're on the run, anything you take outta here, you got to *buy* outright. I'll sell you a good horse at a fair price, like I just done for this here feller." A gap-toothed grin separated the mustache from the mottled beard. "Think you can fork a horse, missy?"

"Fork . . . a horse?"

"He means *ride,*" Morsette said.

"Even more worrisome," Harding added, "will somebody be chasing after you?"

"Of course not." Emily bristled, staring down each man in turn as though he'd taken leave of his senses. "There has been some confusion, some simple misunderstanding, or else—" Harding's attention had strayed to the row of stalls, presumably in search of another horse to sell. Emily turned the last of her explanation on Morsette, but she was losing conviction as her tone softened. "Or else, perhaps Mr. Tanninger has been unavoidably detained."

"Then *perhaps* you ought to take a room at the hotel and wait for him," Morsette suggested.

Emily shot a quick glance at Harding as she stepped closer to the man who had shared the stage ride with her. His methods might have been questionable, but it was thanks to him that she had any money at all for the purchase she was about to be forced to make. "The people I've met here thus far have seemed less than friendly," she confided. "I have asked about Mr. Tanninger, about the location of the farm. Is it too much to expect a simple how-do-you-do and welcome from these people?"

"In my case it generally is."

"But your reputation precedes you."

"What reputation?"

"Your reputation as a fast gun," Emily said solemnly, hushing her tone. "The man on the stage whispered your name in fear. I don't think I've come across it in the stories I've read, but then . . ." She stepped closer. "Did you know Wild Bill Hickok, by chance?"

"Nope. Never crossed his path."

"But you *are* a gunman," she concluded. "Are you, possibly, between jobs?" He arched an eyebrow, offering her the chance to justify her question. "Are you available for hire, that is?"

His eyes brightened, presumably with interest. "What do you need, Miss Emily?"

"I seem to need a guide." She glanced at the toes of her shoes. "And I'm in a rather poor bargaining position since you know exactly how much money I'm carrying."

"I didn't count it." The black horse shifted restlessly. Morsette patted its neck. "I'm just passin' through here. I don't know Tanninger, don't know where his place is, don't really—"

"But I'm sure you could find it." She stepped to the side, turning her back to Harding to shut him out of earshot. "It's not that I'm incapable of managing on my own, and I have read a great deal about the territory, but I think it unwise to venture out without really knowing—" a nervous glance toward the dusty, deserted street betrayed her waning confidence "—where I'm going."

"I think you've already done that, Miss Emily."

"Mrs. Tanninger," Emily corrected.

Wolf smiled.

"This mare's easy-ridin'," Harding called out from the second to the last stall. "Let her go for thirty bucks, plus another thirty for a saddle."

"Forty-five for the lot," Wolf said. "The lady's new in town, Harding. Show some hospitality."

"Take it you learned horse tradin' at your daddy's knee," Harding grumbled. "And horse *thievin'* from the other side."

"Careful, old man. The mention of my name strikes terror in most men's hearts." His friendly wink surprised Emily. More astonishingly, it pleased her. "Guess my reputation hasn't preceded me this far."

"Don't ask no names, don't know no names," Harding recited as he led the mare from her stall. "That's how come I've lived this long. I'll take your price if you pay in gold."

"Half in gold," Wolf said. "That's as good a deal as you've seen since spring, Harding. And if that mare's hard mouthed, you're gettin' her back. Which way to the Tanninger place?"

"West of town about fifteen miles. Follow the trail into the hills out there, you'll run right into it." Harding accepted Emily's money in exchange for the dun horse. "Tanninger generally fires off a couple of shots at anyone who comes too close, but he don't shoot to kill."

Morsette handed Emily the black horse's lead in a wordless invitation for her to hold his horse. She accepted without question. "You sure he knows you're coming?" he asked as he took the mare from Harding.

"Of course. He . . ." Emily hoped. She *trusted*. "He knows."

Morsette slid one hand along the mare's foreleg and lifted the hoof for a quick inspection. "We'll have to do some hard ridin' if we're gonna cover fifteen miles before nightfall. You sure you're up to it?"

"We haven't agreed on your—"

"Sounds like the place is on my way." Continuing his inspection of the mare, he felt through the thickening winter coat for saddle sores. "Maybe your husband will put me up for the night if I bring his bride to him, safe and sound."

"I should hope so." Emily gave a tentative nod. "I should certainly hope so, Mr. Morsette." He turned to her with an admonishing look. "Wolf," she corrected.

"Shh," he warned as he drew on a rawhide glove. "Somebody'll be wantin' to draw down on me, just to build up a reputation like mine."

"Indeed? Perhaps you need an alias."

"Why don't you think one up for me?" He smiled. "One for the books."

THE AUTUMN season had been one for the books this year. Wolf had spent the summer in Dakota Territory, picking up jobs where he could find them. He was Métis—a mixed-blood Cree who also had French and Scots relations in the Red River Valley on both sides of the Canadian border. He'd been a buffalo hunter, trapper, guide, interpreter and, yes, a hired gun on occasion. But ever since the Sioux had whipped Custer at Little Big Horn, the whites had got real touchy about Indians, and the Indians—all the different bands who had lived on the Plains as far back as anyone could remember—were being herded from one little square on the map to another.

It was hard for a man like Wolf Morsette to figure out which way to turn from one job to the next. He was a wanderer by nature as well as by trade. Or *trades*. He was adaptable. If a handsome woman needed a little shepherding, hell, he didn't mind helping her over the hard spots. She was, he thought—eyeing the open front of her jacket and admiring the way her breasts bounced to the rhythm of the mare's mincing trot—an entertaining diversion. A plucky little wayfarer whose dilemma had given him an amusing way to turn, at least for a day or two.

"Couldn't we either speed up or slow down?" The question bounced exactly the way her breasts did, and Wolf's laughter brought a scowl to her face. "I'm neither properly dressed nor properly equipped for this, and it's quite uncomfortable."

"Don't wanna play the horses out," he said with a smile. "Don't wanna drag our tails, either."

"How much—" she grabbed the saddle horn and adjusted her seat "—farther?"

He nodded toward the clear blue horizon. "I'd say just over that hill."

"The *next* hill? From here it's hard to tell where it begins and ends."

"Maybe it doesn't. It's a big hill." Feeling a little devilish, he nudged the black's flanks with a moccasined heel, extending the trot. "But you can handle it, Miss Emily."

"Certainly, I can." She lifted her chin. *"Certainement."*

"Bien." Again, he flashed her a smile.

HER FIRST GLIMPSE of the log house gave her an eerie feeling. The queer chill in the back of her neck had nothing to do with the numbness in her fingers and toes. Neither was it due in any way to the fact that the house was considerably smaller than she'd pictured it, nor to the unharvested squash and pumpkins that were visible amid the frost-blackened vines in the garden at the side of the house. But the large bird circling over a distant grove of pines lent a sense of heaviness to the silence in the brown and yellow valley.

"Turkey vulture," Wolf said, his eyes following it, too. "Sick livestock, maybe."

"That must be why he couldn't come to town."

"Must be." Wolf raised his voice as they approached. "Hello, the house!"

The front door opened just a crack. Twin shotgun barrels appeared.

"Don't look like your new husband's got much height on him," Wolf muttered as he reined in his horse and signaled for Emily to let him ease in front of her. "Take it easy, now," he called out. "You sent for a bride, and here she is."

The shotgun protruded farther through the crack.

"If this ain't the Tanninger place, we'll be on our way." Wolf raised the palm of his gun hand to show that it was empty while he eased his weight toward the left, visualizing the move he'd have to make if the situation turned any uglier. Dismount, scare the mare to the trees, and cover the woman's back as she fled for safety.

"Mr. Tanninger, it's—"

"Just sit real tight, Miss Emily," Wolf warned softly. "We'll go or stay, whatever you say," he called out. "But put up your gun. It's makin' me a little nervous."

"Who are you?" a small voice shouted from the house.

Wolf glanced at Emily, who seemed, impossibly, to recognize the voice, to warm to it instantly and take it to heart, though its owner's face was yet unseen.

"I'm Emily Lambert," she said eagerly. "Emily Lambert *Tanninger*. Are you little Lisette? No, you must be Marie-Claire."

"Lisette's hidin' under the bed," the voice reported.

"This is Mr. Morsette," Emily explained. "He was kind enough to help me find my way here. Please put the gun down, Marie-Claire. We're not strangers. I have letters from—"

The double-barreled gun was slowly lowered and laid across the threshold, then the door squeaked on its iron hinges. A young girl emerged. She had a woman's eyes set in a childlike face. Her eyes were the same dark color, the same hooded almond shape as Wolf's, and her skin was nearly as brown. He dismounted as she descended the single wooden step.

"Mr. Morsette, I believe I need some assistance," Emily said quietly. "My legs feel a bit unsteady."

Without a word he reached up to help her down. The slight weight of the woman in his arms and the fear he saw in the child's eyes combined to stir some protective part of him. The woman had come a long way to be a stepmother to mixed-blood children. He glanced from her face to the girl's and back again. If it had come as any surprise to her, it didn't register on her face.

"Now that I have purchased a horse, I shall practice daily." She turned to the girl, who stood waiting, tears slipping silently down her cheeks. "Marie-Claire and I shall practice together. Do you enjoy riding, Marie-Claire?"

"I think she's glad you're here, Miss Emily."

"And I am most certainly . . ." She pulled off her glove and gently touched the girl's jaw with the backs of her fingers, then cupped her hand over the side of her head, smoothing a straggly braid. "Lisette is hiding under the bed, you say? We must allay her fears at once. Would you mind if we—"

Wolf held both horses' reins. "Where's your papa, Marie-Claire?"

The girl took a swipe at her tears with one hand and pointed past the house toward the stand of pine trees with the other.

The black-and-gray turkey vulture wheeled overhead, stretched its wings in a shallow V, then flapped once, twice, easing its dismal descent toward the treetops.

Chapter Two

"TAKE MISS EMILY inside, and tell your sister it's gonna be all right," Wolf said quietly.

Marie-Claire couldn't seem to pull her focus away from the pine trees. She drew a long, shuddering breath, and her lower lip trembled. "I put him by Mama, but I didn't make it deep enough."

"I'll see to it." Wolf untied one of his saddle packs and gave it to Emily, along with a shuttered look. "There's food in here." He glanced at the stone chimney. "Is there no wood for a fire?"

"I can find some," Marie-Claire offered. Clad in a long-waisted calico dress, she wrapped her arms around herself as though the reminder had given her a chill. "We ran out, and I was kinda scared to go lookin'."

"I'll bring wood. Is your sister sick?"

"No."

Wolf nodded once, and his eyes finally betrayed something—relief, maybe—as he mounted the black horse and instructed Emily. "Water the mare and tie her up somewhere. I'll hobble them both where they can graze, soon as I see to—" He pulled his hat lower, hiding his eyes as he finished softly, "Mr. Tanninger."

Wolf returned to a roaring fire, a kettle of hot water, and a cake of lye soap, which he sorely needed. Two little girls with wet hair and clean faces were chewing on his hardtack and jerky, and Miss Emily was buttoning her own cuffs. Without a word, she filled the basin for him while he hung his capote and hat on a peg near the door and began stripping himself down to the waist and his parti-colored *l'assomption* sash, which was the badge of his heritage.

The need to wash himself was so strong it nearly made his hands shake. Imagining what Marie-Claire must have gone through in trying to lay her father to rest had nearly undone him. The child's best efforts to do the impossible had fallen short, leaving Wolf's namesakes to do their worst. There had been little left of Mr. Tanninger, and the smell of death had been hard to stomach, even on a cold night. He hadn't been a young man—that much Wolf had discerned—nor did it appear that he'd been shot.

Wolf leaned over the basin and scooped handfuls of warm water over his thick hair, then rolled the soap in his palms and scrubbed hard. He closed his eyes and worked the soap over his shoulders, his arms and his chest, straightening after a time and letting the water trickle down his weary back even as he kept washing.

"I'll help you rinse when you're ready."

His eyes flew open. Three pairs of female eyes stared at him. Miss Emily was ready with a bucket of water. She glanced away, but not before she'd given his bare chest a quick appraisal. The spark of admiration in her eyes made his chest swell. He wanted to smile.

But instead he bent over again. "Douse me good," he told her.

The water sluiced over the top of his head, splashed into the basin, over the tabletop and across the rough plank floor. A rivulet ran down his back and got trapped in the wide sash, but it felt good. He couldn't remember the last time he'd had warm water for bathing. A quick shake of his head showered the room with drops and made little Lisette giggle.

It was that sound that made Wolf smile.

"It feels like it's raining inside," the little girl said.

"That might be for the best." Emily took after the puddle with a broom. "The house needs a good scrubbing, top to bottom. I found wood for a fire, but there's not much food here."

Wolf gave Lisette a passing wink as he moved closer to the fire. "No jerky left for a hungry man?"

"Oh, yes, there's that, but not much else."

"We don't need much else. I see squash outside. We could make soup."

"We have some beans and some salt pork," Marie-Claire reported. "But a wolf got the chickens after Papa took to his bed."

Wolf ruffled his thick hair with both hands as he sat on his heels and hunkered close to the fire. "When did he get sick?"

"He's had a pain in his belly for a long time."

"You mean, more than a few weeks?" Emily asked.

"More than a year."

"Did he go to a doctor for it?"

Marie-Claire shook her head. Her voice barely rose above the crackle of the fire. "Papa said no doctor could fix it. Either it would go away after a while, or it would kill him. It never went away. Just got worse, and finally he took to his bed. He said our new mama was comin' soon, and that I should be there to meet the stage when it came. But the horses ran off, too. Or else somebody stole them." She looked at Emily, apologizing with her eyes, as though she had failed to keep a promise. "And then I forgot what day it was that I was supposed to . . ."

Emily laid a comforting hand on the girl's slight shoulder. "It's all right, dear. Mr. Morsette found the place with no trouble."

"While I was tryin' to look after Papa and Lisette, the place just went to pot. I couldn't keep up."

"How old are you?" Wolf asked.

"I'm eleven now," Marie-Claire boasted. "My sister's almost six."

"I'd say you've done just fine." Wolf reached for the hardtack and jerked meat Emily offered. Her fingers brushed his, and their warmth distracted him for a *moment*. Their eyes met, and he read her wish that she could make more food—or better food, or hot food—the kind of nourishment that gave a woman a sense of satisfaction, he supposed. He felt an unsettling sense of pleasure simply in taking it from her hand. Softly he thanked her. Flame shadows danced across her face, and her smile was even softer.

Turning his face to the fire, he reminded himself that he'd just buried this woman's husband—husband at least in name—and that she was suddenly a widow. And then he reminded himself that he was Métis.

"What did Mr. Tanninger tell you of his first wife? Anything at all?"

"Only that she died when Lisette was a baby."

He turned to Marie-Claire. "Your mama, was she Métis?" When the girl didn't respond, he lifted one end of his *l'assomption* sash. "Was she a half-breed, like me?"

The girl shrugged as she glanced away. "We ain't supposed to talk about that."

"Look at me, Marie-Claire." If the sash meant nothing to the child, surely his deeply tanned face would make his point. "Was she dark-skinned, like me?"

"She was part Cree." Marie-Claire glanced from Wolf's face to Emily's and back again, as though this bit of information must go no further. "We never went to town much because people there say things about us."

"You're a very pretty girl," Wolf told her. He smiled when Lisette stopped gnawing on her jerky long enough to analyze her sister's prettiness. "Both of you."

"That's what Papa said. He said the new mama would teach us woman things. I already know how to read." Marie-Claire shrugged and reconsidered. "Well, pretty good. Papa was teaching us because they wouldn't let us go to school. They said we had to go to an Indian school."

"Where's the Indian school?" Emily asked.

"I don't know. Wherever the Indians live, I guess."

"And you don't know where that is," Wolf concluded.

Marie-Claire looked at Emily. "Are you disappointed?" she asked. Quickly she elaborated, "Papa said when you got here, things might not be the way you thought, and you might be disappointed."

"I regret Mr. Tanninger's passing. I regret that very, very much." She knelt beside the two girls, touching Marie-Claire's knee, smoothing back Lisette's damp hair. "Tomorrow, we must make plans, and for that we shall all need a good night's sleep."

THE GIRLS WERE asleep in the tiny loft. Wolf spread his bedroll near the hearth while Emily hovered nearby, almost as though she expected to share his bed. Of course, he knew better. But the only place left for her to sleep was on the rope bed with the straw mattress in the far corner. It was to have been Emily's bridal bed, but presumably—Wolf pivoted in a squat, his hand braced on one knee, and scrutinized the cheerless piece of furniture—it had been Charles Tanninger's deathbed.

"Would you rather sleep here, close to the fire?" he asked her.

"You're welcome to use the bed if you wish." She dragged one of the cabin's two ladder-back chairs across the floor and set it at the foot of his bedroll. "I thought I'd sit up for a while and just . . . ponder all this."

She sat in the chair. He sat cross-legged on the bedroll and began filling his small clay pipe.

She tried to watch the fire, but her gaze drifted to the bed, and she stared, entranced. "He sent me his picture. He wrote wonderful letters about Montana. He made everything sound so . . ." She pressed her lips together, then gave her head a quick, dismissing shake. "He should have *told* me."

"He needed a mother for his children. You wonder why he didn't send *their* picture?"

"No, of course not. That never occurred to me." *That* was left unclarified. "But he should have told me that he was ill."

"Would you have come sooner?" Perversely he preyed on the guilt he saw in her eyes. "Or not at all?"

"Do you think he knew he was dying?"

"I'd say he must have had it figured weeks back." He poked the glowing end of a piece of kindling into the bowl of his pipe and puffed several times before adding, "Maybe months."

"Was there no help for him close by? Why wouldn't anyone help?" When he offered no answers, she sighed and concluded, "He probably didn't tell anyone."

"I'll take you back to town in the morning."

"I don't suppose we could—" she surveyed the cabin's sturdy rafters and its plank floor "—stay here."

"We?"

"I am Mrs. Charles Tanninger. Legally." Tentatively she added, "This . . . this *is* my home."

"Does it feel like home to you?"

She shook her head. "But I could—"

"No, you couldn't." Abruptly he tossed the kindling into the fire. "There's nothing here to eat. It's November." He eyed her sternly. "No, you couldn't."

"We'll find a place in town, then."

"Wonder if Tanninger left any money behind." Either the prospect, or the notion that he'd come up with it, seemed to surprise her, but out of habit he interpreted the look in her eyes as an accusation. "For his *family*. I'll do what I have to do to get by, Miss Emily, but I won't steal from a woman or from children."

"I didn't think you would, Mr. Morsette." She looked at her small hands, primly folded in her lap. "I shall seek employment."

"What can you do?"

"I have been a governess." At a glance she could tell that not only was he unimpressed, he wasn't even sure what that was. "Or I can be a schoolteacher."

He raised one eyebrow, acknowledging the latter as a legitimate vocation.

"I shall take care of them." She squared her shoulders and looked to him for approval. He only puffed on his pipe. "We shall find a place in town, and in the spring perhaps we shall return here, replant the garden, buy some livestock . . ."

Her voice drifted for lack of any practical mooring, but he had no reassurance to offer her. "I admire your spunk, Miss Emily. But you know damn well you haven't got a prayer of makin' it work." He leaned back on one elbow, stretched out his legs and eyed her pointedly. "Not without a man."

She bristled. "Mr. Tanninger discovered himself unable to make it work without a woman."

"With two little girls to raise, it didn't take a genius to figure that one out. The wonder is that he didn't go lookin' in the real obvious places." He plucked the pipe from his mouth. "Wonder how he met up with his first wife and why he didn't go back to the same place for a second one."

"He was originally from New York."

"That explains it," he said, discovering the need for another light. He reached for more kindling. "Likely he learned a lesson about stickin' with your own kind."

"I don't know about that. Sometimes a person who seems to suit one perfectly . . ." Intent upon watching him relight his pipe, she seemed to briefly lose her train of thought. "Sometimes that person isn't suitable at all."

"It helps to start out with certain things in common."

"What would those things be? Proximity, family background, an interest in education and children, and dreams of . . ."

A wistful smile crept into her eyes, and he was drawn into it, trying to imagine a very young Miss Emily strolling on the arm of a dapper gentleman. He'd met a few such men in St. Paul, and he'd taken no pleasure in their company. "A list like that oughta get you started," he allowed, soothing unexpected bitterness with a puff of smoke.

"Not if a prettier face with better breeding comes along."

Wolf gave a caustic chuckle. "You mean there's better breeding than full-blooded white?"

"There are all kinds of breeding and all kinds of blood."

"There's red . . ."

"And there's blue. Yes, indeed, sir, I once had a beau." The forced lightness in her voice was counterpoint to his dark scowl. She smiled too brightly. "'Had while he was mine,' to paraphrase Mr. Shakespeare."

The thought appealed to him less with each passing moment. "Then along came a demoiselle whose papa made your beau a better offer?"

"Just so." She gave a small, self-deprecating shrug. "Accepting the proposal of a man I had never met seemed, from my experience, no more hazardous than trusting a man I *thought* I knew." A fluttering gesture dismissed her remembered folly. "For, you see, in the end, all that we had in common was not worth a fig."

"There is one very important thing you and Mr. Tanninger lack in common." She allowed him to make the obvious point. "You're alive, and he's dead."

"I must look quite the fool." She laughed and gave her head a quick shake. "You wouldn't buy a horse without assessing first that it was sound. I, on the other hand, have traveled two thousand miles, only to find—" She waved her hand toward the empty bed. "Perhaps all it takes is desperation to turn an intelligent human being into a fool."

"And Mr. Tanninger was desperate."

"Perhaps I thought I was, too." She lifted her chin, then her gaze, toward the loft and spoke solemnly. "But now I cannot afford foolishness. I must remember that I am, first and foremost, an intelligent human being, and I must decide how best to provide for these children."

"You won't do it by staying out here." He sat up and leaned closer. "Did you see the look on that child's face when we first came, Emily? That was desperation. You try to make a go of it out here, she'll have that look on her face again, real soon. And so will the little one." He paused, assessing the concern in her eyes. It was, he truly believed, all for them. "And so will you."

She nodded like a chastised young girl brought to her senses by the reminder that she was, after all, a woman. For all her courage, physically she was still quite vulnerable. "If you would take us back to Billings tomorrow that would be very helpful, Mr.—" She looked into his eyes and nodded almost imperceptibly. "Wolf."

MARIE-CLAIRE rode behind Wolf, and Lisette sat in the saddle in front of Emily. The cold, crisp air turned their breath to steam, and the pale gray sky seemed to droop overhead as the day wore on. By the time they reached Billings, Emily's bottom was so sore she made a private vow to spend an entire night in a hip bath once she secured lodging. Lacking adequate transport, she had previously stored her baggage at a hotel with the intention of returning to collect it with her new husband's wagon and able assistance. The remembrance of her naïveté almost made her weep. It was as though years had passed since she'd last laid eyes on the hotel sign.

"I'll be makin' arrangements at the livery," Wolf told her. "The girls will help me get the horses bedded down while you get your room."

"Won't you be renting a room, too?"

"Like I said, I'll be makin' my arrangements at the livery."

"If it's a matter of adequate funds, I certainly owe you—"

"It's nothing to do with money." He glanced contemptuously at the hotel's pretentious false front. "I'm used to sleeping out under the stars most nights. There's a wood stove over at the livery stable, and I've got a friend there. This ain't my kind of town, I can tell you right now."

"After we get our bearings, the girls and I will seek out long-term lodging, but for now—" the thought made her smile "—food, a tub of hot water, and a bed will do nicely."

"I'll be taking my supper at the saloon."

"Oh."

"And I'll be leaving tomorrow. Headin' north."

"Oh." She couldn't ask him to do otherwise, but the announcement gave her a strange, hollow feeling. "You won't leave without saying goodbye, will you?"

"I'll be hung over and feelin' mean, Miss Emily. Sure way to ruin your day, so, uh . . ." He dismounted and wordlessly offered to help her down, leaving Lisette in charge of the mare.

Emily's rubbery legs were in no hurry to carry her away, and Wolf's hands were in no hurry to let her go. They stood between the horses—she looking up, wondering, he looking down, resolving. "I'll be claimin' my goodbyes right now."

"You'll be—"

He lowered his head slowly, so that she might have backed away if such a thing had occurred to her. But there was no threat in the dark depths of his eyes, and the idea of the impending touch of his generous lips to hers was suddenly more enticing than the thought of food. She heard his heels slide against the hardpan street, and through her skirt she felt the pressure of his thighs. She closed her eyes and drummed up the notion that there was no wantonness on her part if she couldn't see it coming.

His lips lit softly, like a butterfly, and his kiss invited her to take flight. The soft groan could not have been hers, for she had no breath for sound. The hungry response could not have been his, for his tongue had found its way past her lips, taking its fill of the taste of her.

Then it was over, and she imagined fleetingly that she had dreamed it all. But his laughing eyes laid claim to every nuance of her dream.

She stiffened with counterfeit indignation. "Mr. Morsette!"

"Wolf," he reminded her with a lopsided smile. "Miss Emily Lambert."

He chuckled to himself as he transferred Marie-Claire to the other horse. "You girls can ride double on Miss Emily's mare while she gets you set up with a place to stay." He mounted the black while Emily stepped back, still staring, still trying to recover. "You might want to take your meals in your room," he advised as he neck-reined his mount. "There might be some objection to, uh, children in the dining room."

EMILY SAT IN the hip bath soaking the soreness out of her lower half until the water turned cold. It took some time to dry and coif her long hair, dress and prepare to enjoy a hot meal. All the while she mulled over her problem—or *problems,* each one sure to create two or three more—and cast an occasional glance at the street below, wondering what had become of Marie-Claire and Lisette. It was nearly dusk, and still they had not returned from the livery stable. After supper it would be their turn for a bath, and then . . .

And then what? Without ever having been a wife, Emily was suddenly a stepmother and a widow. It was simply too much to handle all at once. She would have to take it apart and deal with each piece separately—the death of her husband, the woeful condition and legal circumstances of his property, the arrangements for herself and the children—all matters that would not easily be resolved. She had limited funds and few resources. But she had one advantage. She was accustomed to earning her way.

Chapter Three

"MR. MORSETTE?"

The big barn was quiet but for the sound of horse jaws working over a mouthful of grain in one of the far stalls. Dim lamplight glowed behind the single door that stood ajar. Emily pulled it open cautiously.

"Wolf? Are you . . ." Three pairs of dark eyes beamed up at her. "What's this?" she asked, but she could see that this was where Mr. Harding kept his tack and his potbellied stove, his worktable and apparently his guests. "What are you doing? I thought—"

"I'm feeding the girls some supper," Wolf said, explaining the obvious as he soaked up the last of his stew with a hunk of bread.

"But I thought they were coming over to the hotel after they helped you take care of the horses."

"They said we couldn't stay with you at the hotel," Marie-Claire muttered as she, too, turned her attention to the contents of her tin plate.

"Who said that? I told the clerk that I had two children with me who would be along any time, and that they should be directed to—" Emily gestured toward the hayloft, then folded her arms around herself tightly "—my room."

Marie-Claire spoke with her mouth full. "The man said no Indians could stay there."

"Are we Indians?" Lisette asked.

"Mama was mostly an Indian, so that means we're mostly Indians."

"Well, we shall see about this. I paid for a room, and it is certainly my prerogative to—"

Wolf finished off his bread, then set his empty plate on the workbench. "What name did you register under?"

"Why, Emily—" She remembered her signature, and her voice dropped considerably. "Lambert."

"Old habits die harder'n old husbands," Wolf said as he fished around under his capote for his pipe bag.

"Mr. Morsette!" She cast a pointed look at the girls, then stared him down vehemently. "Why should it make any difference whether I registered under my maiden name or—"

"Because if you'd used your *married* name, you probably would have been told there was no room at the inn." His curt nod served as punctuation. "Miss Emily."

"There *is* room."

"Don't push it. The girls can stay here."

"The girls most certainly may *not* stay here, Mr. Morsette. Why, that would be *most*—" tucking the pipe bag under his sash, he took her by the arm and scooted her out the door before she could finally utter "—improper."

There in the shadows it was his turn to stare her down, nose to nose. "Miss Emily, you have a room at the hotel, and if you wanted to take a man up to that room, strip down and bang the bedstead against the wall all night long, nobody'd try to stop you. They wouldn't think there was anything improper about that at all."

Her mouth dropped open.

"But they won't let you have those two little Indian girls sleep up there with you. No way in hell."

"That's absurd."

"Maybe so. But that's the way it is."

"What about you?"

"I can go into a saloon in one town, order up a drink, have myself a game of cards, no questions asked. Go to another town, they might point to the No Indians Allowed sign and send for the sheriff. All depends on what they want to see when they look at my face." He squared his shoulders, swept his long coat back and hooked his thumbs in his beautifully woven sash. "Or whether they think I might be in a mood for trouble."

When she caught herself admiring his hands, she quickly looked up and found the challenge in his eyes equally disturbing. "And if you are in such a mood?"

"I once held a barkeep at gunpoint while I drank a whole bottle of Taos Lightning, then walked out the front door without missing a step." He gave a jaunty smile. "At least, that's what they tell me."

"You don't remember?"

"I remember the halfway mark on that bottle and the way that barkeep's Adam's apple kept bobbin' up and down every time I lidded his temple with my gun barrel." She stepped against the wall, and her eyes widened. He braced his shoulder next to hers and gave her an off-center grin. "Tell you what, though. I can get myself a room in any jail house in the territory without even askin'."

"Mr. Morsette, *you* are a rogue."

"And *you,* Miss Emily Lambert—" she closed her eyes against his admonishment "—have a lot to learn."

He laid a warm fingertip against her temple, and she wondered what a cold steel barrel would feel like there.

Not good, she decided, and her eyes flew open. "If you knew all along that we might have had this problem at the hotel, why didn't you—"

"I didn't think they'd—" He drew his finger away, then rolled his shoulders against the wall and rested his head. "Those two pretty little girls. I thought maybe they'd get past the desk on your good name and their innocence after you were checked in."

"I've already paid for the room."

"Then use it." He straightened, gesturing toward the outside door. "I'll pass up my visit to the saloon. They'll be fine here. Harding gave us some blankets. We've got a stove and plenty of wood." He encouraged her with a smile. "All the comforts."

Emily shook her head. "It wouldn't be proper."

"*For you* it wouldn't be proper." With one hand on her shoulder he guided her toward the door. "Go on back and get some sleep. We'll figure something out tomorrow."

"Figure something out," she grumbled as she marched away from the livery and across the dark street. Piano music tinkled several doors away, and rowdy laughter poured into the street. Wolf would rather be there, she told herself. That's the way he would prefer to spend his evening, and who could be certain that he would not, once the girls were asleep? Who could predict anything in this cold, austere, unfriendly, *unruly* locale? *She,* Emily Lambert, certainly could not.

Nor could she predict the weather. When next she marched across the street, lugging two carpetbags, it was snowing.

THE GIRLS WERE asleep, and Wolf was having a smoke when Emily appeared once again in the doorway. She plunked both bags on the threshold at once and adjusted her bonnet as though the gesture itself were some kind of an announcement.

Wolf pulled his pipe from the grip of his teeth as he levered himself off his straw-cushioned blanket. "Don't tell me the hotel gave Miss

Emily Lambert the boot."

"They did not. I informed them that the accommodations were unsuitable. I demanded that they refund my money—all but the twenty-five cents for the bath."

"Did they?"

"No."

"They will." He indicated the straw pallets. "Are these accommodations more to your liking?"

"Under the circumstances, I believe certain practical considerations must take precedence over comfort. Marie-Claire and Lisette need an adult female chaperon." Primly she straightened her wool jacket. "So you may consider yourself relieved of duty, Mr. Morsette, if you feel an urge for . . . sport."

He wasn't sure where it came from—maybe the blue-gray evidence of fatigue beneath her eyes—but he felt an urge to bed her down next to the girls and simply watch over them all while they slept.

"We were listening to the music a little while ago, while we watched the first snowflakes fall," he told her as he snatched his blanket up, stepped over her bags, and led her away from the warmth of the small room toward the heavy door that faced the rutted street. He draped the blanket over her shoulders. She thanked him with a look.

They stood together in the doorway, a block and tackle hoist dangling overhead from a roof beam that jutted from the loft.

"It's been an open winter so far, but we're gettin' it now."

"It's pretty." She looked straight up and watched until the dancing flakes made her dizzy.

"You like snow?"

"Tomorrow is the first of December. It's time for snow." She pulled the blanket close, shawl fashion. "Soon it'll be Christmas. I had hoped and really planned to hang pine boughs and decorate a spruce tree in my own home this season." She tipped her head to the side, as if the angle gave her a better view of her dream. "I thought I'd light the yule log in my own hearth and sing carols. We wouldn't have missed having a piano or a violin after I'd served Thomas Lambert's secret grog recipe."

"Grog?"

"It's a hot drink, made with a bit of rum," she admitted as she watched Wolf light his small pipe. "My father was an old sailor, then a shipwright. He used to recall how the sailors would grumble whenever the captain would cut the rum with water. They called *that* grog. But during the holiday season, a bit of rum mixed with hot lemon and sugar water was a part of his merrymaking." She smiled, remembering. "My mother never disapproved as long as he permitted her to do the mixing."

"Maybe he added an extra kick to his own on the sly."

"Perhaps," she allowed as she untied her bonnet. Her smile was for him this time. *"Peut-être."*

"Peut-être," he echoed as he puffed on the clay pipe. "My great-grandfather was a *voyageur,* a man who plied his trade on the waterways up north. But his boat was a canoe, and his language was mostly French. My grandfather was a Métis trip man, who manned the oars of a york boat on the big Canadian lakes."

"And your father?"

"Ah, that's where my boating heritage came to an end. My father worked for the Hudson's Bay Company for a time, but as the forts and the jobs became fewer, many of the Métis lost their jobs, and he was one of them." He leaned against the big, rough-hewn doorframe. "And so what French I know comes from the schooling I had off and on from the priests who followed our camps when I was young. My people call their language *Michif.* It's a little like French and a lot like Cree."

He stole a glance at her between puffs on his pipe. "My mother was Cree. My father brought her from Canada to Dakota."

"Are you American or Canadian?" She looked up, as though seeing him for the first time. "Or Cree, or . . . or is that the same as Red Indian, or . . ."

"I am Métis. Mixed blood." He suffered her bold perusal of his face, wondering how she saw him now, what she thought. He saw no judgment in her eyes.

He gave a nod over his shoulder. "And so are those little girls. What do you intend to do with them?"

"I intend to provide for them somehow." She looked at the bonnet she'd taken off and fingered the satin ribbon on the brim. "Perhaps we might return to Boston."

"Not before spring." His pipe had gone cold. He jerked it out of his mouth and gestured into the snowy night. "I'm headin' north. I've got an urge to dance to some fiddle music and drive a *cariole* through the snow and feel welcome at any fireside."

"You're going home, too, then? North to Canada?"

"From what I hear, I've got some relations living this side of the border on the Milk River. That's where I'm headed." He shifted his weight from one foot to the other, feeling pressed to say something he was far from sure was the right solution.

Trouble was, he'd thought long and hard, and it was all he could come up with. "I can take the girls with me and find a family for them."

"Among your mixed-blood relatives?" He had managed to astonish her. "How do you know they would be welcome there?"

"They are Métis." He slapped his pipe against his palm, and the ashes scattered. "We know one thing for sure, Miss Emily. They're not welcome here."

"You've only *heard* about these relatives of yours? You don't know them?"

"There were some families that left the Red River Valley a few years back and headed west, following the buffalo. Families I'm related to."

"Following the buffalo? They sound like nomads." He questioned the word with a look, and she assumed he needed a definition. "Wanderers. They have no home."

"Home is wherever your people are. Your relations. The people who open their doors and tell you to come on inside, no questions, no charge." It was the kind of reception he'd yearned for since the autumn chill had set him on the move.

"Do these Métis people of yours *have* doors?"

He smiled patiently. "Working together and with a good supply of logs, they can raise a cabin in a day."

"How do they get their living?"

"We hunt, trap, trade, sometimes farm a little plot of land. The game used to be much more plentiful, but now that it's harder to find, we make do." There was no need to elaborate. He knew the art of wandering better than she did, and she knew that the tools of the hunter had many uses. "We find ways."

"I should think I would be able to find ways, too."

"Tanninger's land must belong to you now," he suggested cautiously. "I don't know how much he had, but it must be worth something. You could sell it."

"Whatever it brought would rightfully belong to Marie-Claire and Lisette."

"That's pretty generous thinking." He touched her hand. She glanced up, and he smiled. "You ought to be thinking about what you'll need to see you through the winter here and get you back to Boston in the spring."

"Winter . . . here?"

"Here in town," he said, directing her attention to the hotel at the other end of the street. "Come wintertime, nobody usually goes

anywhere. Indians have their winter camps. Métis have *hiverant* camps."
He shrugged. "You've got this town."

Where she didn't know a soul.

"How far is the Milk River?" she wondered, listening absently to the
merry tinkling of the piano.

"It's a good distance. Probably take us ten days to a fortnight, if the
weather holds."

She assumed the full measure of her height, tipped her chin up and
looked him in the eye. "I cannot let you take those two little girls, Mr.
Morsette. It would not be proper for them to travel in your company
without a chaperon."

"You got a better idea, Miss Emily?"

She nodded once. "I shall have to accompany them."

"What for? Come spring, you'll be free to light out on the first stage
and never look back."

"Knowing that I had shirked my duty, I would never be able to stop
looking back." She paused to take a brief, silent inventory of her feelings
about her decision, then gave a nod. "You're right, Mr. Morsette. The
girls need a good home, and clearly there is no acceptance for them here.
Nor, I think, for me." Which, she realized, didn't bother her in the least.
"I'm going with them."

"And after we reach our destination, what will you do then, Miss
Emily?"

"I'm not certain. I only know that Mr. Tanninger was counting on
me. And he did write fine letters. He may have omitted a few details, but
he gave me such lovely things to dream about." She glanced down the
street and confided quietly, "I do not relish the notion of spending
Christmas alone in that hotel, Mr. Morsette."

The dismal prospect was one that had haunted him, too.

"You keep forgetting my name," he said.

"Wolf." She smiled, feeling braver now that she was set on a course
of action. "I confess, the name Wolf does give one pause. Since you say
that it suits you, I am given to wonder how."

He returned her smile. "If you travel with the Wolf, you will see for
yourself."

Chapter Four

IT TOOK SEVERAL days to prepare for the journey. Wolf and Emily pooled their resources to buy a packhorse, a gentle mare for the girls, and supplies. Following a two-day hunt, Wolf traded fresh kill for cured pelts, sinew and pemmican, which was counter to his customary trading practice. Pound for pound, bargaining with raw goods went against his grain, for a Métis hunter knew the value of cured pelts and dried meat.

But he had no time for the intermediary steps. He needed to fashion fur-lined mitts and moccasins for his three female charges. In time he planned to make a few more items from the materials he had left, but the hands and feet needed immediate protection. Embracing the challenge ahead, he assured Emily that in her situation she could do worse than hook up with a "born nomad." Every drifter had his methods, but the Métis had honed their wandering skills to perfection.

They set off early one brisk, rosy morning, while much of the town still slept. Harding Livery's resident rooster perched on a corral post and crowed farewell to his fellow boarders. Emily had no idea where she was going, but she was not saddened to leave this frontier town behind. She told herself that in putting her life in the hands of this handsome nomad—she used the word with a deferential smile—she was risking no more than she did whenever she consigned her safety to the driver of a coach or the engineer of a train. At least Wolf was not a total stranger.

An enigma he surely was, but perhaps that was simply a function of his being male.

They were headed almost due north. The wind in their faces sometimes made their eyes tear. There was snow in the draws, but the hilltops, swept clean by the wind and bathed in winter sun, were nearly bare. As long as the weather stayed mild, Wolf resolved to ease Emily and the girls into the routine of strenuous travel, progressively increasing the amount of time they spent in the saddle. At first, even though they stopped several times a day for a brief rest, the three were exhausted by the time they made camp at dusk. They were all healthy, Wolf assured himself as he continued to push hard. They would adjust to the demands of the trek sooner or later.

Each night he asked that they gather the firewood and prepare the food while he built a shelter that was as cozy as any cocoon. The four of them slept in a tight bundle, children snug in the middle, their feet warmed by the embers of the camp fire. When it burned too low, Wolf would build it up, then return to his place. He would lay his arm over the children, and in her sleep, Emily would reach across them, too. Their arms met, forming a warm, protective arch, and Wolf smiled as he permitted himself to drift on the outer shell of sleep.

"TONIGHT WE WILL make bannock bread and tea," Wolf announced triumphantly several days into the ride. He brandished his string of grouse, unabashedly seeking female approval. He had been rationing the flour, but roast fowl was a particular favorite of his, and his girls were in store for a feast.

"I know how to make bread," Marie-Claire offered.

"And I know how to make tea." Taking a turn around the birds, Emily silently speculated that the tea would be the easy part.

"But here's the important question." Wolf's eyes danced as he handed Emily his catch, pretending not to notice the way she grimaced and held them at arm's length. "Which one of you is the best poker player?"

"Poker?" Marie-Claire shook her head, then brightened when she thought of an alternative. "Papa taught me to play whist with a blind man as a partner."

"You notice they're gutted," Wolf told Emily in an aside. "All we have to do is roast 'em, then skin 'em."

Emily uttered a small sound of relief.

Wolf turned to Marie-Claire and merrily challenged her with arms akimbo. "Now, just where would you find a blind man to play cards with?"

"You couldn't see him, and he couldn't see his cards. That's why he played so dumb. But Papa had Lisette for *his* partner, and that was the same as having a blind man."

Lisette wound up to smack Marie-Claire's hip. "I ain't the same as no blind man!"

"Well, you were practically a baby then," the older sister chided, forestalling Lisette's hand.

"I ain't no baby!"

"I knew a blind man once who played poker with marked cards," Wolf said. "Marked them himself with little pin pricks you could hardly notice. He never got to deal, so he never touched anyone else's cards until they laid down their hand. Then he got to check and see what they had."

"Couldn't you feel the marks when you dealt the cards?" Emily asked as she carefully laid the string of birds on what had been designated the table rock when they'd made camp.

"Nobody knew what they meant. You could hardly even find them. He had fingers like an eagle's eyes." Wolf chuckled, remembering. "Skinned the pants off me every time, that ol' blind man." He cast Emily a repentant glance. "So to speak."

"I'm not sure that poker would be a proper pastime for two young ladies," Emily averred, accepting his contrition with the properly prim nod.

"It will where we're goin'." Wolf rubbed his hands together, warming them by the fire. "Everybody plays cards. Everybody plays the fiddle, and everybody dances. You know how to do a Red River jig, Lisette?"

"I know how to skip-to-my-Lou." She demonstrated, skipping around in a circle until she drew a round of applause. Then she bobbed a fitting curtsy.

"Very nice," Emily said. "That last part will be quite useful in many dances."

Clearly torn between taking up skipping in the hope of earning a similar response or practicing mature restraint, Marie-Claire asked, "When we get to where we're going, will there be dancing?"

"Plenty of dancing," Wolf said.

"Whoopsie!" Dizzy from her performance, Lisette planted a fur-mitted hand on the table rock to steady herself. "I want to see Wolf dance with Miss Emily."

"Oh, yes, will you?" Marie-Claire asked him.

"Tonight!" Lisette demanded.

"I'll surely ask her." Thoroughly charming Emily with his smile, he asked the girls in an aside, "What do you think she'll say?"

"Yes!" they squealed in unison.

"I'm sure I shall need instruction," Emily allowed. "I believe I was fairly adept at Lisette's dance when I was a girl, but I've not learned much dancing since."

"Let me teach you a step or two after supper."

"Teach me, too!" Lisette pleaded.

"We can watch," Marie-Claire suggested, recovering her sensible-older-sister tone. "Let Wolf first teach Miss Emily."

Wolf gave a lesson in coal-roasting game birds, sparing them the finger-freezing job of plucking the feathers. Then the girls helped Wolf make the bannock bread, while Emily played the novice onlooker. The recipe was simple enough, but Emily was not accustomed to the heavy texture and bland flavor of skillet bread.

"Fills the hollows," Wolf said as he watched her taste it. "I've had raised bread before, mostly when I've been in places like St. Paul and St. Louis. I'll bet you like raised bread better."

"I do, but this is a clever way to make it on an open fire." She scooted closer to the warm flames, immersing herself in the simple joys she'd once taken for granted. "The roasted bird is wonderful. I don't believe I've ever had it cooked this way."

He laughed. "You're finally tasting the best there is, then." His expression turned boyishly hopeful. "You know how to make raised bread?"

"Yes, I do. Several ways." She eyed the skillet and the remains of the flat bread. "But I've only used an oven to bake it."

"How about a Dutch oven?"

"I could try that. Do you have one?"

"Not on me. But I'll get us one if you'll make us some raised bread." He flashed her a quick smile, laced with rare shyness. "Sometime."

She imagined a kitchen.

He envisioned a tripod standing in a big stone fireplace.

She wondered whether they'd both heard the word *us* in the same intimate way.

"It might take some practice," she said, "but I'm beginning to think I can master almost anything."

He grinned as he set his empty plate aside. "How about a two-step?"

She studied the bits of brown leaf floating in her tea and shook her head. "I've always tended the children while other people danced."

"Tended them where? Don't the children come to the dances, too?"

"Not in Boston."

"Not in St. Paul or Deadwood, either," he recalled. "At least, not that I saw. Not that I was invited to many dances. But at the Milk River camp, I will be. We all will be. Big people, little people, young and old." He braced his palms on his buckskin-clad thighs as he stood. "So we'd best get ourselves in practice. Stand up, you two, and learn from the nimble-footed Wolf."

The girls leapt to their feet.

Emily clutched her tin cup in both hands, searching one face after the other for a sign of good sense.

Wolf swept one side of his open capote behind his hip and made a courtly bow. "Miss Emily, may I have the honor?"

"Without music?"

The tune he hummed was not one she recognized, but his deep, sonorous voice rendered the melody irresistible. Emily abandoned her search for good sense. With a smile she rose gracefully and allowed him to take her in his arms. He provided the music and the pattern of movement, but she was half a step behind at every turn, for it was a lively dance.

"One-two, one-two, that's it," he instructed, and then resumed the tune.

Her next misstep elicited a giggle from the sidelines.

"You two smarties follow along," Wolf ordered. "This arm so, this arm so, and one-two, one-two." There were more giggles as the girls copied the pose. "Come on, I can't count and provide the music both." He entreated Emily with a charming smile. "One-two, one-two."

"One-two, one-two," she recited, even as her feet faltered in the snowy grass.

"Or here's a waltz. A little slower, now. One-two-three, one-two-three, yes." And he hummed a gliding tune.

Emily might have caught on faster had his lithe step not been so distracting. Only their arms and hands actually touched, but she could feel the power in his thighs simply in the way he moved, and the arms that carefully guided her felt impossibly strong. He was doing all the work, and she could not help but follow, if stumblingly.

"Is this right, Wolf?" Marie-Claire led Lisette in a close approximation of the dance step. "One-two-three, one-two-three."

He continued to hum as he nodded.

"Sing the words," Lisette pleaded.

Wolf made a funny face and shrugged, still humming.

"There is only the melody," Emily interpreted. Wolf nodded. "Our Wolf is a complete orchestra."

Our Wolf. His eyes brightened. His hum became a bellowing "da-da, da-dee" as he whirled Emily round and round on the energy infused in him by the heady claim she'd made on him.

Marie-Claire laughed. "I think he's turning into a tornado!"

"Ouch!" Lisette hopped on one foot. "You stomped on my toe."

"Just as I have done to my poor partner," Emily confessed. Wolf spun her in a circle. Her head flopped like the lid of a tobacco tin, dislodging her hat. Still tied beneath her chin, the bonnet dangled down her back, doing a wild dance of its own. "Oh, but our Wolf is so busy being an orchestra, he can't howl in protest."

"Ayooooo!"

The dance party dissolved into fits of laughter.

"The Wolf can always howl," he assured them as his spinning slowed to a halt. "And the only instrument I can be is a fiddle. Don't I sound like a fiddle?"

"You have a wonderful voice." Emily pressed her hand to her chest in a reflexive attempt to check any unseemly rise and fall. "That's why Lisette wanted to hear the words." On a deep breath she wagged a finger at Wolf. "But now, before you come up with more ways for me to make a fool of myself, I think we must stoke up the fire and put these children to bed."

Emily used warm water from the leather boiling bag to clean the girls up while Wolf arranged their bed, stripping pine boughs of their needles to make an insulating mat inside the lean-to. Once the girls were tucked in, he and Emily lingered near the waning fire, sharing the last of the tea, enjoying the quiet beauty of a starry winter night from their comfortable seat on the fire-warm flat rock that served as their only piece of furniture.

"Did you feel foolish, dancing with me?" Wolf asked, the vast darkness nearly overwhelming his hushed voice.

"Only because you're so good at it, and I seem to have wooden feet."

"If we practiced together, we would learn to move one with the other. You wouldn't have to count. You wouldn't even need to think. Your body would learn the rhythm from mine."

His words made her feel a delicious flash of warmth. She closed her eyes briefly and let the feeling flow through her.

When she opened them again, she encountered his knowing smile.

She cast about for subject matter. "Do you play the violin?"

"I fiddle a little." His rhyme made her smile in return. "Or used to. Haven't touched a fiddle in a long time. Not since I left home."

"Which was a long time ago in a land quite far from here," she recalled.

"Sometimes, my childhood home was far from here. Sometimes not. We traveled across northern Dakota, into Canada." As he gestured expansively, he noted the interest in her eyes, the earnest attempt to understand *home* as he described it. "You and the girls and me, we take this camp with us as we go. We set up in a new spot, and we make it ours for the night." He considered the serenity he saw in her face—the sleepy eyes, the fire-flushed skin, the dewy mouth. "You feel good here tonight. I can tell."

"How can you tell?"

"By the way you smile. It comes more easily than it did when I first met you." He edged closer. "Do you remember when I kissed you?"

"You were saying goodbye."

"This time I'm saying thanks." He took her shoulders in his hands and drew her to him. "*Merci*, Miss Emily."

His kiss was slow and smooth, never faltering, at once bestowing blessings and gratitude. Then abruptly it was withdrawn.

"For what?" she managed to ask, self-consciously turning her face aside.

"For the dance." His lips skimmed her cheek, his breath warming her skin. "Now this is my thanks for the kiss."

His second kiss claimed her breath, her brain, and all her senses. He engulfed her in an embrace that made her feel marvelously warm and safe. It surprised her that she could take comfort from someone whose size and strength so completely overwhelmed her. But she could. She *did*. And she thrilled to the pressure, the stimulating motion, the delightful taste, and the unexpected softness of his lips.

"This could go on and on," she said breathlessly when he permitted her to speak.

"That's the idea. One kiss leads to another."

Stubbornly she kept her eyes shut tight. Perversely she croaked, "It can't."

"Of course it can," he said silkily. "Exactly the way you know you want it to."

She groaned. Her shoulders sagged in the parenthetical grip of his hands. She shook her head quickly. "You do understand, it simply cannot lead from one to another because . . ." She searched for some innocent way to express what she imagined his far-from-pure thoughts to be. "Because I think you would want more."

But when he released his hold, it only left her in doubt.

Too quickly, she sought reassurance. "Wouldn't you?"

"I would." *He did.* "But wanting and having ain't hardly the same." He levered himself off the rock and stood up, making a production of stretching his long legs as though he'd just had a pleasant nap. "And right now, I have other matters to attend to."

"Oh?"

He gave her a sly smile.

She hopped down from her perch and straightened her skirt. "I mean, *good.* We should . . . we *must* attend to other matters, so that we do not think about . . ." Flustered, she snatched up a stick and poked it into the fire, stirring flame from the coals. "About matters that we should not think about."

"Thinking and *doing* ain't the same, either." He chuckled behind her back. "And you can't stop a man from thinking about one matter while he's attending to another."

THEY BOTH HAD matters to attend to that neither wanted the other to see. They were private matters that would spawn surprises when the time came. Christmastime. It meant something a little different to each of them, but it also meant something miraculously, wondrously the same. Not wanting or having, but giving. And in order to create something special to give, they both had work to do.

It wasn't easy. They had been on the trail for eight days. If their luck held out, they would soon reach the big bend in the Milk River, and it would be none too soon, for in this country, fair weather could not hold through December.

Wolf was making himself a pair of snowshoes, so by all apparent accounts his creative efforts were being poured into that undertaking. Each night after supper, he set about shaping the frame and stringing the web of sinew while he sang snatches of French voyageur songs that had been passed down through generations of Métis who no longer plied the north country waterways.

Meanwhile, Emily ducked into the back of the lean-to he put up each night. The shadowed firelight barely illuminated her work, and her stiff fingers were barely useful in manipulating a needle, but there she applied careful stitches to the muslin and flannel she'd bought in Billings. When the girls announced that they were going to take a peek and see what she was doing, Wolf bade them join him in song. It was an invitation they could not resist, and patiently he taught them strange new words and lively old tunes.

After Emily called the girls to bed, it was Wolf's turn to craft in secret. He expected his fur hats to be a welcome change from flimsy felt bonnets and woolen shawls. He had some ideas for toys, too. It had been a long time since he'd done any whittling, but he successfully revived the knack he'd once had, and all done in cheerless silence so that he would not wake the children. Or the woman.

Ah, the woman. She was a rare breed, no doubt about that. She had as much courage as any man he'd ever met, and she was far more honest than most. More honorable than just about anybody he might care to name, including himself. But they had as much in common as fish and fowl. He knew it was a mistake to let a woman like her get under his skin, even slightly, even briefly.

But be damned if he could think of anything better to do. Except maybe find a way to get under hers.

WOLF RECOGNIZED the signs of a Métis community. The twenty-five cabins were built in a circle around a larger building. The circular arrangement of the camp was inspired by their Indian heritage. The clay-plastered walls and stone fireplaces he knew he would find within most of the cabins were proof of their European ancestry. The dance hall in the center was pure Métis.

But the lack of smoke issuing from the chimneys was not a sign of any heritage. It was, he feared, a sign of nobody home.

Emily and the girls could feel the emptiness, too. From a distance, the abandoned village looked peaceful, as though everyone might be asleep. But as they drew near, the winter landscape silently attested to complete desertion. That they had come all this way only to be greeted by utter quiet was unspeakably heartbreaking.

And so, for long moments, no one spoke.

The horses' dogged plodding announced their arrival. Not one face appeared in a doorway. Finally, Wolf called out, *"Métis ici? Mou nou si Morsette."*

"Don't they speak English?" Marie-Claire asked.

"If they were here, many of them would. They would jabber your ears off." With the broad sweep of an arm he voiced the bitter irony of their journey's reward. "You wanted a house of your own, Miss Emily? Take your pick."

"They've all moved away?"

He dropped his arm to his side. "Sure looks like it."

"But why?"

"Wish they'd left someone behind to tell us. Doesn't look like they did." His hand signal forestalled her dismount. "Let me check things out first."

He moved from house to house, flinging doors open, kicking the last three out of frustration. *"Rien,"* he called out, shaking his head dejectedly. "Nothing. Not a soul."

He headed back to one of the first cabins he'd checked, signaling with a jerk of his head that they were to follow him. "This one's clean as a church, and they left the bedsteads behind."

They unpacked, gathered firewood and found that there was plenty of grass for the horses—a sign, Wolf said, that the camp had been abandoned all summer.

After sharing a somber evening meal and arranging bedrolls over the rope webbing on the beds, Marie-Claire withdrew quietly to bed. Lisette had fallen asleep on the floor, with her head in Emily's lap. Wolf lifted the little girl into his arms and tucked her into bed with her sister. It would be a tight squeeze if Emily chose to sleep with the children. She would. As he stepped away from the bed, Wolf took visual measure of the sliver of space left and made a silent bet with himself on it.

"One thing bothers me," he mused, joining Emily on the floor by the fire. "We haven't cut much sign in the last couple of days."

"Sign of what?" She handed him a tin cup of hot tea.

"Anything moving, either on hoof or wing. Anything living or breathing."

She sighed. "You're saying, nothing to eat."

"I'll go out and find meat tomorrow. If it's out there, I'll find it."

"I know you will. With you as our guide, the girls and I haven't had to worry about food or shelter. Things I once took for granted, but now . . ." She dipped herself a cup of tea from the boiling bag, then sat back and savored the scent of the steam and the warmth of the cup in her hands. "I see that it's a mistake to take life's essentials for granted. If suddenly they're not there, the pampered individual has no notion of how to provide."

"If they're *not* there, only God can provide."

"Indeed." She looked at him curiously. "I would not have taken you for a religious man, Mr. Morsette."

"You would not have *taken* me at all, Miss Emily. I was your last resort. Just like the livery stable, and just like . . ." His observation made them both uncomfortable. He glanced away, finishing on a doleful note.

"This hapless journey. Your guide has brought you to a ghost town."

"There is ample precedent for finding hope in a stable, Wolf. And for persevering even though the prospects seem limited. Tomorrow there will undoubtedly be manna from heaven. Or deer." Her optimism drew his gaze to her, and her smile instantly buoyed his spirits. "Or a heavenly hare, how would that be?"

She touched the back of his hand. He was unprepared for the way his heart suddenly skittered against his ribs.

He cleared his throat and effected a diffident shrug. "The Métis are given to moving on. They might have left just because they were tired of the place."

"I thought Mr. Tanninger was my last resort." Her fingertips stirred over his hand. "You, Mr. Morsette, are something else entirely."

"And what is that, Miss Emily?"

"I don't quite know. An unexpected—" she smiled wistfully "—messenger, perhaps. Pathfinder. Conveyer. Catalyst. A bit of sand working his way into my shell."

He leaned closer. "If I break through, there'll be hell to pay when I whisper my message in your ear, Miss Emily."

"Is that so?" She stayed her ground, her nose only inches from his. "You've yet to answer the question about whether you are a religious man."

"You didn't ask a question. You made a statement." And it was he who retreated, staring into the fire as he spoke. "Anyway, I don't have an answer. See, I'm a mixed blood. There are two sides to me. The Métis always have a Black Robe around telling everybody to get married and get their children baptized. If you were to ask the Black Robe, he'd tell you I'm a sinful man. On the other side—the Red Indian side, as you call it—hell, I'm just a man like any other. I do believe in God."

He turned to her and spoke so quietly she had to strain to catch every precious nuance. "I guess if you're wondering whether a man's got any religion, you've got to watch how he behaves, see if there's love in him somewhere."

"What if he's hiding it?"

"If it's there, you can find it. You just have to know how to look. You have to keep in mind who he is and where he comes from."

She took a deep breath and released it slowly. "What if he holds a gun to someone's head right before your very eyes?"

"What if he doesn't pull the trigger?" They exchanged a look of frank acknowledgment devoid of common ground. Then Wolf turned his attention to the fire. "Sometimes a man's hard-pressed when it comes to standing up for what needs defending."

"Sometimes he goes too far."

"Sometimes he doesn't go far enough." Again he shrugged. "Either way, I guess that's why he needs some religion. Because sometimes he's just too damned weak and too damned hard-pressed."

"This is harsh country. That much I can surely see."

It was his turn to touch, experimentally, the curve of her skirt-draped knee. "Too harsh for a gentle woman like you?"

"I have two sides, too," she said quietly. "I'm finding more strength than I knew I had."

He stretched out close to her, bracing one elbow on the floor, his face only a hand's breadth from the lap where he longed to lay his head the way Lisette had earlier.

"What sort of a house do you want?" he wondered. "What kind do you dream about?"

She tipped her head slightly, considering. "One that's mine to put the trimmings on."

"Woman frills." With a forefinger he touched the bit of lace that encircled her wrist at the end of her otherwise plain white sleeve. "My mother always beaded everything. Anything she could sew a bead to ended up covered with flowers."

He pictured a leather wall pocket beaded with blue and red blossoms sprouting from curly green vines.

She imagined yellow wallpaper flocked with tiny pink rosebuds.

"I would have curtains in the windows and rugs on the floors," she said.

"How many floors would you need?"

"One." She caught his eye with a teasing smile. "In each room."

"How many rooms would you need?"

"I would only *need*—" she gestured with an easy flourish "—the essentials, now that I'm no longer a pampered individual. But I would make it comfortable."

"So comfortable you'd never want to leave?"

She nodded.

"Not even if someone said . . ." He lifted his hand to her cheek and cradled it in his palm, entreating softly, "'We have to go, Emily. You can take your curtains and your rugs along, and I'll build you another house, but we have to leave this one behind.'"

"It would depend on who that someone was." She stroked the back of his hand. "And whether I could depend upon him to keep his promise."

AFTER WOLF STOKED the fire, he turned to find that Emily had, indeed, wedged herself in with the girls. So he went to bed alone and watched the fire shadows flit from rafter to rafter until the darkness finally swallowed up all but the glow of embers. He closed his eyes and wished for sleep, but he was cold. In all the nights he'd spent sleeping under all kinds of circumstances, he'd known plenty of cold. But not like this.

"Emily?"

"Hmm?"

He was deep-down glad she hadn't managed to fall asleep, either.

"I was gettin' sorta used to us sleeping close," he confessed, knowing damn well how forlorn he sounded.

"I'm not far away."

"Feels like you are."

Silence.

"I like being able to touch you, just to know you're there." He sounded like a lovesick kid, and he knew it. But it was worth a try.

She was so quiet, he wasn't sure she was breathing.

Finally, she whispered the word he longed to hear. "Wolf?"

"Hmm?"

"The truth is, I like that, too."

He smiled. The rope bed groaned as he turned toward the sound of her voice.

"But I'm staying over here."

Chapter Five

WOLF WAS BUSY setting a rabbit snare when his sixth sense told him he wasn't hunting the river bottom alone. He hadn't heard anything. He hadn't cut any sign. He just knew. And he knew his company had to be one of his kind—either Indian or mixed blood. Otherwise the proof of the presence would have been more substantial. He cocked his pistol and turned slowly.

"You *bonjour* man?" The watcher appeared to be Ojibwa or Cree, but he could very well have been a mixed blood himself. The man had some nerve, Wolf thought, calling *him* the disdainful term some Indians used for the Métis.

But since, for all Wolf knew, this man might well have friends close by to back him—and since Wolf had not a one, save a gentlewoman and two little girls—he gave a grunt that might be taken as assent, and he lowered his gun.

The newcomer opened his buffalo wearing robe to show that he meant no harm. His knife was sheathed. His rifle was still in the scabbard, strapped to the Appaloosa standing behind him. "Berger coming back already?" the man asked.

"Berger . . . Back from where?" Wolf had an uncle from Pembina named Pierre Berger. He wondered if the Indian could be referring to the same man.

"Back from a better place."

Wolf scowled. "What, heaven?"

The Indian laughed. "When I find a place *that* good, I keep it for myself." He gave a chin jerk, indicating the river bottom. "There is no game here. Last spring, those *bonjours* down there, they were looking—" he nodded toward a pine sapling "—pretty skinny. Even their dogs. So I told them, better hurry up and get to gettin', before the whites get every good place there is."

"Do you know where they went?"

"Sure, sure, I showed them." He pointed westward. "Not too far. Maybe five days' ride without those *bonjour* wagons." He clapped his hands over his ears and mimicked the infernal squeal of the Red River carts' greaseless axles. Wolf's hearty laughter didn't fit with the pistol, so he put it away.

"Hurt your ears, do they?" Wolf gasped, the last ripples of laughter still tickling his belly.

"Only a man who has no enemies makes such noise."

"Must be why it's been so long since I drove a Red River cart." Absently toeing the rawhide loop he'd been triggering as a trap, Wolf scanned the frozen river's lazy curve. "There's still no game here?"

"Hard to find any."

"So why are you here?"

"Saw your smoke. Thought Berger came back, maybe. Or maybe somebody wants to trade."

"I've got nothing to trade." He jerked at the loop with his heel, spending his snare in disgust. "I was looking for relations, come over from Dakota. Or so I heard."

"I can take you there."

"We've already come a long way. I have—" Wolf nodded in the direction of the village and gave what seemed the simplest, safest account "—my family with me."

"They go hungry this winter, you stay here. I can take you to Berger, leave tomorrow." By way of explanation, the man grunted in disgust. "The missionaries come to our camp and make Christmas."

"Oh, ho, I see." Wolf planted hands on hips and gave an appreciative chuckle. "You'd rather hear some fiddle music."

"I like to kick the heels with the *bonjours*."

"And New Year's is the best time for that." With a wave of his hand, Wolf invited the man to mount up and follow him. "We'll see what Emily says."

EMILY'S RESPONSE was unequivocal. "I will not be moved."

"Thank God I left Bear Catcher standing outside. I told him . . ." He gestured in exasperation. "I told him you were my woman. Told him we had two daughters. Where are they, anyway?"

"They're fetching water in which to boil the meat you promised you would bring back with you."

"I tried creating antelope out of clay, but I thought it might fall apart in the pot."

She would not be intimidated by sarcasm. "Who is Bear Catcher, and why on earth would you tell him that you have a wife and children?"

"Because I thought it sounded good!" He raised his palms in abject surrender. "All right? I wanted to see what it felt like to say it, so I said it." A gesture indicated the man beyond the door. "He offered to lead the way. I didn't want to explain it all, so I just told him . . ." He glanced away with his confession. "The first thing that popped into my head."

"How interesting that a lie should be the first thing."

"Yeah. Interesting." He realized that the *nature* of the lie was more than interesting. "It would save me some embarrassment if you would act—" He looked her in the eye and tried not to demean himself further with an unbecoming plea. "If you would go along with me, the way any good wife—"

"Good wife! I beg your pardon, Mr. Morsette, but you have persisted in addressing me as *Miss* Emily. Fairly rubbing my nose in my status, despite the fact that *legally* I *have* been a married woman, however briefly. And now, you make a mockery of that fact, blithely claiming me as *your woman,* when we have not even . . ."

"We have shared a bed," he reminded her quietly, taking mean-spirited satisfaction in shattering her usual decorum.

Her eyes widened in horror. "Are you going to compromise the integrity of that experience, as well?"

"I said you were my woman. Any details would be just between you and me."

She stared, tight-lipped, clearly doubting his word. His heart hardened again. "It's not like the details would be something you'd never take part in. You *did* come out here looking for a husband."

"I *had* one."

"You had a dead one." He turned away, muttering, "Now you've got me."

"From a dead husband to a fake one," she clipped acidly.

He spun on his heel faster than any of her fanciful gunfighters. "I'm no fake *anything.*"

Undaunted, she squared her shoulders. "And I'm expected to comply with *your* wishes to save *you* embarrassment."

She was infuriating. She was unreasonable. Damn her, she was . . . *woman.*

He glanced at the door, hoping no one would come through it and witness his mortification. He paced the length of the room and back again. The place had suddenly become too small, too tight a fit, to contain the two of them. Damn! What would the girls do if he resorted to trussing up their dignified Miss Emily and tossing her over the back of his horse?

Not a good plan, he told himself.

"Let me tell you a story," he said, and his controlled tone helped to calm them both. He took her hand in both of his and drew her to sit beside him on the bed he'd tossed around in the night before. "The Lakota tell a story about a woman who would not obey her husband when he told her it was time to break camp and move on. She sat down and refused to budge, so he had to leave her, because . . ." He searched for a reason she might accept, but he wasn't sure one existed. His gesture appealed to her simply to grant him the obvious. "Because it was time to go. And she's still sittin' there to this very day." He paused for effect, then looked her in the eye for the same purpose. "She turned to stone."

Emily responded with a dismissive shrug. "Like Lot's wife, who turned to salt."

"No, there was a difference. The Lakota woman had a child strapped to her back. The child shared her fate."

He knew he had made his point when he saw her lower lip tremble. He'd backed her into a corner. But somehow he felt no joy in it.

She stared at their hands, still clasped on his knee. "I don't understand this *time to go*. We just got here." Her dejected sigh nearly undid him. "And I'm so tired."

He wanted to give in and make more promises he couldn't keep, but he remembered the way his father used to answer that heart-rending complaint. "Only a little farther and we will find what we're looking for."

She looked into his eyes, hers frankly pleading. "I hardly remember what that was."

"People who will take us in."

"It's almost Christmas." She turned her attention to the fireplace on the opposite side of the room. "I could make this place feel like home, and we could at least have Christmas before we—"

"Get it through your head, Emily, this place can't be home. I can't let you think of it that way. There's no one here because there is *no food* here." He squeezed her hand. "It's best that we go now. You have to trust me, Emily. I may not be much to you . . ."

He gave her a chance to object, and when she did not, he released her hand, rose from the bed and walked away. At the door, he paused, steeled himself and offered her a cocky smile. "I may not be your true husband, *Miss* Emily, but I'm all you've got. We're leaving in the morning."

"And I have no say in the matter, no choice at all."

"You can choose to remain a woman . . ." He nodded toward the stone hearth that seemed to hold such an attraction for her. "Or become a rock."

ALL RIGHT, SHE would go, Emily told herself as she stuffed her belongings—what he'd allowed her to take with her when they'd left Billings—and the girls' into her two carpetbags, preparing them for the packhorse. She hadn't seen him since they'd had their talk, but the girls had dashed in and out a couple of times, once for a piece of charcoal and once to deliver Wolf's instructions that she make a batch of bannock bread.

Wolf suddenly burst through the door, the look in his eyes as jubilant as that of a boy who had just made his first ringer in horseshoes. "We've got something to show you, the girls and me. Come on outside."

"I'm not finished here," she said in a small, tight voice.

Surely he could see that she'd done as he'd asked. He might have told her that he was glad to see that she'd decided to be, in his eyes, sensible. But he did not. He waited. When she finally looked up, she was sure she detected an uncharacteristic touch of humility in his eyes.

"It's kind of like a peace offering," he said quietly.

A peace offering.

Magic words.

He hooked one hand over the top of the door, braced the other on the doorpost and stood there awkwardly, as though he wasn't sure whether to come in or stay out. She might have mentioned the cold air coming in, but she didn't. It wasn't important now. They shared a look that would have served well between true husband and wife, apologies and forgiveness passing both ways.

"The girls helped, remember. So . . ." He rocked the door back and forth, making the wooden hinges squeak. "So, just so you know. They heard us arguing."

"Oh, dear."

He shrugged, almost boyishly. "It's nothing. People argue sometimes."

"But the girls will feel better when they know we've put it aside."

The look in his eyes said, *So will I.*

She read the message and nodded, then smiled. "Show me this peace offering."

It was a sleigh. A *cariole*, he explained, but he'd made it from parts that had been scattered and left behind. "I found the runners stuck up in some rafters. Somebody must have forgotten that he'd stored them away." He took a turn around the conveyance, proudly pointing out each resourceful feature. "Found some pieces of harness, a wagon tongue. And I fixed up the box off a broken cart. Filled it with some straw I found stored in a rack. Bear Catcher helped the girls make some paint, and *voilà!*"

The girls stood to one side of the sleigh with their latest instructor, Wolf to the other. All eyes were on Emily, all awaiting her approval.

Approval was surely too small a word for the emotion that flooded her heart.

"Oh, it's beautiful!" She approached the creation cautiously, as though she were afraid she might scare it away. "It's just perfect. Such wonderful, wonderful . . ." She examined one of the metal runners, the supporting uprights, the wooden platform, then the box itself, decorated by novice painters. "Oh, look, snowflakes," Emily marveled. "And flowers. A combination of seasons. How lovely!"

She held out her arms to the girls, and they came running, each claiming a side so that she could squeeze them both at once.

"What about me?" Wolf demanded jovially. "Peace offered deserves peace given in return."

The girls nudged Emily in his direction.

"Yes, of course . . ."

"Right here." He laid a forefinger against his lips. "The kiss of peace would sit well right here."

She stepped up to him, stood on tiptoe and gave his lips a matronly peck.

He arched an eyebrow. "Did that look as halfhearted to you girls as it felt to me?"

"Do it again, *longer* this time," Lisette advocated, clapping her hands for good measure.

"Lisette," Marie-Claire admonished. "Behave like a proper lady."

Hearing the echo of her own teaching gave Emily a warm sense of satisfaction. She thought of another bit of wisdom, and offered it gently, her eyes never leaving Wolf's mock stern face. "When a gentleman shows such consideration, a proper lady responds wholeheartedly."

She slid her arms around his neck and pulled his handsomely chiseled face within her reach, then gave him the kind of lip-melting kiss she'd never have guessed to be part of her repertoire.

"Peace," Wolf said when he caught his breath.

Smiling, Emily responded, "Peace."

THE SLEIGH COMPLICATED their travel at first, for the mares did not readily pull as a team, and the harness Wolf had improvised kept breaking. He was patient. He put on his snowshoes and fairly skated over snow and ice alongside the mares, coaxing them to work together. When something broke, he fixed it, grumbling only when he thought no one was listening.

At times Emily thought he was almost *too* patient, for there were some moments so frustrating that she wanted to beg him to leave the infernal contraption behind and get on with the journey. But then she would look into the faces of the two girls and remember their efforts, as he had asked her to do, and she would steadfastly hold her peace.

But after a few days the going got easier. Between Bear Catcher and Wolf there was always a hunter to provide something for the skillet or the spit. The sleigh finally proved to be an asset, especially when long stretches of frozen river offered a level path. And then, what fun! Emily taught everyone to sing "Dashing through the snow," even as they did so, and the air turned less cold, the days less tedious, the travel less arduous.

Spirits rode high until Christmas Eve came before they had reached their destination. To make matters worse, the wind at their back was picking up, and the small white clouds overhead began to bump into each other, blend together and turn gray.

"We will find them soon," Bear Catcher promised. "Before we reach the mountains. Berger does not make camp in the mountains."

"He is Métis," Wolf agreed. "A man of the prairie. He travels until he finds the best hunting, then makes his camp."

"You can see that the deer are thick here," Bear Catcher said. "The camp is not far. This is where I told him to come."

"I'll ride on ahead to look for some kind of sign. Find us a good place to camp, if nothing else." Wolf could tell that his proposal didn't sit well with Emily, but she kept her concerns to herself. He offered what encouragement he could. "Either way, I'll bag us a good Christmas dinner."

THEY FOLLOWED Wolf's tracks until they trailed over the top of the river bluff and disappeared. Bear Catcher stayed the course along the river bottom until late afternoon, when Emily began to worry aloud. "He must have found them by now," she said. "Otherwise he'd be back, don't you think?"

"He waits for us."

Emily chucked the horses with the reins. "Do you know where?"

"A good place."

"A good place," Emily echoed. "A good place, a good place. He is testing me. He asked me to trust him, and now he thinks he must test me. And on Christmas Eve, of all times, testing my confidence, testing my . . . my faith."

The girls huddled close to her in their straw nest, all three swaddled in the blankets that made up the bedrolls. Including Wolf's. At least he had no plans to make camp without them, which surely meant—Emily scolded herself for thinking of it, even in the negative—he had no plans to desert them.

She looked up, seeking more substantial assurance from the new friend who had taken over Wolf's shepherding duties. "You believe he's somewhere up ahead, waiting for us, just . . . *waiting* for us?"

Bear Catcher's expression was both intent and inscrutable. "*Bonjour* man always finds a good place."

"I hope it's the place we're looking for," she muttered as she flicked the reins again. "I hope he's finally found those people."

"He finds *something*." Bear Catcher nodded downriver, toward a place where the high bluffs seemed to support the sagging clouds. "Look there."

At first only the smoke was visible. Then the cave in the rocky river bluff came into view, its tall, narrow portal festooned with pine boughs. Close by, Wolf could be seen tending something on the fire. When he saw them, he waved and motioned them over, grinning like a man who had found treasure. And to be sure, he had, for in the face of a gathering storm, the cave was as welcome a sight as the house of Emily's dreams ever would be.

It might have been a castle. A yuletide fortress, really. Wolf had trimmed it, inside and out, so that the scent of pine filled the interior, and the fire held the chill at bay. If Emily wanted an extra room, she had it now, for there was a second opening, where he'd built the fire, and enough space to accommodate the horses.

"You're awfully big to be a Christmas elf," Emily teased happily.

Wolf laughed as he welcomed them into his glorious find. "Do you mind spending Christmas Eve in a cave?"

"I believe there's some traditional precedent for a cave that shelters both man and beast." Her cheerful tone obscured the anxious look meant only for him. "No sign of the Berger encampment?"

"This is as far as I've gone. It was far enough for you to travel today." He slipped his arm around her shoulders and drew her close. He was still shaken by the overwhelming sense of relief that had flooded him the moment he'd caught the first glimpse of them, moving slowly down the river. He'd hated leaving them, but his choices had been limited, and he hadn't been comfortable with the one he'd made until he had them in his care again.

"The Métis are close by," he assured her. "I know it. Only a little farther."

"This is wonderful, Wolf." Emily surveyed his work, breathing deeply of the scents of pine and fire. "It's so festive. It feels like Christmas."

He squeezed her shoulders, and he laughed when Lisette suddenly grabbed his leg and hugged for all she was worth. "I don't want you girls getting attached to a cave, now, so tell me if you start thinking it feels like home."

"I think it does, a little, now that we are all together." Emily looked up and then reached out to touch his smooth chin. "With the ominous clouds gathering overhead, I did wonder . . . did fear for your safety, Mr. Morsette." He scowled, and she smiled softly. "Wolf."

"I'm not about to stray." Reluctantly he backed away, for there was still work to do, but he lifted an admonishing finger her way. "And I'm not about to forget that I made you a promise."

"What promise?"

"Have *you* forgotten, then?" He shook his head, offering Bear Catcher a man-to-man look. "When a promise slips his woman's mind, a man should keep his mouth shut and count himself lucky. It doesn't happen often."

"A woman's head is made to store these things," Bear Catcher agreed.

"You see, Emily? What is between a man and a woman is the same no matter where they live or what clothes they put on." Such talk drew him back to her for another quiet word, fingers laid briefly against her cool cheek. "Or the color of their eyes or face or hair. We never get to see your pretty hair, Miss Emily. It's always covered or knotted up somehow."

"I like to keep it neat, and, um . . ." He was pushing her bonnet back, touching her hair as though he had a sudden need to make sure it was still there. "Wolf," she whispered, desperately torn between propriety and the soft glow in his eyes. "My goodness."

"Your goodness." He gave a quick nod. "That's something I don't doubt."

It was her turn to back away, for this time the sense that all eyes were on her made her feel flustered. Awkward. She wasn't sure what response would be appropriate. Surely not the ardent kiss she was half-inclined to bestow upon his dear, welcome face.

"Look at this Christmas feast," she exclaimed dramatically, taking into account the sizable chunks of spitted meat dripping over the fire. "With all this—" her gesture included the spruce tree he'd stood in one corner and the pile of boughs he'd stripped to be made into beds "—you have certainly outdone yourself, Mr. Morsette."

He tucked his thumbs into his sash and grinned. "Your goodness must be rubbing off on me."

"And yours," she said, touching his arm, "on me. I have another song for tonight, and I have surprises." She smiled at the girls. "Gifts."

"So early?" Wolf asked.

"What is your custom? Do you save them for Epiphany?"

"It's been so long . . ." Wolf shook his head and laughed. "The priest would hold Mass and tell us, 'No fiddles, no dancing, you Métis! This is a night for quiet prayer.' And so it was. But then came the visiting from house to house, and gifts and music and racing the *carioles*. We know how to make a celebration last."

"It sounds wonderful, doesn't it, girls?"

"We have some fun in store," Wolf promised. "We'll unload the straw and bed the horses down. Is everyone hungry enough to eat my cooking?"

AFTER SUPPER EMILY taught the lyrics to "Silent Night." Wolf's strong voice lent rich, haunting depth to the hymn. In the distance, a whole choir of wolves joined in, and the horses' patient presence reminded the group of the part the animals played in their lives, this night and every night. Wolf and Bear Catcher were hunters, as their fathers and their fathers' fathers had been, but they never took the meat or the hides for granted, and their horses were like brothers to them.

And so when Emily told the story of Christmas, she made special mention of the donkey, the ox, and the lamb. In all the years that she had heard the story, she had been most thrilled by the vision of golden angels and most charmed by the serenity of mother and child. The "lowly manger" had been a familiar but meaningless phrase before this night.

Now she understood what it meant to huddle together—man, woman, child, and beast—simply for the need to stay warm. She looked at her companions, and for the first time in her life she understood what it meant to be a stranger in one's own land, now ruled by a conqueror who lived in a faraway place. Never before had she traveled so far, made do with so few comforts, and sought nothing more than a safe haven and unqualified acceptance.

And, after the long day's journey, never before had she been so content to be where she was with what she had.

When Wolf came to bed, he discovered that Emily had claimed the cold berth, the one close to the wall, leaving him the spot nearer the fire, with the girls to be snuggled, as usual, between them. Not tonight, he decided. He tucked the blankets around Marie-Claire's feet, then stepped over the three. The pine needles rustled beneath the cozy nest as he insinuated himself between Emily and the cave's rock wall.

She stirred and made a soft sound of protest, lifting her head just enough so that he was able to give her his arm for a pillow.

"Shh." He positioned his lips close to her ear, put his other arm around her and pulled her against him. "Tonight the Wolf shall lie down with the lamb."

"Oh," she said, and he could tell that she wasn't sure whether he was man or dream.

He brushed her hair aside and kissed the edge of her ear. "You'll sleep warmer this way, and I'll sleep happier."

"But, Wolf—"

"Hold my hand," he suggested as he trailed it down her arm, seeking her hand. "Hold it tight, now, don't let it stray, the way it will in my dreams."

"Wolf, you are such a . . . wolf."

"Shh, love, you could tame me," he crooned in her ear. "I could be your lapdog." He traced the curve of her ear with the tip of his tongue and felt a shiver shimmy through her. "Your watchdog. I would let no man come near you." Delicately he nipped her downy nape, and she gasped. "Your hunting dog," he whispered. "I could provide for you."

"What must I do in return?" she whispered.

"Don't make me sleep outside."

"Oh, Wolf . . ." She squeezed his hand and tucked it against her belly. "You once told me that you were accustomed to sleeping under the open sky. You said—"

"Did you know that it was a woman who first tamed the wolf for a pet?"

"It was?"

"The wolf found her sleeping in the woods one night, and he thought she was beautiful. He lay down with her to keep her warm." Wolf snuggled as close against her back as he could get with their clothes in the way. "Like this. Just before the sun rose, he slipped away. Each night he would seek her out. Some nights he would find her in the woods, and he would curl up next to her. On cold nights when she slept inside, he would stay outside her door. During the day he went into the hills, but at night he wanted to be near her. Soon he began to long for her company, day and night.

"He hid in the trees one day and watched her gather cherries until she filled her baskets. Then she tried to lift them, but the weight of the full baskets was too much for her. She stumbled and spilled the cherries. When she picked herself up and started collecting them off the ground, the wolf noticed that she was crying, and he knew he had a choice to make. He could either go back to his own kind, to the wolf people, or he could stay with the woman and ease her burden.

"In his heart the choice had already been made, but when he came out of the woods, he frightened her. She'd never seen him in the daylight, and he looked quite fierce. He thought she was repulsed by him, and he wanted to die. But she did not hiss at him or throw rocks to make him go away, the way a man might do. Instead she stood very still. Then, finally, she held out her hand, palm up. He came to her and licked the salt of her labor from her hand, licked her until her calluses melted away. And he offered to carry her baskets on his back."

Emily gave a soft sigh. Then she moved his hand slowly, slowly, letting it trail lightly along the center line of her body until his fingertips touched her chin. She lowered her head and pressed her lips to the back of his hand.

Wolf closed his eyes and finished his story in a husky whisper.

"To this day, the dog is a friend to the women of the Cree, the Lakota and the Ojibwa. He bears their burdens, and he asks little in return."

"What a wonderful story," Emily said softly. "Tomorrow you must tell it to the girls."

First one giggled, and then the other joined in.

"We heard."

"I didn't hear the first part," Lisette insisted.

"You didn't have to make up a big story, Wolf," Marie-Claire admonished. "Miss Emily would never make you sleep outside."

Wolf chuckled. "I didn't make it up. The grandmothers tell that story."

"My grandmother told it another way," Bear Catcher informed them from his corner of the cave.

Emily had to bite her lip to keep from laughing aloud. Wolf could feel her shaking with it. He playfully nipped the back of her neck, but still she managed to contain herself, which was more than he could say for himself when she reached back and tickled him in the ribs.

The night wind whistled and stirred the snowfall, while inside the warm cave the voices in the dark took turns telling stories. First Bear Catcher launched into his grandmother's wolf tale. Then Emily whispered a fairy princess tale, followed by Wolf's dream-catcher story.

It was Christmas Eve. No matter whose customs they would follow, it was gift-giving time.

And the best gifts of all were the stories.

Chapter Six

CHRISTMAS DAY HAD a dreary dawning. The world outside the cave was ruled by wind and snow. But inside there were two young girls who took no notice of the weather. They were too busy exclaiming over the miraculous appearance of gifts made especially for them. There were fur hats and wooden string puppets whose legs jackknifed when their strings were pulled. There were two soft-bodied dolls with calico dresses and pretty muslin aprons, one for each of them.

Emily helped them try on their Cossack-style hats and showed them how to tie their aprons. She admired the little puppets' remarkable mechanism and praised the cleverness of the carver who had fashioned them.

The two men quietly smoked their pipes, enjoying the proceedings with male reserve until Wolf announced that it was Emily's turn to be surprised.

The girls sat her down on their bed.

"Close your eyes, Miss Emily."

Emily could hear Wolf whispering to each girl. Intrigued, she shut her eyes even tighter and listened closely, trying to imagine what he was handing them and which girl approached her from the left and which from the right. A fur hat was the first gift. Emily could easily guess by the careful way she handled the fitting and hair arrangement that Marie-Claire was the designated giver. Emily lifted her hands to touch, parted her lips to praise, but Wolf's voice delayed her response.

"Don't open your eyes yet. We're not finished."

She sensed that it was little Lisette who came up behind her and draped something soft and fuzzy around her neck, topping it off with an exuberant hug and a whispered "Merry Christmas."

"Say it the way Wolf told you," Marie-Claire instructed.

"Joyeux Noël!" Lisette shouted, jumping with considerable joy of her own. "Open your eyes! Open your eyes, Mama!"

Lisette didn't notice the startled expressions in the faces around her, but her innocent excitement bridged the awkward moment, and Emily quickly fell to petting the fur pieces and fawning over the girls, who hovered close by.

"Lisette's just a baby," Marie-Claire whispered apologetically. "She never knew our—"

"It's all right," Emily said, warming Marie-Claire's hand in hers. "It's perfectly all right."

"You look like the beautiful fairy princess," Marie-Claire said. "Doesn't she, Wolf? From the story last night."

"I don't know much about fairy princesses. She reminds me of the woman in *my* story." A smile danced in his dark eyes. "The one who tamed the Wolf."

"But I wouldn't tame him and then take his fur."

"These are made of fox fur, not wolf. The skins were small. I only had enough for—" Laying a hand on her shoulder, he smoothed the triangular fur scarf the girls had arranged about her neck. "What would this be called?"

"I think they used to call this a fichu." Emily tucked her chin into the fur, looking down her nose to admire as she patted and primped. "They used to wear them when the dresses had very low necklines."

"I don't know much about ladies' fashions."

"I shall be happy to revive this fashion. It's wonderfully warm and soft." She looked up at him and smiled. "Very practical. Thank you."

"When my cousins see you, the women will all want one of these. When we find them . . ." He knelt beside her, bracing his arm over his knee like a suitor, eager to offer credible reassurance, which he knew to be the gift she needed most. "*When* we find them and we get settled in, I'll make you a cape. Or a coat. Which would you like?"

"I'm very pleased with what I have."

"What you need is a wearing robe, like Bear Catcher's."

Emily's gaze followed Wolf's, and together they included the man who still lounged on his sleeping pallet, smoking his pipe. "Why, yes, I have admired—"

"Careful," Wolf warned quietly. "He's liable to give it to you if you tell him how much you like it."

Bear Catcher laughed. "I like very much your saddle and two of your blankets, *bonjour* man."

"Just trying to make you look good," Wolf teased.

"I'm looking plenty damn good already." Bear Catcher tapped a forefinger to his temple. "Plenty damn smart, too."

"Well, I have a gift for *you,* Bear Catcher," Emily announced. She opened one of her carpetbags and produced two flannel shirts. "And one for Wolf."

The shirts looked exactly alike—both red and black, both collarless, buttonless boxy styles, but they fit. And the men seemed genuinely pleased.

"Oh, my, you do look handsome, both of you. You could pass for brothers."

"Half-brothers, maybe." Wolf tapped Bear Catcher's shoulder. "You think the Indian agents would believe I'm your brother, Bear Catcher? This side of the Canadian border, there's no Métis. There's either white or Indian." He held out his hand, displaying the back of it for proof. "And I sure ain't white."

"*Half*-brother, maybe," Bear Catcher allowed.

"See, so that makes me Métis. Not *bonjour* man." Playfully he jabbed an elbow into Bear Catcher's ribs, and Bear Catcher returned the gesture, adding a sparring maneuver. In their look-alike shirts they might well have been two rowdy boys. Their audience rewarded them with feminine giggles.

"'Course the government's making reservations for you Indians. Your half-brothers don't qualify." Wolf slapped Bear Catcher's shoulder. "Where's your agency, Bear Catcher? Is there room for me on the rolls?"

Bear Catcher shrugged. "If I go back to Dakota and put my name in their book to be counted, they say I will have an agency and annuities."

Emily considered the curious requirement. "You mean, you're supposed to return to the country where you were born so that a census can be taken?"

"Just like in the Christmas story?" Marie-Claire asked. "Just like Mary and Joseph?"

"Governments have their business to do. Since time immemorial they have made it a project to count people and determine their . . ." Emily searched for the proper word. "Origin, I suppose."

"When they come to count us, we'll be with the Métis." Wolf chucked Marie-Claire under the chin, drawing out her soft, sweet smile. "Right, girls? If they don't have Métis on their list of choices, they can count us as Indians who play the fiddle and dance a Red River jig."

"And wear beaded moccasins and hunt buffalo," Emily supplied, admiring Wolf's moccasins, then Bear Catcher's.

"Buffalo are gettin' harder to find these days, but not beads." Wolf stuck out his foot for a better view. "We've still got the beads. So they can call us Ojibwa or Canadians or *bonjour* men if they want, but we'll still be Métis."

"And where shall I be?" Emily wondered.

"For the rest of the winter, you'll be with us. After that . . ." He shrugged, his glance skittering away from her face and purposely avoiding the two girls'. "I guess you *can* be wherever you want to be."

"If we find your people—"

"*When* we find them."

"When we find them," Emily obliged, "are you planning to finally settle down?"

"I'm used to makin' my way as I go. I've never done much planning." He planted one hand on his hip and gestured in her direction with the other. "Well, look at you, Miss Emily. You made your plans, and they didn't work out. Looks to me like a plan ain't something you can always depend on."

The crackling fire was the only sound filling the abrupt, awkward silence.

"I guess you're right about that." Taking her own time, Emily rose to face him.

But not in anger. She mirrored his stance, arms akimbo, and challenged him with a fierce smile. "Guess that's why a man needs some religion," she drawled in a passable imitation of Wolf Morsette. In her natural voice, she added pointedly, "And I guess that's why a woman does, too."

Wolf was momentarily dumbfounded.

Emily stood her ground, still smiling.

He laughed. Then he looked at her, shook his head and laughed some more. "Hell, that sounds like something a wise man once said."

"He has his flashes of wisdom, along with his moments of weakness." Emily lifted Lisette into her arms and gave her puppet string a quick tug. "And from the looks of it, he's been planning for Christmas for some time."

"Damn right. I might not know just where I'll lay my head from one night to the next—" he ruffled Lisette's hair and treated Emily to a wolfish wink "—but I know what I'm givin' my girls for Christmas."

When the storm abated, Bear Catcher rode out with a promise to locate the Berger camp. When he didn't return, Wolf roundly cursed the man's entire ancestry.

But Emily was worried about their friend. "Perhaps he's lost."

"Lost? Indians don't get *lost*. He doesn't wanna miss any part of the

New Year's celebration, so he's just takin' his time, just fillin' up his belly." Wolf kicked at the last of the firewood. "He's probably keeping his mouth so full he hasn't gotten around to telling anybody that we're out here waitin' on him."

It was easier to grumble than to think of bundling the women up and taking them out on what could well prove to be another fruitless journey.

"I don't think Bear Catcher would let us down." Emily laid a consoling hand on his arm. "You don't, either."

"We'll see." From the cave door he scanned the frozen stretch of river below. "The weather's on our side now."

And so was the granter of Christmas wishes. They'd traveled no more than half a day when they came upon a party of Métis hunters. Riding in the lead was their friend, Bear Catcher.

"You don't trust my word, *bonjour* man?"

Unable to suppress a broad grin, Wolf rode up beside his Indian friend and clasped his arm. "Hell, I thought somebody might have mistaken you for a renegade Sioux and shot your damn tail feathers off."

Bear Catcher laughed. "Not even a one-eyed white man could mistake a Ojibwa for a sneaky Sioux."

"Then again, I thought you might have gotten caught up in the fiddle music. But Miss Emily knew better."

"They got a Black Robe, these *bonjours*." Bear Catcher smiled at Emily as he gave Wolf fair warning. "If she's not your woman, she will soon be mine."

"You *wish*," Wolf said, his sense of humor suddenly in short supply. His horse pranced restlessly as he wheeled to greet the party of horsemen strung out along the riverbank.

"Are you Wolf Morsette? Joseph Morsette's son?" A man with a salt-and-pepper beard offered Wolf a handshake. "You sure favor your mother, boy."

"So I've been told."

The older man motioned for the rest of the party to gather in close, then leaned back in his saddle, taking in Wolf's appearance from head to toe. "Heard you made yourself a reputation with a pistol. What kind of a thing is that for a Métis? A little six-shooter. A man needs a good buffalo gun. A good rifle."

Squinting into the bright winter sun, Wolf agreed, indicating his rifle scabbard with a nod. Next to his pipe and his knife, the rifle was a Métis man's most prized possession.

"You got the law on your tail, son?"

"Not that I know of."

"I'm Pierre Berger. Don't know if you remember, I'm a half-brother to your father, from over by—"

"I remember my uncle Pierre," Wolf said, smiling.

"Where you been keepin' yourself?"

"Been knockin' around the Territories since I can't remember when. Thought I'd head up this way, look up some of my relations."

"See you brought your family."

"I, uh—" Wolf backed his horse up a couple of steps, reining his head toward the sleigh. "This is Emily. The little ones are Marie-Claire and Lisette. What we need is—"

"What we need is some fiddle music, Mr. Morsette." Emily took off one of her gloves and extended her hand to the elder man. "Please say we haven't missed the celebration, Mr. Berger."

"Missed it?" Berger dismounted in order to greet Emily properly, taking her hand in both of his. "No, no, we've got plenty to celebrate. This place Bear Catcher told us about, this whole basin, the game is plentiful. Good land here. We got twenty-five families, and the trader, Janeaux, he says he'll put us up a trading post." He looked at Wolf. "We're calling it Spring Creek."

"Spring Creek," Emily repeated, as though the words were almost sacred. "Oh, Wolf, it has a *name*. Girls, your new home is called Spring Creek."

JUST AS WOLF had promised, they had found people who would take them in. And, as Pierre Berger had promised, the holiday celebration was still in progress when they reached the camp, which looked quite similar to the one on the Milk River. But here the hearths were warm, the laughter merry, and the big hall was jumping with music.

The dancing was even livelier than anything Wolf had demonstrated. The men, especially, were the most tireless dancers Emily had ever seen. The new dance hall's as yet only partially mud-plastered log walls fairly trembled with the rousing hoots and yelps that punctuated the music of fiddle, washtub and clacking spoons. The plank floors shook from the stomping heels. The parti-colored *l'assomption* sashes tied about most of the men's waists whipped around the room like trailing banners. Emily would have judged Wolf the most agile, most graceful, surely the most remarkable dancer in the crowd, but he termed himself "rusty." She could see why when the contest winner was able to perform thirty different jigging steps.

Bear Catcher had his own version of each dance, but the Indian influence on the blended heritage of the Métis was readily apparent in his steps. One young woman seemed particularly interested in teaching him to waltz. And even the smallest children were fine dancers. There was no shortage of dance teachers for Marie-Claire and Lisette, who had known a dearth of playmates in their young lives. But that was about to change.

For Emily there was only one dance partner. She thought perhaps Bear Catcher's comment had given Wolf pause. He had come home at last. Not to a place, but to his people, with whom he had a lot of catching up to do. Still, he was as attentive to her as the most ardent suitor. She loved the feel of his hand on her back as he guided her effortlessly about the floor. She would have been pleased to spend the rest of her life dancing with him thus.

"Nothing would please me more," he whispered in her ear, "than to dance with you until the sun comes up, Miss Emily."

The declaration surprised her, so close had it come to her own thoughts. He looked into her eyes and smiled knowingly. Unless he was a mind reader, she'd unconsciously made her wish aloud.

"Or until you agree to be my wife," he said. "Whichever comes first."

"Marriage means settling down, doesn't it? Making plans?" She gripped his shoulder tighter than she meant to as she recalled his every infuriatingly evasive word. "You said that in the spring . . ."

"There will be no spring. Not unless you marry me." The hand at her back slid to her waist, taking a possessive hold. "At least, not for me. I've had winter in my heart for such a long time, I didn't know any better." He glanced over her head, then quickly back, his eyes pleading with hers. "Marie-Claire and Lisette belong with us, Emily. Don't speak of leaving me."

"I was thinking more that . . . *you* might not stay."

"Woman, don't you know how much I love you?"

They stood together in the middle of the floor, dancers whirling in the periphery of her stunned awareness. *He loved her?*

"And . . . I promised to build you a house."

She found only a small piece of her voice. "For all of us?"

"And then some. As many rooms as it takes to make you happy." He pulled her against him and whispered, for her ear only, "And as many babies."

"Oh, Wolf, I love you. I didn't imagine . . . I dreamed, yes, but I could not think or hope—" she tipped her head, needing to see his face through the tears gathered in her eyes "—that there might be a husband for me and love, too."

He touched her cheek solicitously. "How else would you have it?"

"No way else," she declared, hugging his neck, seeking his lips. "No one else. Oh, Wolf . . ."

"They've gotten started kissing in the New Year," someone shouted.

"*Sacre coeur,* wait, wait . . ."

A hand on each of their shoulders drew them out of a blissful kiss. Like two dreamy-eyed children they blinked at each other, then at Uncle Pierre's laughing face. "What is this, you want to start your own tradition?"

"What tradition?" Emily's question ended in a funny little croak.

Wolf laughed and squeezed her affectionately.

Pierre waved his hand in the air. The music had stopped, and the room was filled with chatter, both *Michif* and English, flavored with hearty guffaws and happy giggles. "Father, we should have the blessing," Pierre announced.

"I think these two must have the blessing." A priest robed in a black cassock appeared at Pierre's side. He addressed Wolf solemnly. "If all you have is a country marriage, my son, I can give you the Church's blessing tonight."

Wolf took no offense at the priest's assumption. He simply grinned at his bride-to-be. "None too soon for me, Father."

"Wolf." She rose on tiptoe and whispered in his ear. "We ought to have a proper wedding."

"She's right." Tucking her hand under his arm, he turned to the assemblage to make his announcement. "Miss Emily has tamed the Wolf. She is a very proper lady, and she deserves a proper wedding. And a proper house." He gestured with his free hand. "And all this family."

Cheers filled the dance hall. The fiddler added his chords of approval, and the washtub player rattled a resounding tattoo.

"People who will take us in," Emily said with a smile. "No questions asked."

"Considering our special circumstances, Father, would you mind dispensing with the banns and such?" Wolf entreated Emily, making no attempt to mask the eagerness in his eyes. "Let's have our proper wedding after we kiss in the New Year. New Year's Day is a good time to make vows." Then he whispered, "The sooner we marry, the sooner you will have your house."

"Then let's turn this party into a wedding feast," Emily agreed.

AS THE HEAD of the group, Pierre received the priest's New Year's blessing, which he passed on to his wife and each of his own children in the form of a kiss. Once the New Year's kissing started, it continued throughout the group, a blessing joyfully shared. The mood was right for a wedding, then, and Pierre's wife brought out a treasured length of cream-colored embroidered cutwork linen, which served as Emily's veil. Pierre magnanimously offered the use of his cabin for a honeymoon.

THE HOUSE-TO-HOUSE visiting, the *cariole* races, the dancing, the music—all the festivities continued without the newlyweds. For three days they listened to the sounds of the celebration going on outside the walls of their borrowed lovers' bower. Food appeared regularly on the doorstep, and, periodically, someone outside would shout in *Michif* a close approximation of *Toujour l'amour!*

"You're missing the Métis festivities," Emily teased as she fed her husband a bite of the raised bread she had baked for him and dipped in stewed plums. He licked the plum juice off her fingers and then shared the sweet taste from his lips to hers.

"I'm *making* Métis festivities," he told her. He smiled lustfully as he dispatched the buttons on the yoke of her white flannel nightgown. "Would you rather make them here by the fire this time, or under the bed covers?"

"If you touch me there . . ."

"Where?" His thumb flicked across her nipple. "There?"

The sweet ache he'd been tutoring her to love took her breath away, made her eyes drift closed, made her smile.

"Yes, I think so," he whispered against her neck. "I think you want me to touch you there."

"I think so, too," she said. "And I think it's too late to move to the bed."

There were races going on outside. Wolf had half a mind to race a little, too. On a bet he knew he could shuck his sash, pants, and moccasins before she could get her nightgown over her head. But his

Emily liked it better when he took her slowly. When he teased her and touched her and kissed her until all her thoughts were quite improper—that was the way his Emily loved to be loved.

He smiled when he heard another victory shout. "Noisy fellow," he grumbled. "Maybe I should just go out there and give him a run for his money, hmm?" He bit her nipple gently and sucked air between his teeth until she shivered with the tingle he took pleasure in creating for her. Chuckling, he pushed her nightgown over her shoulders and down, down until he'd stripped her bare.

And bare she lay on the soft fur rug. He knelt beside her, grinning at the lovely picture she made, her skin already flushed from the fire and from his ardent attentions.

"Would you mind if I ducked out now, just for a little race?"

She tugged on his sash, drawing him back to her. "Not if you wouldn't mind sleeping outside."

He gave a wolfish whimper as he nuzzled her, rooting around her breasts. Moments later he growled as she took her time freeing him from his pants.

And finally, as the moon rose over the New Year's festivities in the Métis winter camp, Miss Emily's Wolf gave a thrilling, thoroughly heated-up howl.

Within a month, Miss Emily had a house of her own.

And within nine more, Marie-Claire and Lisette had a baby brother.

The Twelfth Moon

Prologue

THE LONG GREYHOUND topped the rise and dropped Luke Tracker's stomach over the hill ahead of the rest of him. For at least the tenth time since he'd left Fort Leonard Wood, Missouri, he asked himself why he'd taken the bus. The answer that came back was, That's part of coming home, remember? Jets flew over Wakpala, South Dakota, but passengers saw nothing except the winding white scar of a river and maybe the lights of Mobridge, ten miles away.

Luke sat up and peered over the top of the seat in front of him. The town of Mobridge sprawled across the flat below, with the Missouri River throwing a cozy loop around it on the south and west. The Mobridge he remembered wasn't much of town, either. The old Brown Palace Hotel was the dominant building on Main Street, and it only stood three stories high. Main Street itself looked like a movie set for a Western, with its row of storefronts and its tacky saloons gathered at the west end. Jets flew over Mobridge, too, and freight trains rumbled through without stopping, but there was a bus stop here. Luke wasn't sure he actually wanted to get off, but he'd damn sure be glad when the bus came to a stop.

He settled back to watch the fields fly past the window as the bus drew near the edge of town. Golden stubble poked through a crusty, bright snow shell. It was always hard to tell how much snow they'd gotten, because the wind seldom let it pile up. The sky out here was high, wide, and handsome, and the winter sun bounced its brightness off the white ground cover, reminding Luke that nature had a practical reason for endowing his race with hooded eyes and high cheekbones.

The bus pulled up in front of the Brown Palace. Luke's own reflection in the window superimposed itself over the assortment of faces that looked up from the street below. He dismissed the fuzzy Scotch caps with earflaps and the black felt cowboy hats as he searched the crowd. Then he caught a glimpse of Frankie's blue-black hair, done up in a fashionable French braid, and he smiled.

Her eyes brightened when she saw that he'd finally picked her out of the crowd. She sank her chin into the pile collar of her bright red down-filled jacket, happily puffing out mist as she flashed a row of white teeth. She was such a pretty sight, it made Luke's heart swell. He grabbed his green overcoat and his dress cap from the aisle seat and stepped off the bus to greet his sister.

"Damn it, Frankie, if you don't look just like a woman." He grinned as he dropped an arm around her shoulders and edged her away from the crowd. Even after three years, there would be no showy public embrace from Luke and no delighted shrieks from his younger sister. Certainly not here in an off-reservation town. He gave her braid a sly tug. a gesture subtle enough to be shared on the street as they stood aside and waited for the luggage to be removed from the bus's underbelly.

"Don't call me that, Luke," she pleaded, although she knew she had little chance of shedding the nickname with her oldest brother. "It's Frances."

"Or Miss Frances? Or, better yet, Miss Tracker?" He gave the shoulder under his hand a quick squeeze. "I can't believe you're a teacher now."

"Why not? Anybody can be a teacher," she reminded him with a smile. They were his words. All of them. "All you have to do is finish high school, go to four years of college—"

"And practice your BIA—Bossing Indians Around," he finished with a laugh. It was their old joke on the Bureau of Indian Affairs.

"I'm glad you wore your uniform," she said. "Daddy loves to see you in it." She watched him step forward to claim his army green duffel bag. He hitched the canvas strap over his shoulder, and she pointed across the street. "That's my car." He heard the note of pride in her voice. The little blue Chevy was the first car she'd bought nearly new.

"Nice," he said. He looked up and down the street as he stepped off the curb. "You know, this place looks just the same."

"It isn't. They've opened a new restaurant and at least two new grocery stores." She took two short steps for each of his long strides as they crossed the street together. "It's been seven years since you were home, Luke. Things have to change some in that much time."

"It's only been three since I've seen the family." He had to get that in. Seven years sounded pretty negligent.

"But that was in Vermillion, when you came to my graduation. You haven't been home in seven years." She unlocked the hatchback, and he tossed his duffel bag into the car. "Mama's at home, cooking to beat the band, and Daddy wanted to come with me, but Mama said it wouldn't be fair, because she couldn't come. So my instructions were to take the shortcut to get you home."

They wanted him home. That was the worst of it. It wasn't as though he were the black sheep of the family who stayed away because he wasn't welcome. He stayed away because nothing ever changed. Except him. He'd changed, and he was sure he wouldn't fit in anymore. When he'd first enlisted, he used to come home a couple of times a year. He'd wanted to see Monica then. When it became obvious that Monica would never leave home, not for him or for anyone else, his visits had dwindled to once a year—Christmas, for sure. Then, maybe Christmas. He was good about calling, and he even wrote once in a while. But he'd left the Reservation, and he wasn't anxious to return.

"I'll bet you're good at bossing Indians around." Once she had her brother's attention, Frances handed him her car keys. "Or anybody else, for that matter. You look one-hundred-percent government issue." And he wore it well, she thought. He was the right man for the uniform. The shiny black brim of his dress cap pulled down low over his brow gave him an eagle-eyed look, and his square jaw was the perfect complement to his square shoulders.

"I don't suppose you'll take orders from me anymore, now that you're a big teacher." He smiled. "You've gotten so damn pretty, Frankie. I think I oughta teach you a little self-defense."

"Are you kidding? I grew up the same place you did, remember? I learned that long ago." It surprised her when he opened the car door for her. It wasn't something she'd seen him do for anyone except their mother.

"So tell me, little sister, what's new in Wakpala?"

Frances gave him a mysterious little smile as he pushed the driver's seat back from the wheel. "You'll have to find out for yourself. I will tell you this, though. Your parents are getting old, and they shouldn't have to wait so long between visits from their oldest son. And"—she turned her attention to the windshield—"your ex-girlfriend moved to Billings with some truck driver."

"She did, huh?" He turned the key in the ignition, and the little car's engine roared. Luke chuckled. More power to her. She'd turned out to be stronger than he'd thought. "You sure you want me to drive this thing across the river?"

"Sure I'm sure. The ice is thick enough." She raised a challenging eyebrow his way. "You're not chicken, are you?"

Luke grinned. "Baby sister, we are taking the shortcut."

Chapter One

HO-HO-HO!"

The initial "Ho" sent the table knife flying out of Hope Spencer's hand. She grabbed the oblong cake pan before it toppled over the edge of her desk and clattered the way of the knife. A tentative giggle rippled through the group of nine-year-olds that had gathered for chocolate cake, but there were several faces registering such wide-eyed, gap-toothed awe that Hope hesitated to crane her neck toward the doorway.

"Merry Christmas!"

Two small hands latched on to Hope's belt. She laid her hand on the quaking shoulder, holding her first two fingers straight out to avoid smearing chocolate frosting on little Carol Two Horses' sweater. "It's okay, Carol," she said softly as she turned her head toward the classroom door. "It's only Santa Claus."

Hope's friend, Frances Tracker, had delivered the man with the booming voice to the door. He did look like Santa Claus. Sort of. The plush red suit had obviously been in storage for twelve months, and it was a little short for a man his size. The tall black combat boots were an interesting touch. Hope wondered how soon the children would notice the contrast between his white beard and his thick black eyebrows.

"Here he is!" Frances announced. From the gleam in her eyes, she might have brought some hot screen star. "Santa brought treats for everybody. My second graders are sure enjoying theirs."

Santa looked the group over and scowled. "What sort of boys and girls are *these*, Miss Tracker?" He gave Frances a dramatic over-the-shoulder look. "Are they *good* boys and girls?" Again he surveyed the group, huddling closer now behind the teacher's desk. "Or are they *naughty* boys and girls?"

"You'll have to ask Miss Spencer that, Santa. They're probably a little of each," Frankie said.

"A little of each, hmm?" Santa raised one eyebrow and stepped into the room. In each hand he carried a flowered pillow case that presumably contained the promised treats. "Guess I'll have to find out for myself which is which."

"I have to get back to my bunch," Frances said, smiling so hard her face must have hurt. "Have fun, Miss Spencer."

Most of the children were jostling for position behind Hope. Only a few brave souls stood their ground and watched as the tall man approached. Feeling a little wary and childlike herself, Hope quickly licked the sweet chocolate from her fingers.

"I think what Miss Tracker meant, Santa, was that they've all had good days and bad." Hope shrugged as she offered a tentative smile. "Don't we all?"

"We definitely do," Santa agreed. "I have them myself."

A stubby arm clamped itself around her waist, and she reached down to smooth Courtney Brown Bear's mop of hair. "I think we're all wondering, uh, which it might be today, Santa."

He turned his rich, deep laughter into a Ho-ho-ho, then said, "I've come a long way, and I'm very tired. Will you bring your chair out here for me, Miss Spencer?" He patted the saggy stuffing under his wide plastic belt, then pointed to the array of small chairs throughout the classroom. "I certainly can't sit in one of *those* little things."

"Of course." It took some maneuvering to give herself room to do the job. "Excuse me, Carol. Courtney, here, just let me . . ." Courtney dove under the desk as Hope lifted the chair and used it to clear a path. "I'm not going anywhere, Patty. Santa needs to sit down so he can—"

As she broke free of the cluster, one of the braver youngsters grasped her by the wrist. "What is it, Cowboy?"

"That ain't no Santa Claus," the boy confided quietly. "I saw Santa Claus at the Ben Franklin store in Mobridge, and you can just tell this one's a fake."

She knew she shouldn't ask, but it slipped out. "How can you tell?"

"Well, he's not white."

Hope's face reddened, while Santa Claus enjoyed a belly-shaking laugh. On the heels of the laughter he asked, "What makes you think I always have to be white, Cowboy?"

"Well, every time *I* see you . . ."

"Have you ever seen me after I just got back from down south?" Santa boomed. "I just made a run down to Brazil. Gotta see those kids down there, too, you know. Don't you get darker in the sun?" Now as wide-eyed as the rest of the children, Cowboy nodded. "So do I," Santa said. "I tan real easy. It's summertime in Brazil." He kept his eyes on

Cowboy as he reached for the big armless oak chair. "Or didn't you know that, Cowboy? Haven't you been doing your geography homework?"

"We haven't gotten to South America yet," Hope put in.

"You haven't, huh?" Santa made a production of seating himself with a weary groan, settling his sacks on either side of the chair and planting his hands on his knees. "Bunch of real nice kids down there in Brazil," he said absently. Then he pointed a white-gloved finger in Hope's direction. "You be sure and teach these little guys all about South America, Miss Spencer."

"Yes, I . . . I certainly will."

"Now." Santa slapped both knees at once as he eyed the crowd. "I want each and every one of you children to come over here, sit on old Santa's knee—whichever one you want—and introduce yourself properly so I know whether to give you something from this bag—" he nodded to the right "—or this other one. Who wants to be first?"

There were no volunteers.

Hope stepped closer to the formidable visitor from the North Pole via Brazil. "Santa, maybe I could just help you distribute the gifts—"

"Nope." The bell on the point of his cap jingled as Santa shook his acrylic white wig. "I came here to shake hands with each and every person in this room, including that one." He pointed at the big brown eyes that were peeking out from under the desk. They vanished immediately. "And that's just what I'm gonna do." He lifted a challenging eyebrow as he turned his face up at Hope. "Maybe we should start with the teacher."

The children's giggles seemed encouraging. "Shake hands?" she said. "Why, of course." She extended hers, and it was lost in his white glove. She felt the strength in the warm hand beneath the velvety fabric.

"So tell me your name," he demanded.

"I . . . I'm Hope Spencer, Santa Claus."

"Very nice name." He planted his feet wide apart on the floor and hooked his hands at his hips. "Well?"

Hope blinked. "Well, what?"

"Which knee do you prefer, Hope Spencer?"

Hope stepped up close to Santa's side and lowered her voice. "I really don't think that's necessary, Santa. I'm a pretty big girl."

"They say there's a kid in all of us at Christmas." He turned his head to the side and muttered from the corner of his mouth, "Do you want these kids to play the game or not?"

Hope stared at the red-clad thighs. They were long and looked completely sturdy. "Did Miss Tracker sit on your lap, Santa?"

"'Course she did. She's getting a new pair of boots for Christmas, too, so sit right down here, Miss Spencer." His eyes danced as he slapped his thigh. "Let's see what ol' Santa can do for you."

Hope stepped between his knees and seated herself gingerly, as though his thigh might be connected to the radiator along the wall. He cupped his hand lightly at her waist, smiled and then let loose with a Ho-ho-ho that didn't begin to express his utter delight with the situation.

"I think that if you'd tone that down," Hope muttered with a forced smile, "you might have better results."

"I think I'm getting pretty damn good results," he mumbled back. "How do you like it so far?" Before she could answer, he Ho-ho-hoed again, and Hope just rolled her eyes toward the ceiling. "Are you a good girl, Hope Spencer?" Santa demanded.

"I try hard to be, Santa."

"I'm trying hard to be Santa," he mumbled into his beard. "You just try hard not to look so terrified." Then, in his stage voice, he announced, "I'll bet you do. I'll bet you're a very good teacher. *But . . .*" He raised his white-gloved index finger. "Do you eat your vegetables?"

"I love vegetables," she managed evenly. She was beginning to enjoy this man.

"Of course you do." He glanced at the children, who were gradually venturing forth from the stockade of the teacher's desk. "That wasn't a fair test, was it, you guys? She's an adult. Adults *all* love vegetables. Most of their taste buds have died." There were some nods, some shaking heads, and some giggles. "*So,* Hope Spencer. Do you make your bed every morning?"

"Yes, well . . . most of the time."

"With the blanket tucked tight enough so I could bounce a quarter on it?"

"I don't know." She frowned and then shrugged. "I've never tried bouncing—"

"And what about your desk over there?" He held his hand in front of her face, and his challenge rumbled deep in his chest. "If I ran this glove over that desk, would I find dust?"

"Probably," she confessed.

"Hmm. Two demerits so far." He tapped his fingers against his thigh as he weighed the evidence. "*Now,*" he barked, "let me see your shoes."

"What?"

He waggled his fingers above her knees, which were covered demurely by a drapy Christmas-green skirt. By this time the children were laughing easily. "Get 'em up here. Let me see how long it's been since you polished your shoes."

She turned slightly and stretched one leg out in front of her. "You sound like a drill sergeant," she muttered, and he answered with a chuckle. She saw that his visual inspection took in her calf, her ankle and finally her black pump.

"Pretty dull," he judged, and he noticed a little stiffening in her back as she lowered her leg. "Didn't you use any spit?"

"I used the stuff that comes in the can."

"The stuff in the can, huh?" he nodded thoughtfully. "I don't know, Hope Spencer. I'd say you're a *pretty* good girl." He reached for the pillowcase on the right. "But when I come back next year, I expect to hear that you've made some improvements." He pulled a small, gaily-wrapped box from his sack and handed it to her. "I expect to see some shine on those shoes. That stuff in the can, that's not good enough. You've gotta use a little spit."

She lifted her toe into the air again and studied the shoe. "Doesn't eating my vegetables count for anything?" she wondered.

"'Course it does. 'Course it does. That's why your gift came from the *good* sack. Now tell me what else is on your wish list." Hope opened her mouth to speak and felt his hand tighten at her waist as he leaned closer, his eyes dancing. "Whisper your wishes into Santa's ear, Miss Spencer."

With a look that told him she could handle the challenge, she cupped one hand around his ear, lifted her chin and shared her Christmas wishes. Then she leaned back and smiled. Just when she was getting comfortable, he roared another, "Ho-ho-ho," that made her spring off his lap. He looked up at her, somewhat regretfully. Santa had been getting comfortable, too.

By the time Santa left, he'd gotten all of the children, including Courtney, to shake his hand, sit on his lap, and tell him their Christmas wishes. Everyone got something from the *good* sack, which left them to wonder, after he'd disappeared down the hall with a parting "Ho-ho-ho," what the *bad* sack had contained. Hope dutifully admired every trinket and sweet that had come from Santa and had so enlivened the class Christmas party. Through it all she couldn't quite rid her mind of the burning question for the day. Who *was* that bearded man?

HOPE LOADED A box of gifts into the back of her car, and Frances heaved Hope's suitcase over the tailgate. "I let my brother use my car today, but it's just as well. You'd never find our place by yourself."

"You must really have the Christmas spirit, Frances. I thought you said you never let anyone else drive your car."

"Oh, well, Luke's different. Luke's my older brother."

"The one who's in the army?" Hope shut the tailgate and adjusted her sunglasses as she sorted mentally through the gifts she'd brought. When Frances had invited her to spend Christmas vacation at the Tracker ranch, Hope had begun to make subtle inquiries about brothers and sisters and their ages and interests. It was easy to choose gifts for children, especially the younger ones whom she knew from school, but Frances hadn't known which of the older siblings might be home. Hope had brought a couple of generic gifts, just in case.

"The one who's finally come home for Christmas after seven long years." Frances grabbed Hope's arm as she started for the driver's side. "You want me to drive? It's mostly gravel roads."

"I need the practice," Hope said.

"Yeah, but . . ."

The two friends looked at each other, black eyes searching blue, and Hope finally handed the keys over with a laugh. "I don't guess we want to spend Christmas in the hospital."

"You *are* getting better," Frances admitted, grateful for the keys. Several weeks ago, they'd hit a spot in the road weathered like a washboard when Hope had been driving them out to meet with the parents of one of her students, and they'd had to flag down a pickup to pull them out of the ditch. "You've got such a great car, but these roads take some getting used to."

Hope's four-wheel-drive wagon had been a gift from her father, who had insisted she leave Connecticut with a vehicle built for the wilderness. He was certain she was headed for the ends of the earth, but, as always, he bought her something grand and wished her well. He had his younger second family to worry about, and, as he often marveled whenever he saw Hope, she'd "suddenly become a young woman" when his back was turned. Since Hope's mother had married a widower with three children, Hope didn't really consider herself a part of any family. The family she'd once thought she belonged to had disintegrated in divorce.

Perhaps it was because both her parents had been so completely unhappy with each other that she'd been their only child. She'd been shipped off to prep school when she was thirteen, and each of her parents had begun fashioning new lives. She'd fashioned her own. She'd been teaching for five years, but this was her first year in South Dakota. Her interest in Native American culture had prompted her to apply for the position in the tiny town of Wakpala on the Standing Rock Sioux Indian Reservation. Because so many of the children lived in remote areas, St. Elizabeth's Mission provided dormitories where the children stayed during the winter months while they attended the public school in town. Hope's apartment at St. Elizabeth's, some five miles from the school, was provided in return for her counseling and tutoring services.

The peacefulness of the countryside was one of the many pleasant aspects of Hope's new situation. Fall had become winter without the fanfare of color to which she was accustomed, but the brown prairie had been blanketed quickly, and the rolling white landscape was as soothing to the eye as the endless sea. She liked its timelessness. The network of gravel roads did little to insult the land, and it was easy to drive ten, even twenty miles without seeing a house. Maybe that was why people seemed so willing to include each other in their lives out here. The Trackers were a family of twelve by Hope's count, but Frances had assured and reassured her that they were anxious to have one more for the holidays.

"You never did tell me who Santa Claus was," Hope reminded her friend as they approached a two-story white house flanked on the north by a stand of cottonwood trees and chokecherry bushes.

Frances grinned. "What do you mean? Santa Claus was Santa Claus."

"He was quite a character. He nearly scared the wits out of the kids when he first came in."

"Those department store Santa Clauses are no fun. No sense of humor. Did you sit on his lap?" Frances asked.

"Didn't you?"

Frances shut the engine off and handed Hope the keys with a mischievous smile and a shake of her head. "He told you I did?"

"Yes. I thought it was part of the tradition."

With a merry laugh, Frances threw the car door open and hopped out. "I think Santa likes you. What'd you ask for?"

"Snow on Christmas Eve." Hope shut the door on her side. "And something else. Something I used to ask for every year when I was a kid. Nobody ever took me seriously."

"Really? Maybe you never asked the right Santa."

"My father thinks he's the world's greatest Santa." The curtains moved in an upstairs window, and a small face appeared. Hope smiled and waved, absently adding, "But I never got what I asked for."

Frances took Hope's luggage, while Hope carried her gifts. "I see my car's not back yet," Frances noted. "I wonder what Luke's up to."

Hope greeted George and Emma Tracker, Frances's parents, and a succession of children whose ages ranged from eight to eighteen. A couple of the older siblings were missing at the moment. Everyone seemed to have a nickname, like Sweetie and Tom Tom and Beaver. After Hope had deposited her gifts under the tree, Frances took her upstairs to deposit her luggage. They were to share a room. Hope saw only four bedrooms upstairs, and she was sure the rest of the family would be crowded, but Frances said that her mother would see that everyone had a place to sleep.

Both women turned their heads toward the sound of the opening of the front door and the mighty "Ho-ho-ho!" that followed. Hope's eyes widened as she noted the familiar mischief in Frances's smile.

"I should have guessed."

"He was one of the few people we were sure the kids wouldn't recognize," Frances explained. "Last year we hired a Santa with a German accent, and the kids thought he was Heidi's grandfather. Altogether too tame."

"Your brother can't be accused of that. Well—" she remembered being seated on that sturdy thigh, and she turned quickly as she felt her face redden "—let's go see what he looks like without the beard."

Two of the younger children were relieving Luke of several packages, while a third stripped him of his brown-leather bomber jacket and ran to put it away. Luke wiped his black boots on the mat one more time for good measure and then looked up to the top of the stairs at the two women.

The man who had been Santa made jeans and a blue chambray shirt look like a uniform, Hope thought. His black hair was closely cut, stylish by chance and practical by design. His clothes were crisply ironed, and they skimmed his trim body as though they'd been tailored for him. He was startlingly handsome, but he gave the impression that he would permit only regulation handsomeness. Even so, there was nothing regulation about his slow, easy smile and the glint in his eyes that hinted that he shared some secret with the woman who followed his sister down the stairs.

"Hello, Hope Spencer. Have you recovered from your ordeal with Santa Claus?"

"I wouldn't call it an ordeal," she protested as she reached the foot of the stairs and accepted his proffered handshake. "I'd say it was a learning experience. I take it the 'jolly old elf' image doesn't make it out West."

"Unless things have changed drastically since I was a kid, my version of Santa was a pussycat compared to what's in store."

"I haven't told Hope much about what she's in for," Frances put in. "But I'll let you both in on one secret. If the weather's good, Daddy promised to take the bobsled out Christmas Eve."

"Is that old thing still around?" Luke asked.

"Daddy's not about to give up his team, Luke. You know that."

Luke shook his head in amazement. "He's getting too old to be fooling around with those Percherons, especially in the winter."

"After a blizzard he's able to get feed out to the stock before most people get their tractors started." In the back of her mind, Frances forgave her brother for being so out of touch with his memories. He well knew how little heavy equipment their father used in keeping their small cattle operation going. They had a small tractor with a few attachments, but the summer haying was accomplished largely because the family had so many hands.

"Your dad uses a team to pull a *bobsled?*" Hope asked. "Doesn't it just sail down the hill on its own steam?"

Luke looked at Frances, and they both laughed. "In the Olympics, maybe," Luke said, "but not in Wakpala."

"See, you take the wheels off the wagon box," Frances explained, going through the motions with her hands. "And you put runners on it. It's kind of a sleigh."

"Only we call it a bobsled," Luke added. Yes, *we,* he thought. He remembered how excited the mere mention a bobsled ride had once made him. Even now, he liked the thought of hearing the jingle of the harness again and knowing his father held the reins. He reminded himself to hold the sentimentality down to a minimum, and he changed the subject. "So who helps Dad take care of the stock?" he asked Frances. "Gorgeous?"

"Imagine Gorgeous George being any help." Frances laughed. "He works when Mama tells him no work, no supper." She turned to Hope.

"Gorgeous is my other older brother. His birth certificate says he's twenty-seven years old, but he's still trying to find himself."

"He never had much trouble finding himself in the mirror. Give me a few weeks with him in boot camp. I'll help him find himself." Luke sniffed the air. "Is that coffee I smell? And maybe frybread?"

"It is," Frances said. "And we'll probably be able to have some, if you promise Mama you'll be nice to Gorgeous when and *if* you see him."

"If? I haven't been home in seven years," Luke pointed out as he led the way to the kitchen.

"And your brother's visits are no more predictable than yours, although they're certainly more frequent." Frances tossed Hope a conspiratorial wink and continued. "Who's to say whether you can be worked into his busy schedule?"

"Busy my a—"

"Luke!" Emma Tracker—short, graying, and clearly accustomed to being in charge of her children—turned from her crackling skillet. "Mind your mouth. I don't want our guest thinking I raised any boys who cuss all the time."

"Yes, ma'am," Luke responded with a smile as he took a chair at the long table. "I always tell recruits I was born to whip them into shape. Raised by the original female drill sergeant."

"Then you *are* a drill sergeant," Hope said as she joined him at the table.

"Drill instructor," he corrected. "A teacher, like yourself."

Frances set three mugs on the table and poured the coffee. "I wish I could get my second graders to jump to attention," she said as she put a carton of milk in front of Hope. "Maybe if I told them I was a specialist in martial arts and I'd been a Green Beret like my brother . . ."

"Go ahead and tell them," Luke teased. "I'll vouch for you, Frankie."

Frances laughed. "You had enough trouble getting them to believe you were Santa Claus."

"The uniform didn't fit right. Get me in parade dress, and I'll have your little darlings saluting smartly and saying 'yes, ma'am' before you can recite the Pledge of Allegiance."

Hope shook her head as she tried to imagine the scene. "If you came into my class and started barking orders, I have a feeling there'd be eighteen children fighting for space under the teacher's desk."

Frances readily agreed. She had never regarded her oldest brother as anything less than a hero, and the worshipful eyes of a child still glowed in her womanly face when she looked at him. Emma treated the three to hot frybread and persistently shooed the younger children away to give them this time to visit. She knew she had Frances to thank for convincing Luke to come home for Christmas. Luke was the son who had to leave home as soon as he had come of age, and Frances was the daughter who had to bring her education home to the children who needed her. But there had always been a special bond between the two.

DECORATING THE church for Christmas was a community project. After supper the Trackers crowded into all available vehicles and headed for the old church at St. Elizabeth's Mission. Hope's car was packed with excited children, who scattered when they arrived, while the adults set about trimming the church. The arrangement was time-honored, and it was clearly important to recall exactly the way it had been done in previous years. There were real poinsettias for the altar, as well as plastic blooms that were saved from year to year and tacked to the pews. Red candles, white linen, and gold garland brightened the church's dark wood. A spruce tree rose to the ceiling in the center of the basement parish hall, its green needles gradually disappearing as decorators piled on the multi-colored lights and silver tinsel.

Hope enjoyed watching the activity as much as being part of it. She was a coffee fetcher, a tack hander, a bow tier. It was nice to be included. She was also an observer, and, during her break from handing Frances tacks, she sat in a pew at the back of the church and listened to the rhythm of the women's voices as they exchanged stories, mainly in English. Some of the older people spoke with one another in Lakota, but few of the young adults knew the language. Even so, Lakota words and phrases would slip into the conversation, and there were local expressions of unknown origin that enriched these people's English with a special spice. Listeners encouraged the storyteller with an occasional *"E'n it?"* which roughly meant, "Really?" Or, if the story became totally incredible, the comment might be *"Dwah-lay!"*

A steaming Styrofoam cup appeared at Hope's shoulder. She looked up as she accepted it with a smile and slid over, hoping that Luke would join her. She sipped the coffee and wondered where he had found creamer in this land of drinkers of strong black coffee.

"How would you be spending Christmas if you weren't in Wakpala?" he asked as he sat down beside her.

Hope's indifferent shrug said a great deal about how little it had mattered. "I'd have to pay a visit to each of my parents at some point, and I'd probably have dinner with friends." She considered his expression and realized that, after seven years, he'd become an observer here, too.

"Married friends?"

She nodded. "Usually. I like to watch the kids."

"Me, too. It's probably the only time of year when I miss all this—" he gestured, cup in hand "—togetherness stuff."

"So how have you been spending Christmas for the last seven years?"

"Dinner in the mess hall," he told her. "It's good for morale. And, you know . . . friends." His voice drifted, echoing in the hollowness of the years. "'Course, in the military, they come and go. You don't get too attached."

"If I had a family like yours, I'd come home every Christmas." It was a spontaneous comment, born of a wish, but she knew once she'd said it that it sounded like a judgment.

Surprisingly he gave her a one-sided smile. "You would, huh? Just drop everything on the twenty-third or so and trot right home?"

"I'd try." His eyes unnerved her. They were too dark, too deep, and too compelling. "I really think I would, unless something came up and I just couldn't get away."

He chuckled, appreciating the fact that she'd decided to give him an out. "The longer you put it off, the harder it gets," he confessed. "After a while, all it takes is an ingrown toenail, and you can't get away."

"But don't you miss them?"

"Sure, I miss them." He looked around at the familiar arched windows of one of the oldest buildings in the area. "I even miss the town sometimes, which scares me. When I was growing up, my one goal was to get out of here any way I could. Nothing ever changes here. Nothing ever will."

His goal was understandable. Hope knew how little employment there was on the reservation, and how much poverty. "But your family's here," she reminded him. "Pictures of you are hanging all over your parents' house. Frances thinks you could fight off an invasion single-handedly."

He smiled as he caught a glimpse of his sister ducking behind the bishop's chair with a dust cloth. "Frankie's a dreamer."

"She tells me you helped put her through college."

"Did what I could." He tossed off the recognition of his efforts with a shrug. "She made damn good grades. I wish she'd take her dreams and get out of here. Go someplace bright and pretty, where it's Christmas all year long."

"Don't send her to Connecticut," Hope admonished with a smirk.

"Missouri, either." He thought for a moment, then shook his head. "I've been to Texas, South Carolina, New Jersey, Germany. Didn't find Christmas all year long in any of those places."

There was a buzzing of voices up front, and Frances's laughter rang out from behind the big wooden chair. "Maybe once a year is enough for her, Luke."

"I guess it's better than once in seven years."

His smile stirred a warmth inside her that gave new meaning to her own idea of Yuletide spirit. She glanced away and remembered the job she'd been given when she saw the two plastic wreaths she'd set on the pew. "I guess I'm shirking my duty," she said as she reached for the wreaths. "I'm living in the dormitory apartment just across the way, but I confess I haven't used the church facilities that much. I'm supposed to tack these up on the bathroom doors, but I can't find the bathrooms."

Luke tipped his head back and laughed as heartily as Frances just had. He set his cup down and took Hope by the hand. "Get your coat, Hope Spencer. The bathrooms are out back."

Chapter Two

IT WAS THE FIRST time in his life that Luke remembered being impressed by brown hair. Black hair, of course, was beautiful, especially when it was long and thick like Frankie's. And he'd done a double take a time or two when a sunlit head of yellow hair had crossed his path. As he lifted Hope's coat over her shoulders, she swept her pretty brown hair up in her hand and dropped it over her collar, and he was captivated. The color was mink rich, and he could smell the floral fragrance of her shampoo. She turned a glittering blue-eyed smile on him as she clamped a set of fur earmuffs over her head. Real mink. Just a shade darker than her hair, and they rivaled each other for shine. Luke was looking forward to this hayride.

"Hey, Luke." Ten-year-old Crystal turned worshipful eyes up at her brother. "Can I sit next to you?"

"No, me!" little Sweetie demanded, cuing a chorus of pleas from children who stretched to their full height like puppies clamoring to be picked from the litter.

Luke had to think fast. "We have to put all you little guys in the middle of the box, so you won't bounce out. Big guys around the outside." He turned to Hope. "Ever been on a bobsled?"

"No, I haven't. This is so exci—"

"Listen, you guys, Hope's never been on a bobsled, and she's pretty nervous." With a face full of concern, he laid a hand on each of two little shoulders. "I think I'd better sit by her, just in case. After all, she's our guest."

"In case what?" Hope asked.

Luke's smile reminded Hope of Frances's. They both had Fourth of July sparklers in their eyes when they teased. "You never know," he told her. "Wolves, thin ice. Full moon tonight. Anything can happen."

"But I haven't been on a bobsled, either," Sweetie insisted as she tugged on Luke's leather sleeve.

He swung the little girl up in his arms. "Yeah, but you're a cowboy. Hope's just a dude. Boy, you've gotten big, Sweetie."

"They grow a lot in three years." Emma came from the kitchen with two large Thermos bottles. "If you had children of your own, you'd know that. Here, take these," she ordered, thrusting the supply of coffee into the arms of one of the older children.

The Tracker matriarch obviously lacked enthusiasm for this Christmas Eve outing, but she hadn't spelled out her objections to her husband. Instead, she grabbed, shoved, stomped around, and grumbled.

"A woman my age should have grandchildren," she muttered, looking Luke's way. When she got nothing but an impertinent chuckle from her eldest offspring, she pulled her plaid wool scarf down tightly over her head and whipped it into a knot under her sagging chin. "A woman my age should ride to church in a car," she grumbled as she threw the door open. "Tell Frances to hurry up with the rest of the blankets, Sissy," she ordered over her shoulder as she headed out into the night. "Go help her."

Long-legged Sissy leaped into action, taking the steps two at a time. In another moment the two sisters descended the steps, each bearing an armload of quilts and blankets. "This is it," Frances announced. "Some of us will have to share."

Luke took part of Sissy's load and gave Hope a slow smile.

It was impossible to believe that the moon didn't produce its creamy brilliance on its own. Hanging like a medallion on the sky's black velvet breast, it brightened the crusted snow. What had seemed like such a crowd of people within the confines of the house became only a small group of travelers surrounded by endless land, sky, and night.

George Tracker held the reins of his two-horse team as two of his sons helped their mother climb into the seat beside him. The box of their buckboard had been removed from its wheels and set on runners for winter use. It was filled with loose hay.

"Climb aboard." His eager tone hinted that he was about to share something wonderful with his family. "The cats chased all the mice out of the hay," he promised.

Emma grumbled something to her husband, but no one paid attention. There was too much excitement. The younger children took their blankets and dove into the hay in the center of the wagon. Dolly and Beaver, who were well into their upper teens and, like their mother, preferred cars—though for speed rather than comfort—sat together behind the driver's seat with a cache of potato chips. Sixteen-year-old Lana sat beside her mother, and Tom Tom, who couldn't decide whether he was really ready for encroaching adolescence, opted for childhood and took to the center of the box, where the best wrestling matches would take place. At the tailgate Luke was comfortably flanked by two women—his favorite sister and the friend he predicted he would know much better by the end of the night.

"Your mother doesn't seem to be a fan of hayrides," Hope suggested as Frances took pains to pack hay around their hips.

"This was the only transportation we had for a long time," Luke told her. "Frances and I grew up going to church in the bobsled or the buckboard. For Mom, it's like going back to the washboard after you've had a ringer washer."

"Washboard? You mean, for doing laundry?" Hope had used a ringer washer for the first time in the laundry room at the Mission. Fully automatic washing machines couldn't withstand the corrosive effects of the artesian-well water, which was used only for washing. Drinking water had to be hauled in. But washboards and horse-drawn wagons seemed farfetched, given how young Frances was.

"Where've you been hiding yourself, Hope Spencer? Connecticut?" Luke chuckled. "What would you use a washboard for in Connecticut?"

"We tried to find one for a jug band once when I was in college," she said innocently. "We found kazoos, but no washboards."

"Welcome to Wakpala, South Dakota."

"Oh, Luke," Frances protested, "most people have cars now. Daddy uses the bobsled to feed the stock when the weather gets bad, but he never takes us to church in it anymore. This is Sweetie's first ride in it, and she's already eight."

"So we've made progress."

"I don't think you should ever give this up," Hope said happily. "It's a beautiful night, and it's Christmas Eve, and I can't think of anything more perfect." She smiled at Luke. "I'm having fun already."

The light in her eyes illuminated her pretty face and kicked Luke's metabolism into high gear. "So am I," he admitted as he unfurled his woolen army blanket. "The trick is to keep warm, so if both of you scoot in, I'll share my blanket with your legs."

"You notice he gets the best of the deal," Frances pointed out as she scooted over and ducked her head under his arm. "He's in the middle."

"My mama didn't raise no fool," he quipped. He moved more gradually to bracket Hope's shoulders, and she slid more cautiously than Frances had. When she'd aligned her thigh against Luke's, he urged her to lean into his side with the steady, gentling pressure of his strong right arm. She looked up and saw the pleasure he was taking in her company in the soft expression on his face.

The Trackers were among the last to arrive, but no one seemed to be worried about starting at a certain hour. The socializing was well underway in the church basement, and supper would be served when people were hungry. The coats were piled high on a bench near the wall. George headed for the coffeepot, and Emma sought the consolation of her sisterhood of friends, who would understand what a trial life with a "crazy old Indian" could sometimes be. The young children's anticipation became tangible energy as they raced, tussled, and teased in every corner of the large basement room.

Except for the tinsel and colored lights, it was a stark room, with its bare gray floor and whitewashed walls. There was a small kitchen alcove with a stove, but there was no running water. An old fuel-hungry furnace provided a background roar. The air was blue with smoke, but heat was too precious to be vented into the night through an open window.

Hope had been part of the community for several months, but the only social event she'd attended had been school-sponsored. This was different, certainly interesting—and a little scary. She felt a need to stay close to Frances and Luke, to belong here with someone. When someone asked Frances to take charge of the cigarette bowl for a while, Hope flashed a quick look of alarm at Luke, and he responded with the soft expression she'd seen earlier. He would be with her. Standing at her side, he found it easy to give her hand a subtle squeeze.

"What's the cigarette bowl?" Hope asked.

"They fill a bowl with cigarettes, and the girls offer it around all night," Luke explained. "At a celebration like this, no one ever has to bum a cigarette."

"How, um . . . how thoughtful." She looked up at him and made a squinty face. "I guess."

He laughed. "We have an ancient love affair with tobacco. It's one vice we can't blame on you guys." When Frances offered him the bowl, Luke shook his head. "I've quit. I was tired of getting winded twenty minutes into a workout."

"You should see his karate moves," Frances said. "Poetry in motion."

Hope looked up and caught his quick frown. "So you really are a martial-arts expert."

Luke shoved his hands into the pockets of his jeans. "The army spreads the term 'expert' around pretty freely."

"I wouldn't call black belts in jujitsu and karate anything less than expert," Frances insisted with pride. "Luke's an instructor."

He tugged at her long black braid as she turned to walk away. "Big mouth," he teased. "What, are you trying to sell me or something? Why don't you just let her count my teeth?"

"Because she wouldn't be impressed," Frances tossed back when she was safely out of range. "I knocked one out with a well-aimed rock when you were fourteen years old."

"You really know how to ruin a guy, Frankie." With a dramatic sigh, Luke rolled his eyes toward the ceiling. "Yes, I really do have a false tooth. So I guess in order to save face, I have to confess that she's right about my karate moves." He grinned, knowing that Hope was trying to figure out which tooth it was. He gave her a wink. "Pure poetry."

Suddenly a booming "Ho-ho-ho" filled the stairwell and echoed through the room. Hope had never seen so many children take cover so quickly. They scurried behind folding chairs that were occupied by comfortably familiar adults, or dove underneath the benches along the walls.

Hope looked up at Luke, who raised his hands, as if empty palms somehow proved his innocence. "That didn't come from me."

"This is the strangest reaction to jolly old Saint Nick I've ever seen," she murmured.

"You oughta hear some of the ghost stories they tell us as kids," he whispered as they watched a genuinely rotund Santa descend the bottom step, set two white sacks on the floor, settle his gloved hands on his ample hips, and survey the room. He could have been Matt Dillon bringing instantaneous order to the Long Branch Saloon.

"Boy, when you say, 'You'd better watch out, you'd better not cry . . .'"

"We mean the man is not about to tolerate any pouting or sniveling," Luke concluded for her. "It's part of the game, just like the ghost stories. Part of growing up."

"Were you scared, too?"

"Damn right." He jerked his chin toward a heavy wooden table in the far corner. "That was my favorite spot."

"Don't you guys got any kids in here?" Santa roared. "I thought I heard kids' voices down here."

"Looks like they don't want any Christmas presents, Santa," said one smirking parent.

"Guess not," another chimed.

"I do!"

"Shh, quiet!" warned a voice from under a bench.

"But I want—"

"Get out there, then. Go on!"

"I'm not scared." A six-year-old in bib overalls scrambled from his hiding place. "I want a Christmas present, Santa."

"And I want that kid in another twelve years," Luke whispered. "He'll make a hell of a soldier."

By twos and threes, the children came out of hiding, and, while their parents looked on, each was given a gift. Most of the children anticipated little more in the way of material gains at Christmas than this gift, but the level of excitement that was reached as they tore into red-and-green paper was contagious. It combined with the smell of food to add a festive luster to the barren walls and the most sober elder face. Santa never completely abandoned his gruff guise, and his parting "Ho-ho-ho" was as formidable as his greeting.

When it was time to eat, the older people took to the head of the line, along with many of the men, who, traditionally, were served first. Hope noticed that people had brought their own plates and utensils, and Frances distributed those the Trackers had brought. Luke waited with Hope until the line dwindled, and then they took their place with the next wave.

"Have you been to a feed yet?"

Hope shook her head.

"You gonna try everything?" he asked, watching her eye the kettles on the table ahead of them.

"Of course," she said brightly. "I'm really hungry, and it smells—" She breathed deeply as she searched for a word. There was something boiled and beefy, but there was no identifiable spice. Kind of fatty. A little fruity. "—interesting," she decided.

Luke nodded. "I haven't eaten any *taniga* in a long time. Might be interesting for me, too."

She recognized the frybread and *wojapi*, the thickened boysenberry soup that was delicious when you dunked your bread in it. Emma stood behind one of the kettles wielding a long fork and a butcher knife. "Just like sausage," she told Hope as she fished in the steaming kettle, speared something tubular and grayish and whacked a piece off with her knife. "You like sausage, don't you?"

"Oh, yes." Hope's words were more positive than the tone of her voice as she watched the "something" drop onto her plate.

"You want the book?" the lady at the next kettle asked. Hope raised a questioning look over her shoulder at Luke.

"That's what they call—" he gestured toward the pot with slightly puckered lips "—that stuff."

From her kettle the woman had hooked something that looked sort of meaty, sort of leafy and altogether strange. The strong odor was not enticing. Hope glanced around and realized that a number of people were listening for her answer. Either this was a test, or she was holding up the line. "Sure." Whack! "Not too much," she added after the fact. The stuff quivered as it plopped onto her plate. As she moved on, she heard Frances's throaty chuckle.

The lady at the last kettle stood with her ladle poised over steaming broth. "Soup?"

Hope smiled gratefully as she offered up her speckled blue tin cup. "Yes, I'd love some."

Juggling her supper on her lap, Hope sat between Luke and Frances within a large circle of folding chairs. She probed at the strange meats with her fork. "I don't suppose you'll tell me what this really is until I taste it," she said, glancing from Frances's smirk to Luke's.

"I don't suppose we should," Frances said.

Hope tasted the "sausage" first; it bore some resemblance to sausage, but it wasn't spicy. The "book" was blubbery, and nearly impossible to swallow. "All right. Now drop the bombshell."

"It's just tripe," Luke said.

Frances couldn't leave it at that. "Cow intestines and stomach."

"Geez, Frankie, you didn't have to give her the anatomical details."

"Thoroughly cleaned, of course," Frances hastened to add.

"Of course." It occurred to Hope that Frances's information was harder to digest than the food itself.

"You don't have to eat it," Frances assured her.

"It's an acquired taste," Luke added, "and I think I may have unacquired it." He studied his plate. "I remember when it used to taste really good. Either I've changed, or they just don't make it like they used to."

"Try the soup, Hope," Frances suggested.

Although she would have added salt, more vegetables, and a few spices, Hope found that the soup passed over her tongue quite easily and warmed her insides.

"They're not still using puppy in the soup, are they?" Luke asked casually between bites.

"Puppy?" Hope's hand froze holding a spoonful of soup as she slid her gaze toward Frances.

"Nobody had any around that were fat enough," she said easily, as if he'd asked about a pig or a calf. "We had to go with beef."

"Puppy's usually pretty greasy." Luke was studying the contents of his cup as if he weren't totally convinced.

"You . . . don't . . . eat puppies."

Luke exchanged a look with Frances. "Tell you what we don't eat," he offered. "Horsemeat. I was halfway through a meal once when I was in Germany, and somebody told me I was eating horsemeat. I thought I was going to be sick."

"But you don't *really* eat puppies," Hope insisted. "Tell me I'm not eating a puppy."

"We used to."

"But we don't anymore."

"Hardly ever."

Hope joined in the laughter only after Luke had assured her, "You're not eating a puppy."

When "seconds" were announced, Hope went back to the serving line for more frybread and *wojapi*.

After the meal, the men began to line their chairs against the wall, tip them back on two legs, and light up cigarettes. Then the relaxed mood was shattered by a sudden yelp. A tiny flame shot up from old Gabe Red Horse's bushy white head as though he had a butane lighter hidden in his hair. A quick-thinking friend threw a coat over Gabe's head. When he was uncovered, Gabe's wrinkled face was ashen, and his hair was singed.

"Who did that?" Gabe demanded, wide-eyed with shock. "Which one of you guys, huh?" Still clutching the coat in both hands, he peered from face to face, repeating, "Who did that?"

"Geez, I'm sorry, Gabe." Beaver Tracker's unlit cigarette dangled from the corner of his mouth as he held up a headless wooden match. "I struck it on my thumbnail, and the head just went flying."

"George Tracker!" Gabe roared as he rubbed the top of his head. "You'd better teach this boy of yours to light a match before you let him start smoking."

Across the room, Luke grumbled, "Kid's only eighteen. What's he doing with matches?"

"Lighting cigarettes," Frances informed him. "Just like you did when you were *fifteen*."

Laughter—old Gabe's included—drowned out Luke's vow to make sure his younger brother never looked at another cigarette.

The women had supper cleaned up in time for the midnight mass. The service was a combination of English and Lakota, with familiar carols sung in both languages. Hope found herself giving voice to the phonetically spelled Lakota almost as easily as the English verses. It was Christmas Eve, and all roads converged in the timelessness of such a night. All traditions blended. All voices harmonized, and all good things became one splendor. It happened in Wakpala, as it happened everywhere, because it was Christmas Eve.

"COME OUTSIDE," a deep voice entreated near Hope's ear. "I have something to show you."

Luke had disappeared right after the service, and Hope had found herself wondering where he'd gone. Obviously the men had little to do with packing things up and getting ready to go. His voice made her heart flutter, and she turned to find that he was dragging his jacket zipper up to his chin.

"You're probably going to have to carry some of these kids out to the sled," she told him. She pointed to Sweetie and Crystal, who were curled up in a pile of coats.

"I will. This'll just take a minute." He reached for her hand. "Come on."

He helped her with her coat and pulled her out into the night. There had been a gathering of soft white clouds while they were inside, and now a flurry of flakes whirled through the quiet night like ice dancers. Luke held Hope's hand tightly as he brought her away from the church so they could look back at it. The cross on the steeple was illuminated with blue lights, which made it visible for many miles in any direction across the prairie. At night it didn't matter that the old church needed another coat of white paint. It was a scene that could well have graced a postcard.

"First wish granted," Luke said. His voice was roughened around the edges, as though the role of wish granter might take some getting used to. "Snow for Christmas Eve."

"You must have some pull somewhere. There wasn't a cloud in the sky when we got here."

"Here's your second wish." He reached under his jacket and pulled out a bundle he'd made from his own muffler. It mewed as he handed it over.

"A kitten!" She drew the muffler back and discovered two doleful eyes. It didn't occur to her to claim that she had been kidding when she'd sat on his lap and whispered to him that she wanted a kitten for Christmas. "Oh, Luke, I used to ask for one every Christmas when I was a little girl." In those days, it had been too simple and heartfelt a wish for Santa to grant.

Luke buried his hands in his jacket pockets. "You didn't say whether you wanted a boy or a girl."

"Well, I wanted a—" She peeked inside the bundle again and clucked at the fuzzy little face. "What have we here? Hmm?"

"It's a girl."

She saw how boyish her gift giver suddenly looked, and her heart melted. "I always wanted a girl. I can't believe you turned out to be such a softie, Sergeant Tracker."

"Neither can I. I hope it's your color. You know, the right size and everything." It was a lame attempt at off-handed humor. He couldn't remember ever having done anything so sentimental.

"I know she's perfect." Hope was having none of his easy humor. She had been given bicycles and doll houses, jewelry and cars, but no one had remembered her wish for something live and soft and warm. "I wish I could give you something half this good."

"Be careful with those wishes, Hope."

While they were standing there smiling at each other like two Christmas elves, the church door opened and the voices of the community permeated the stillness with low laughter and sleepy goodbyes.

Luke went back inside and carried his youngest sister out to the bobsled. Little Sweetie slept on as the others bundled around her in the bed of hay. Those who were still awake claimed turns at holding Hope's kitten while the adults loaded up the gifts and dishes. Luke offered to help with the driving, but his father fervently swore that he was good for the duration and that no one could handle his team the way he did. Frances disappeared into the hay with the younger children, and Hope agreed with Luke that two bodies under one blanket would generate more heat than two bodies using separate blankets.

It had stopped snowing. The moon dimmed briefly as a gossamer cloud slid past. Sitting on the tailgate, Luke and Hope surveyed the territory they'd already traveled. They listened as the horses' hooves broke through the crusted snow and the bells on the horse collars jingled. The distant buttes were contoured shadows, dark mysteries at the edge of a lustrous white blanket that rippled over the plains. The soft night wind stirred the topmost branches of a lone cottonwood tree as they passed it.

"It's quiet," she said.

"Mmm-hmm."

"There's no place on earth as quiet as this."

"No place this stark."

"No place this beautiful," she said. Beneath the blanket he slid his hand to the top of her arm and pulled her closer. She felt beautiful. The air she breathed made her nose feel frosty, making it seem all that much warmer under the blanket. They had made a nest for themselves in the sweet-smelling alfalfa hay, and they'd spread a quilt over their legs and tucked it around their hips. "Such a gorgeous moon," Hope added, thinking that all this beauty must be noted.

"In the old days, December was called the Twelfth Moon," he told her quietly, "but it had other names, too. It was the Moon of Frost Inside the Tipi." He felt her shiver, and he nuzzled her mink earmuff, adding, "But it was warm beneath the buffalo robes."

"Mmm, I can imagine."

"It was also called the Moon of Horns Dropping Off, because deer lose their horns then." His nose reached the edge of the fur and found her temple.

"How about the Moon of Frostbitten Noses?" she whispered. "Yours is cold."

"So is your cheek."

She grinned at the white moon, riding high in the sky. "I'm cold in some places, warm in others."

"Close to me, you're warm." His lips brushed the side of her face so lightly that his breath made a more distinct contact. More warmth. Deep, deep inside her.

"Yes. Close to you, I'm warm."

"Put your hand inside my jacket."

Hope gave him a doubtful look. Luke drew his jacket zipper down to half mast. He found her hand and guided it through the opening, where her hesitant fingers discovered a ball of fur. She smiled. "I thought the children had her."

"They passed her around and gave her back. You know how kids are."

Petting the sleeping kitten gave Hope an excuse to keep her hand where it was. Her eyes were level with Luke's lips. She knew that if she tipped her head back it would be an invitation. It felt delicious to think about it and wait. She responded to his comment only because it was her turn.

"Fickle."

"But you're not fickle . . . are you, Hope?"

She closed her eyes to whisper, "No," and lifted her chin on a shaky breath. His kiss was not an order but a tentative, tenderly phrased request. She slid her hand past the slumbering kitten and around his back, flattening her palm and pressing her fingers into his woolen sweater. The catch in his breath reached her ears alone as he tilted his head to kiss her again, to explore the warmth of her mouth and tease her cheek with the cool tip of his nose.

He lifted his head, feeling as dazed as she looked.

So this is shell shock, she thought.

So this is moonstruck, he realized.

He gave her part of a smile, and she gave him the rest of it. "Merry Christmas, Luke," she whispered.

"I think you just got that third wish. That was every bit as good as a kitten."

Chapter Three

CHRISTMAS EVE HAD left a covering of frost feathers on every tree branch and every stalk of prairie grass that poked above the snow. From Frances's upstairs bedroom window, Christmas morning looked crisp, still, and fairyland white. Frances reached across to the other twin bed and shook Hope's shoulder.

"Hope! Wake up and look outside."

Hope burrowed her face in the pillow and groaned before she lifted her head, trying to get her bearings as she squinted up at Frances. What had happened to the pretty little sleigh with the flashy silver runners she and Luke had been riding in a moment ago? Frances was kneeling on her pillow and holding onto the brass headboard with one hand as she drew her arm back from Hope's shoulder and gestured toward the window above the beds. Hope wondered whether this was just part of the dream and Frances was passing the sleigh in her chariot.

"Look what a gorgeous Christmas morning this is," Frances said.

Hope ruffled her sleep-flattened hair with one hand and pulled herself up on the brass rail with the other, imitating Frances's stance. Bright morning roused her sleepy brain. "Wow," she murmured as she surveyed the frosted trees in the shelter belt and the whitened strands of barbed wire that were part of a hilltop fence. "When did that happen?"

"Probably sometime between your wish and Luke's." Hope flashed Frances a look that was suddenly fully awake. "I guarantee I'm the only one who heard. The rest of the crew was sound asleep." Grinning at Hope's reddening cheeks, Frances shook her head. "I couldn't believe he actually got you a *kitten*. Luke! He never gives anybody anything more personal than a card with money in it."

"I'm sure he meant it as . . . kind of a joke. That was the other thing I asked for when he came to my classroom, besides snow, and I think he was just being funny." Hope didn't think anything of the kind. It was a precious gift. She hadn't even wanted to leave the kitten in the box Emma had provided in the kitchen, but, as a guest, she'd had no right to protest.

"I don't think he was being funny at all," Frances insisted. "I think he was being cute, and, believe me, I never imagined Luke actually trying to be cute." She lifted an eyebrow in Hope's direction. "So what do you think?"

Hope saw the empty bobsled standing in the yard below, and her heart yearned for another night like last night. "I think . . . it was a very sweet thing for him to do," she said quietly.

"Ohhh," Frances sighed dramatically as she flopped on her back. "Luke being sweet. Stony-faced Luke. I love it."

"He's not at all stony-faced." Hope sat on the edge of the bed and slid her feet into her scuffs. "He just looks that way because he's so lean and muscular."

Frances jackknifed to a sitting position with a teasing grin. "Lean and muscular. This gets better and better."

"You're the one who mentioned his expertise in self-defense, Frances. I'm simply making an observation. He looks very military, but inside he's very . . ." A knowing smile spread into Hope's eyes as she recalled his kiss. "Very sweet." She frowned quickly. "And don't you dare tell him I said that."

"If you keep smiling like that, I won't have to." Frances leaned over to give Hope's knee a friendly smack. "Let's grab the bathroom before the kids get up. Mama always has caramel rolls on Christmas morning."

The kitchen was filled with the smell of caramelized brown sugar and cinnamon. The turkey was in the oven, the rolls were on the table, and almost all was right in Emma's world.

"That cat's been underfoot all morning," Emma grumbled without looking up from her wrestling match with a balloon of white bread dough.

"Oh, I'm sorry," Hope said as she scooped the little ball of calico fur up from the floor. "I wonder if anything's open today. I'll have to buy some cat food."

"It likes turkey liver," Emma said flatly. "Cooked and chopped up fine."

Hope muttered a shy "Thank you," and she was sure she caught a spark of kitten-weakness in Emma's eye as the older woman nodded toward the refrigerator. "I put the rest of it in there. Should be enough for a couple of days."

"No creature goes hungry in Emma Tracker's kitchen." Three faces turned toward the doorway and were treated to Luke's smile and cheery,

"Good morning, ladies. The kids are up. I told them to stay out of the kitchen until I scouted it out."

"The caramel rolls are ready," his mother reported. "You guys better help yourselves before they disappear."

Hope's heartbeat had shifted into high gear, and she wondered whether it showed. Considering the fact that she hadn't taken her eyes off Luke since he appeared in the doorway, she figured it did. He hadn't stopped looking at her, either. He wore jeans and a white T-shirt, and she could smell the soap he'd just used in the shower. She held the kitten against her breast and stroked its head with her fingertips.

"Merry Christmas." Luke left only a few inches between them. Somehow he found the top of the kitten's head with his thumb without looking for it with his eyes. He rubbed the soft fur, thinking his caress was within temptingly close range of the sensitive flesh he would much rather touch. He made the kitten purr, and his smile promised Hope that he could do the same for her. "Did you sleep well?"

"Sort of," she managed with a dry throat. Somewhere in the periphery she heard Emma complain that she hadn't slept well, either, after being out in the cold half the night, and she heard Frances's giggle. A child's voice asked about caramel rolls, and something clattered in the sink. Hope's feet were rooted to the center of the kitchen floor as she searched for something intelligent to say. "Did you see the frost?"

"Inside the tipi?"

She gave her head a quick shake. "Outside."

"I think that was last month."

"It's . . . it's outside now. It's beautiful."

"Wake up and smell the coffee, you two." They turned toward the aroma and found Frances offering two steaming mugs and a saucy grin. "And help yourselves to caramel rolls, or else it'll be next Christmas before you get another chance."

Hope, Luke, and Frances were on their way to the living room with coffee and rolls when they encountered the hungry pack. Six pairs of ravenous eyes fastened on the huge confections on their plates. It occurred to Hope that most children would have been eyeing the gifts under the tree on Christmas morning, but the Tracker children held Emma's caramel rolls in high esteem.

"Have at it," Luke suggested, and all the living room chairs were suddenly vacant. He gestured with his plate. "Sit anywhere, ladies. Either of you up for a little trail ride this morning?"

Hope appeared to concentrate on the sticky task of uncoiling the roll with her fingers. The last time she'd ridden a horse, she'd been tossed into a patch of poison ivy. In the twelve years since Camp Kekekabic, she had made a point of depriving any horse of the opportunity to humiliate her again.

"I think I'd better help with dinner," Frances said, adding quickly, "but you go ahead, Hope. I'll keep the kitten out from under Mama's feet."

"Oh, no, I want to do my share."

"I'll give you your share to do," Luke promised. "Dad says there's fence to fix. He told me to take Beaver, but then I'd feel compelled to give him a lecture on the hazards of smoking, and I don't want to do that on Christmas."

Hope didn't want to get poison ivy on Christmas, either. Frost inside the tipi notwithstanding, she knew darn well there was a patch of it waiting for her somewhere along the trail if she got on a horse. But Luke wasn't giving her a choice. Between sips of coffee he was getting Frances's advice on which horses to take.

There were gifts to be opened after breakfast. Not many, Hope noted. This family wasn't "making a haul" at Christmas. The children's toys had come from Santa Claus the night before, and the family gifts were both modest and practical. Luke's gifts were the most lavish, but they were still practical. He provided warm parkas, cowboy boots, jeans that had not been worn by an older brother or sister, a coat for his mother and seat covers for his father's old pickup. The tall black boots for Frances were a big hit.

Hope pushed the thought of mounting a horse aside for a moment as she watched Luke unwrap the gift she'd bought before they met. The clerk at the cosmetics counter had told her it was the most popular brand this year, but Hope now doubted he'd ever use it.

"Ah." His eyes were alight as he spun the cap open. "Smell-good, huh?" Cute expression, Hope thought as she breathed a little more easily. He took a whiff of the men's cologne, then splashed some on his smooth cheeks. "Nice stuff."

Tom Tom leaned over and made a production of sniffing his older brother's face. "Whooee! That'll make 'em come to attention."

Luke took the teasing as good-naturedly as he gave it out. He helped clean up the mess, pointedly noting the three gifts left unopened beneath the tree.

"He'll be here for dinner," Frances promised quietly. "Gorgeous George can smell turkey for a hundred miles."

Luke shrugged. "Better hide my smell-good, then. He's liable to use the whole damn bottle."

Hope decided she was anxious to meet Gorgeous George.

"Well, Hope—" Luke flashed her a smile that was no less than gorgeous in itself "—it's time to saddle up."

Her heart took a nosedive and landed in her stomach. She was anxious to view the morning landscape with Luke, but not from the top of a horse. She decided that there was anxiousness and then there was anxiety. She carried the combination like a set of barbells as she mounted the stairs to change her clothes.

"I KNOW HE looks big," Luke admitted as he pulled the cinch tight around the black horse's fuzzy belly. "And he *is*. He's half Percheron. But he's the gentlest horse you'll ever meet. You can put three or four little kids on his back, and he'll take care of them just like a baby-sitter."

He extended a leather-gloved hand to Hope, who hung back several feet for safety's sake. She had estimated the length of the huge beast's hind leg and gave herself a few extra feet. "I don't think I can get up there, Luke. He's much too—"

"I'm going to put you up there. Come on."

She didn't want to look like a sissy. He'd called her a dude the night of the hayride, and she'd had the urge to do something to earn herself a better title. She couldn't think of anything that might elevate her from dude to cowboy, the quintessential South Dakota compliment, that didn't involve horses. Lord help her, she thought as she took a step toward the proverbial carrot, which was Luke's hand.

"I'm not much of a rider," she said.

"We'll fix that. We'll take you out on maneuvers. Up you go." He lifted her as easily as he spoke the words, and she grabbed the saddle horn. Her gloves were too slippery, she thought. She wanted a better grip. But to remove the gloves, she would have to let go of the horn. One dilemma was enough. She didn't need the additional one he was trying to hand her.

"Your reins, ma'am."

How could he smile so easily? Hope summoned her nerve and grabbed for the reins.

"You, uh . . . you aren't scared, are you?"

"No, no." Hope took a stab at smiling. "This is a pretty big animal, but I'm . . . I'm not scared."

"Good girl. Ride him around the corral a few times while I saddle that sorrel and get the tools." He patted the horse's rump, and the big black obliged with a couple of steps. Hope's eyes widened as she jerked the reins and pulled them as taut as a bowstring. The black laid his ears back.

"Like hell you're not scared," Luke mumbled as he moved quickly toward the horse's head. "Whoa, boy. Just drop the reins, Hope. Hold on to the saddle and let go of the reins."

She did as he told her, and he took charge of the reins before the black could execute the move his ears had forecast. Luke touched Hope's thigh with a soothing hand. "You okay?" She nodded quickly. "I forgot to ask whether you liked horses."

"I do. It's just that they don't like me." She gave a small apologetic smile. "One threw me once."

"You give old Blackie a chance. He'll change your mind, but not if you haul up on his mouth like that. A horse'll rear up if you do that."

"I'm sorry. He started to go before I was ready."

He rubbed her knee a little and squinted up at the bright sky and the nervous woman. "Should we take the pickup?"

She wanted to get over this foolish fear. "Not if you'd rather ride. I . . . I think I can—"

"Tell you what. I'll get the wire stretcher, and we'll try riding double—with you in the saddle. Think you can handle that?" She nodded. "Okay, then, just sit there for a minute." He wrapped the reins loosely around the saddle horn. "He won't go anywhere," Luke promised.

Hope was grateful when the horse made good on Luke's guarantee. With Luke sitting behind her and the reins in his right hand, Hope found that she was able to relax somewhat. They followed a gravel road, then a cow path across the pasture. The first time Luke dismounted to open a gate, Hope grew tense again, but by the third gate she'd developed some faith in "old Blackie."

"So what happened to you when you got thrown?" Luke asked. "Were you hurt bad?"

"A sprained wrist, scratches, bruises, but the worst was the poison ivy."

"The old nag picked his spot, then."

Hope laughed. "That's what I thought."

"A couple of boys in my platoon got into some poison oak last summer," he said. "One of them really had it bad. I didn't let him know it, but there were a few days there when I did ease up on him some."

"That was kind of you," she allowed.

"Hey, careful with those insults. No drill instructor ever wants to be accused of kindness. If you coddle those kids like . . . like a teacher would, they'll wash out. Or somewhere down the road they'll get themselves killed and take a whole squad with them."

"Did I hear a critical inflection on the word 'teacher'?"

"Uh-uh." He tightened his left arm around her. "I like teachers. Kindness is great in the third grade. You go right ahead and be kind, Hope."

"You're not in the third grade," she reminded him.

"Yeah, but I'm off duty." He patted his left hand against her side. "Kindly take off this glove and stow it in your pocket."

"Your glove?" She felt him nod near the side of her face, and she did as he asked.

He slid his hand under the bottom of her jacket and curled it around her right side. She shivered. "Is it cold?" She nodded. "You'll warm it for me." He liked the feel of her angora sweater. "Just want to make sure I've got a good grip on you."

"It's not as scary this way, with you holding the reins," she noted. "It's . . . *hardly* scary at all now."

"You're not scared of me, are you?"

"Not really."

"Not really." He chuckled behind her earmuff. "This tickles my nose."

"The mink? They're a little extravagant, I know, but they're nice and warm."

"Not as nice as your hair." He nuzzled the back of her head. "Not as pretty, either."

She smiled at the distant point where the sky touched the earth. She wondered whether they might be headed for that, or points beyond. "Do you *really* have a fence to fix out here?"

"Mmm-hmm. Probably wouldn't have taken more than a couple of hours if we'd taken two horses."

"But—"

"But I'm off duty," he reminded her. "I'm on Indian time. No clocks."

"You probably don't get many chances to ride at Fort Leonard Wood."

"Not many," he agreed.

"And you probably wanted a chance to really ride this morning."

"I wanted a chance to be with you."

It was an admission that echoed in the crisp, clear morning air. Like the mist from their breath, it made a mark—something warm that changed the shape of things entirely. The frost seemed to glitter more, and the icy sheen across the flat seemed brighter.

"I was afraid I wouldn't be able to come," she confessed. "You're to be commended for getting me up here. I'll bet you're very good at what you do. Boot camp must be as scary as horses for those recruits."

"I don't ride double with them, you can be sure of that. Ride herd on 'em, maybe. Crack the whip on 'em, definitely."

"I don't believe you're all that hard, Sergeant Tracker. Not after that kitten."

"Let's keep that a secret."

She laughed. "You'd better tell that to your sister."

"You're right," he said with a groan. "Frankie'll ruin me. It'll be another seven years before I show up around here again."

"Why did you wait so long?" she asked quietly. The question brought silence, and she wondered whether she'd just put a damper on their good time.

Finally he said, "The longer you put it off, you know, the harder it gets. Pretty soon you don't want to face them because you have to come up with some kind of an explanation, and you realize you haven't got one." He sighed. "The simple fact is that I love my family, but I don't like coming home."

"But they don't seem to expect any apologies, Luke. They're just glad to have you home."

"Yeah, maybe." That kernel of truth didn't help. "It's this place, Hope. It holds people down. They get to thinking they can't make it anywhere else. I see a lot of kids from reservations wash out of the army because they want to go home. If they make it through the first year, they're the best soldiers in the world, but, God, that first year. It's like the world's too big for them."

"It's that way for a lot of people," she said.

"There's nothing here for them," he insisted. "No jobs. Plenty of nothing. Plenty of poverty."

"Plenty of people who think the world of Luke Tracker. If I went home, I'd have to decide whether I wanted to be a guest in my mother's house or my father's house. So I guess there's really no home for me to go back to. It's all different, and I don't belong."

"You can come back to Wakpala any time and find the same dog lying on the post office steps. *Nothing* changes. And I don't belong, either." He spotted the place where the fence was down, and he laid the reins against the black's neck and tapped the horse's flank with his heel. "I'd like to see Frankie get out of here before she gets stuck," he said. "I hate the idea of her being stuck here."

"She told me about your girlfriend Monica."

"She did, huh?" Luke retrieved his glove from Hope's pocket. "Monica was part of another life. I don't even think about her anymore." He handed Hope the reins and dismounted with the grace of a gymnast.

"But once you wanted to marry her and take her away from all this."

"I suppose I did." As he spoke, he removed the wire stretcher and the small bag of tools from the saddle without looking up. "At the time she didn't want to leave home. Now I hear she's moved to Montana with some guy." He shrugged. "Who can figure it?"

"She's older now," Hope ventured.

"So am I. Older and wiser." He looked up, shutting one eye against the bright sun. "I suppose you want to get down."

Hope tried to imagine swinging her leg over the horse and sliding to the ground. "Well, I guess what I wanted to point out to you is that . . . I think Frances is doing what she wants to do. I don't think she feels that she's stuck here."

"Uh-huh." He grinned. "You wanna come down here and explain all this to me? I'm interested."

"I'm not sure." She gripped the saddle horn and eyed the ground. Her legs felt as though they'd been through a taffy pull. "I think I'm the one who's stuck."

With a laugh, Luke tossed the tools to the ground. "Come on. Let me give you a hand."

"I might not be able to get back up here."

"Yes, you will." He reached for her, and she managed to swing her leg over the horse's neck and slide into Luke's arms.

"That is the widest horse . . ."

"You're doing fine," he said as he pulled her closer.

"My legs feel like mush." She decided not to mention the fact that the way he was looking at her put her stomach in the same condition.

"Mine, too. I think a kiss may help."

"I think a kiss might—" The words *make it worse* were never uttered. They were negated by the warmth of his lips, the delicate stroking of his tongue, the strength of his embrace. The spicy scent of the cologne she'd given him added zest to the cold air. In the bundle of puffy jackets and gloves, only their lips and cheeks and noses could touch, but it was enough to make their senses soar. And the kiss made all things, for the moment, better.

THEY RETURNED TO the house in time for dinner and the arrival of Luke's much-discussed brother, Gorgeous George. Hope saw the physical resemblance between Luke and George, but noted that self-indulgence threatened to mar George's good looks. At the age of twenty-seven his physical condition had already begun to deteriorate, with the effects of an eat-drink-and-be-merry life-style showing in his puffy face and potbelly.

"So how's Uncle Sam treating you, Sarge?" The jovial tone of the question was a thin veneer, and the handshake was tentative. Luke was the man of the hour. George stood in his brother's shadow and shivered imperceptibly for lack of sunshine.

"Can't complain," Luke said. "I like what I'm doing. How about you?"

"I like what I'm doing, too." George laughed nervously and glanced around for someone to join in. "Which is as little as possible. Right, Frankie?"

"You're still just gorgeous, George," Frances chimed.

Luke clapped his hand on his brother's back and offered a smile. The action seemed to release a pressure valve. "Looks like you're getting fed pretty well, boy." He gave George's spare tire a friendly pat.

"But I'm still good-looking," George insisted, returning the grin.

"Still gorgeous," Luke echoed. "Where've you been keeping yourself?"

George gave a quick shrug. "I've got a girlfriend. Takes good care of me. Real good cook." He stepped back to admire his brother's trim figure. "You're eating too much army chicken, Sarge. Look at you.

Skinny as you were when you first left here."

Luke gave George's chin a playful clip with his knuckles. "Wanna go a couple rounds, boy? Don't worry. If I get too rough on you, Frankie'll go running for Dad, like she always did."

George's smile faded, and he turned away. "Let's just see who can put away the most turkey. I think that's a competition I can beat you in."

Luke saw the curious look in Hope's eyes and the plea in his sister's. He reached for George's shoulder. "We're about even in our old age, brother. Everybody's a winner at Christmastime."

Chapter Four

HOPE TUCKED THE blanket under the corner of the mattress, then smoothed one hand over the woolly surface as she reached for the pink chenille bedspread with the other. Suddenly a quarter flopped on the blanket in the middle of the bed. She looked up, smiling. Luke leaned against the doorjamb and smiled back. Hope saw nothing in those gray sweats and running shoes that could possibly be termed underdeveloped.

"It's supposed to bounce," Luke said.

Hope flipped the quarter in the air. It glinted as it rose past the sunlit window, and she opened her hand to catch it. Luke snatched it out of the air and slapped it on the back of his wrist. "Call it," he said.

"What's at stake?"

"A date for New Year's Eve. I win, I take you to the party. You win, *you* take *me*."

"Does everyone come out a winner on New Year's, too?"

The glint in his eye reminded her of the quarter. "Call it," he repeated.

"Tails."

He took a peek, then grinned down at her. "You win, lucky lady. Good thing, too, since I don't have a car here." He glanced down the hall, then beckoned her with a jerk of his head.

She went to him with a saucy swing in her step. "I win, huh? All week long you've been *letting* me help you with *your* chores." She laid her hands on his chest as he dropped the quarter into her breast pocket and took hold of her shoulders. His sweatshirt was damp, and she felt the hard muscles beneath it. "Like feeding oats to the horses."

"Which gave me a chance to steal a few kisses behind the barn." He decided it was a good time to steal another one.

His kiss was brief, but it left her tingling. "And I helped you pitch hay," she said quietly.

"And I kissed you behind the haystack."

"While somebody pitched a forkful of hay on top of our heads."

"Beaver," he said, his eyes twinkling as he recalled the way he'd caught her by surprise, and then, from the top of the haystack, his brother had surprised them both. "I owe him one."

"If we're not careful, we'll get caught again," she whispered. "Every time you kiss me, the woodwork giggles."

"Why don't *you* try kissing *me*?"

She could only let him hold her gaze for a moment before she lowered her eyes and stared at her own hands. They had spent the week with each other. In the Tracker home, surrounded by his family, Luke and Hope had been together except when they went to their separate beds at night. Each morning she'd wasted no time in getting up and dressed, because she always found him waiting for her with a suggestion for something they could do together. Usually some of the children were included in Luke's plans, which made for both fun and tantalizing frustration. They got closer with each day they spent together, and they talked about everything but what that closeness might mean.

It meant such headiness that when he compounded the feeling by standing this close, Hope couldn't make sense of her thoughts. She saw herself drawing him across the threshold, closing the door and peeling his damp sweatshirt away. If she didn't keep talking, she was afraid she might try something crazier than kissing him.

"What have you been up to?" she asked, because it was all she could think of. "You're all wet."

"Sweaty," he corrected. "I've been running."

She glanced up. "Every day?"

"Every morning. Early." He smiled, because he was still holding her, and, even though it wasn't enough, it was something. "Before you got up."

"I could have gotten up earlier."

He'd needed to run to keep his head on straight. For the last week she'd been the last image in his mind before he went to sleep and the first to enter his head when his subconscious alarm clock woke him before daybreak. Being with her had become each day's only priority. Even if half a dozen other people were in the same room, he was with her. When she was helping to get a meal on the table and he was telling his father a story, he'd made it a point to catch her eye and be with her. Some nights, after everyone had gone to bed, he would run and then take a long shower, letting the water run over him until it got cold because he knew she had gone to bed, and he wanted to be with her there, too.

"I didn't know you were a runner," he said.

"I could be." She smiled. "I have a pair of sneakers."

His hands moved over her shoulders, and she became lost in his dark eyes and his promise. "Just say the word, and I'll take you with me."

Yes, take me with you. "No, I'll take you," she promised quietly. "To this party, wherever it is."

"Such blind trust. It's at the Mission. Haven't you noticed? Everything happens at the Mission."

"I'll tell you what I've noticed," she said. "You enjoy being home, whether you want to admit it or not. You like being part of all this."

Then it is time to go, he thought. If it showed that much, the next thing he knew, he'd be thinking about coming back. Or staying. He'd taken to claiming that the army was his home, but even if he'd been kidding himself on that score, he had to remember that the army was his future. This was no time to get sentimental about home and family, even if it was Christmas. Even if this woman had kindled a strong need for something his career could never give him, he had to remember that it came down to choices. He'd made his. All he had to do was get back on the bus. Until then, maybe he could indulge in Christmas sentimentality, home fires, and family ties. He could enjoy being with Hope every waking minute before the bus pulled out. But once he got on that bus, he would leave all the binding ties behind him.

"I think you enjoy it, too," he told her. "For whatever reasons. I'm sure this will be a far cry from your customary New Year's Eve party."

"It *is* the first time I've won a date."

"You'll have to take me in my uniform. For the, uh . . . sake of the ceremony, I promised my dad I'd wear it."

"What ceremony?"

"You'll see." At the sound of footfalls on the stairs, he stole another quick kiss. "I need a shower. And that bed needs more work, Spencer."

"That's a civilian bed," she told him as he drew away from her. "It's fine the way it is."

THE NEW YEAR'S Eve celebration at St. Elizabeth's Mission began in the church. Supper in the parish hall followed the services, and Hope knew her way around the buffet this time. She helped herself to frybread, politely refused the *taniga*, and headed directly for the soup kettle. This time she enjoyed a feeling of confidence in knowing what was on her plate as she wended her way to the group of folding chairs Frances had staked out.

Hope covered her lap with a cotton bandanna, which she'd had the forethought to bring. Because it was New Year's Eve, she had worn a dress. It was nothing fancy, she told herself—just a winter white knit with a full skirt that flirted when she twirled. She was counting on dancing, and she was wearing one of the few dresses in the room. Frances had warned her that she might feel out of place if she dressed up, but Hope had dressed for her date. Her date had dressed to please his father, but when he turned from the serving table in his crisp green dress uniform, it was Hope's heart that swelled with pride. He searched the room only for her.

There was little conversation as they ate together. Luke's uniform brought him lingering looks from the young women and admiration from the men, and he was uncomfortable with the attention. A part of him belonged here with these people, and that part of him wanted the years to drop away so that he could be home. The other part of him didn't fit anymore, and the uniform seemed to him to be a visible sign of that fact. Hope in her soft white dress and he in his green uniform with his flashy ribbons and stripes—they both stood out like a pair of sore thumbs.

But they were a pair, and Luke liked that.

After the food was cleared away, the party moved to the gym, which was part of the dormitory complex. There, several women, including Emma and her older daughters, loaded tables with quilts, appliquéd pillows, beading, and other handwork. Five men gathered around a big bass drum. Hope anticipated more instruments, but the drum stood alone. Her vision of floating about the dance floor in Luke's arms faded as his father summoned Luke with an imperious gesture.

"Let's get this over with," Luke mumbled as he guided Hope toward what had been established as the front of the room. Hope joined Luke's brothers and sisters while Luke stood between his parents in front of the tables laden with goods. First in Lakota, then in English, George Tracker extolled his oldest son's talents and virtues. He explained that Luke served his country by training young men to be soldiers, and that the ribbons and stripes on his uniform represented wonderful military accomplishments. Luke's stance was formally at ease, but his mind raced as he stared straight ahead. He'd deliberately stayed away, and he didn't want to be honored for it. It had been a matter of self-preservation. Self-defense. His father was explaining how good he was at that.

George Tracker knew the meaning of every decoration his son wore, and the deep timbre of the old man's voice was bright with pleasure as he performed an ancient ritual in its modern form. The people listened, and the men nodded their approval, but Luke wondered what they were thinking. His father called him son, warrior, Lakota, but what kind of Lakota deserted the people he'd grown up with? What kind of warrior feared the welcoming of family and friends? What kind of a son stayed away from home for seven years?

"This is a son to be proud of," George announced. "My family celebrates this night with a giveaway because our brother, our son, is home for a visit, and we are glad."

It was that simple. The questions were swept away as Luke turned and basked in the light in his father's eyes. Luke's vision was cloudy, but his mind was clear as he reached blindly for the old man's handshake. No complaints, no excuses, no apologies. They were glad he was here, and that was enough.

Then came the giveaway. Names were called—respected elders, friends, Luke's boyhood buddies—and the recipients of the Trackers' gifts moved down the line, shaking hands with each member of the family. It is our pleasure to give, was the unspoken message. We share your joy, came the wordless reply. Thanks were not appropriate.

When Hope's name was called, she felt a flush of excitement. She had taken a chair near the front of the room to watch the proceedings, and now she was to be included. Emma displayed the quilt with its star bursting in bright primary colors, then folded it carefully and laid it over Hope's arm. Following the example of those who had gone before, Hope smiled, shook Emma's hand and moved to George. She saw that the old man expected solemnity from her, and she behaved accordingly. Luke was next in line, and her pulse suddenly thudded in her temples as she took his hand.

She longed to embrace him as no one else had done, and she lifted her eyes to let him see her longing. She wouldn't, not here, but the need was there. The black brim of his dress cap sheltered his eyes, which were flooded with emotion. He held her hand for more than a handshake. It was his night, and she was part of it. "Stand here beside me," he said quietly. "You've been part of the family since my sister brought you to . . . us."

One member of the Tracker family was missing. Gorgeous George had not arrived, although everyone speculated that he would. After the giveaway, there was an honor song. Flanked by his parents and followed by the rest of the family, Luke led the circular procession in a slow hesitation step. The five singers chanted in a high pitch and pounded a steady beat on the bass drum. The other members of the community took their places behind the family to honor Luke Tracker, who had come home.

And now there would be dancing. Hope could feel it in the air. The teenage girls flocked together and cast hopeful looks at the boys, whose lanky arms and legs struck various postures calculated to be an expression of "cool." Battered black speakers were brought in, along with a microphone and a couple of guitars.

"Ho-ho-ho!"

The gym became quiet as all eyes turned toward the door. "Santa Claus?" Hope muttered. "What's he doing here?" Luke smiled and brought his finger to his lips.

Once again the children took cover as the man in red stalked through the door. He circled the room, peered menacingly at the children who stood behind the older people's legs and roared, "Happy New Year!" When he came to Luke, Santa Claus stood at attention and offered a smart salute.

"You don't salute sergeants, Santa," Luke said, smiling.

Santa's big belly was a natural protrusion, but he stood at attention like an experienced soldier. "I salute *you*, Sergeant Tracker."

Luke nodded and returned a snappy salute. He knew of no enclave in the country that held its sons who soldiered in such high esteem.

"Ho-ho-ho!"

Hope looked to the doorway again. "Another one?"

Luke offered the saluting Santa a quick handshake. "You guys make this quick, huh, Santa? I wanna dance with my girl."

"I don't blame you." Santa backed away as his rival Santa approached. "But I've got my pride to think of, same as you. I'm not going down easy."

"What's going on?" Hope asked as she and Luke joined the others, who had backed up to widen the circle. "Two Santas?"

"The old year Santa and the new year Santa," Luke explained.

"Shouldn't it be old Father Time and a baby?"

Luke slipped his arm around Hope's shoulders. "Welcome to Wakpala," he said with a chuckle.

She looked up at him and smiled. "Thank you."

While the crowd cheered them on, the two Santas circled each other like professional wrestlers. They tapped each other's bellies, then circled again in the opposite direction. Suddenly the new Santa lunged for the old, and the tussle was on. The old Santa's age and the new Santa's robust youth were part of the act, but when it came to tumbling on the floor or making a quick dash across the room, both exhibited equal measures of awkwardness and agility. When the new Santa tweaked the old one's beard, the elastic snapped, and old Santa howled. Finally, to the special delight of the children, the new Santa gave the old one a dramatic boot out the door, emitted a triumphant "Ho-ho-ho" and disappeared into the night himself.

"It's enough to make you think twice about sitting on Santa's lap."

"Really?" Luke took Hope's hand as the band struck up a slow country-and-western tune. "How about dancing with him?"

"I'll dance with *you*, Sergeant Tracker." She put her arms around his neck as she had wanted to do earlier, and he pulled her close, so that every breath she drew was scented with his spicy cologne. She rested her chin lightly on his strong shoulder, which was crisply upholstered in clean square military style. The buttons on his jacket pressed against her ribs, and she could feel his hard belt buckle.

The quality of the sound didn't matter as they moved with the music from one song to the next. The overhead lights cast everything in bright, garish tones. Most of the younger children were by now nestled in piles of coats and quilts, and the older ones were venturing out on the dance floor. Among the adults there were as many women dancing together as mixed couples. Hope couldn't have been happier surrounded by candlelight and a fairy-tale king's courtiers, and Luke firmly believed he held royalty in his arms.

"Let's go for a walk," he suggested near her ear as he guided her off the floor.

She pushed back his sleeve and turned his wrist up to check his watch. "But it's almost—"

"I know. Let's get your coat." As an afterthought he added, "Better put your boots on, too."

The lack of wind made it a warm night for midwinter in South Dakota. They walked away from the bright yard lights with their hearts set only on a moment of privacy under a starry winter sky.

"How many more minutes?" she asked. Even her soft voice was startling in the silence of the night.

"Four or five minutes until January," he told her. "The Tree Popping Moon."

"Why do they call it that?"

"You'll know when you get a real cold snap. It gets so cold here it makes trees split open."

She shoved her hands deep into the pockets of her coat. "Is there a Lakota term for New Year's Eve?"

"In the old days, the year began in April—the Moon of the Birth of Calves."

"For someone who was so anxious to get away from the reservation, you seem to know a lot about its traditions." She looked up at him as they strolled along the wide gravel driveway that led past the mission's little collection of buildings. With a knowing smile she asked, "Why do you suppose that is?"

"I read a lot," he said. "Try to put what the anthropologists say together with the stories I heard as a kid." He lifted one shoulder. "It's kind of interesting."

"The ceremony tonight was . . . kind of interesting."

He saw that there was no point in trying to bluff his way through this conversation. "I've been dreading that for days, you know. Standing up there in front of everybody like you're some kind of hero, when you never really wanted to come back in the first place. But then I listened to my father, and I felt . . ." Grinning at the moon, he put his arm around her shoulders and squeezed with the exuberance of remembered warmth. "I felt like everything was okay. Like they understood that I can't live here anymore, but I'm still . . ."

"You're still part of them, Luke. They're just glad to have you home, even for a little while."

"I know." *Even for a little while.* A short holiday, he thought. A brief hint of what having someone to share life with could be like. He wanted more than a hint. Don't be a fool, he told himself. You'll drive yourself crazy with that kind of thinking.

"What will they do in there at midnight?" she asked. "Sing 'Auld Lang Syne' and go around kissing everybody?"

"Oh, there'll be 'Auld Lang Syne,' all right, country-style. Lots of handshakes. You won't see too much public hugging and kissing. The lovers like us will have to slip away for a kiss."

She looked at him cautiously, as though she wasn't sure she'd heard right. Was it just an expression? Was it a casual term? His unfaltering gaze told her there was nothing casual about the word he'd chosen.

"Is it okay?" he asked quietly.

"I think it's true," she said. "For me."

They stood near a bluff overlooking the frozen river. He took her in his arms, and she looked up, waiting, loving the heated way he looked at her and the cool white moonlight in his hair.

"I'll be leaving in a couple of days," he said.

It was a subject they'd carefully avoided. "I know."

"I don't know when I'll be back."

"I don't know how long I'll be working here."

"It's midnight," he whispered, his voice hoarse as he lowered his head to take her mouth with his. The night receded as the kiss consumed them both. They strained the limits of the act itself, nipping, pressing, seeking, luring, trading tongues and titillation and groaning with the need for more contact. Hunger became an urgency that threatened to shatter all reason. They drew apart on the strength of what little resistance they'd left each other.

He gripped her shoulders. "If this ground wasn't frozen . . ."

"We could go—"

"Don't say it, Hope, because if you say it, we'll do it, and it's crazy."

"It is," she admitted. "It's crazy. You'll be leaving."

"So let's go back inside where it's safe. Where everybody's watching."

"We can dance," she suggested, remembering what bittersweet torture that had been.

"Yeah." He gave her a tender kiss on her forehead. "We sure can dance."

As they walked back to the gym, a car came up from behind and cruised by slowly. The window on the passenger's side rolled down, and Gorgeous George flashed an even row of white teeth. His tone was suggestive. "What are you guys doing out here?"

"Walking," Luke told his brother. "Where have you been?"

"Celebrating. Why? Did I miss something?" The car rolled to a stop on the end of George's question, which was clearly rhetorical. George knew he had missed a great deal.

"Depends on your viewpoint," Luke said. He felt a squeeze of encouragement on his left hand, and he turned to find that encouragement in Hope's eyes. Make peace for the women's sake, his father had always told him. As he extended his hand, he knew it was for his own sake, as well. "Happy New Year, brother."

George's eyes brightened as he grabbed Luke's hand. "Hey, same to you, brother. Same to you." George reached for Hope's hand as he muttered, "Happy New Year, Hope. What do you think of this brother of mine, huh? He's a hell of a soldier, I'll tell you." Before she could reply, George turned to Luke again. "I couldn't handle it, you know. They've still got my picture hanging on the wall at home beside yours, the one they took after basic training. I wish they'd take that damn thing down." His anguished look said that he felt unworthy, even unwelcome. "I didn't know if you'd want me there tonight, Luke. That's why I stayed away."

"I didn't know if I wanted *me* there." Luke's attempt at a chuckle fell short. "I thought I'd feel kind of foolish, standing up in front of everybody like that, in my uniform and all."

"Did you?"

"No," he admitted. "The only part of it I minded was that somebody was missing."

George's eyes glistened as he smiled. "Next time," he promised quietly.

"Hell, I'm not doing an encore." Luke clipped George's arm with a playful hand. "Next time you get the limelight. Give the girls a thrill."

"Yeah." One word and a tight-lipped grin were all George could manage.

"You going in?" Luke asked.

"Nah, they're probably mad." George drew himself back into the car like a turtle. The unseen driver muttered something, and George said, "Yeah, we gotta get on down the road. I left the ol' lady home, so she's probably mad, too." He stuck his head out again, in need of confirmation. "You're really not mad, though, are you, Luke?"

"I'm really not mad."

"I'll see you before you leave?" Luke nodded. "Well, happy New Year, then."

Luke stared after the car as it disappeared over the hill.

"He was in the army, too?" Hope reclaimed his attention with the question.

"Yeah, he joined up just like I did—soon as he was old enough. He made it through basic, but, God, he was a screw-up." He slipped his arm around her, and they started walking again. "George Tracker, Jr. spent most of his short hitch in the guardhouse. He was dishonorably discharged after he stole a jeep and drove it through the wall of the Officers' Club at Fort Dix."

"Oh, no."

"Oh, yes. His exploits were legendary."

"And embarrassing to his older brother?"

He glanced at her and nodded slowly. "It's time I put that aside, isn't it?"

"Sounds like he couldn't live up to your image, so he created one of his own."

"I went my own way," Luke insisted. "Nobody asked him to follow."

"Nobody had to. He wanted to be like you, Luke."

"Then it's time he put *that* aside."

"Hey, Luke!" They turned their attention toward the gym door. One of the musicians was on his way out with a snare drum. "Your dad said to tell you they had to get the kids home. Frances left her car for you."

"Is the dance over?" Luke asked.

"Everybody's packing up."

Luke glanced down at Hope. "Damn. I was looking forward to one more dance."

"Me, too. Walk me over to my apartment?"

He surveyed the dark array of buildings. "You sure you want to stay here tonight? Looks pretty deserted."

"The students will start coming back tomorrow," She told him. "School starts again on the second."

They went back to the gym to get her quilt, his cap, and her shoes, and then he walked with her in silence to her back door. She had stopped in earlier to turn the heat up and bring her kitten home, but the mission had had many visitors that night, and Luke insisted on checking her apartment for safety's sake. When he brought her luggage in from her car, he smelled coffee. She came around the kitchen island in stocking feet and began unbuttoning his overcoat. He covered her hands with his.

"I can't stay, Hope."

"Just for coffee."

He shook his head. "I haven't the slightest desire for coffee."

"Something else, then. I think I have—"

"You know damn well what I want." The look in her eyes said she would postpone his leave taking at all cost. She raised her chin just a fraction of an inch. "I can't even kiss you again," he said softly. "I can't kiss you now and walk away. And I have to walk away."

"Why?"

Because she was so beautiful, and his heart would tether itself to her, and he would never be able to stand on his own two feet again. He held both her hands in one of his and reached to touch her cheek with the backs of his fingers.

"I can't stay," was the only explanation he could give.

Chapter Five

HOPE HAD MADE the coffee because she had felt like having a cup. The fact that she'd made twice as much as she intended to drink was—yes, okay, it was irritating. She felt a little foolish about it. She told herself that anticipating a man's wants was probably bad business for a woman. A trap to be cautiously avoided. If she'd made the coffee before she was sure he wanted some, then she deserved what she got—a second cup that would either go to waste or keep her awake the rest of the night.

Something small and soft slid past Hope's ankle. Tears burned in her eyes as she stooped to scoop up the kitten. "Do you have time for a cup of coffee, sweetheart? You can stay, can't you? Or do you have to be off doing kitty things?"

She held the kitten's tricolored velvet body next to her flaming cheek, hoping to be soothed. A tear slid into the feline fur. "Oh, I'm sorry," Hope whispered into the cat's tiny face. "You don't like to be wet, do you?" She petted the damp spot while the cat cast her own hazel-eyed bid for sympathy up at Hope.

"We spent a nice holiday, together, that's all." She took a swipe at another tear with the side of her hand. "He's a soldier, and we all know about soldiers. I'm just lucky he didn't give me some song and dance about being shipped off to the front in the morning." She cuddled the kitten to her breast and promised, "I wouldn't have fallen for it. He thinks he's cornered the market on self-control, but I've got news for—"

A sudden knock brought her head up. She stared at the back door. "—him. He didn't really leave," she whispered as she slid the bolt on the door. "He just went to get his tap shoes."

He looked cold and humble standing out there on the step with his collar turned up. She decided to let him stand there until he said something.

"I, uh . . . I couldn't get the damn car started."

"Funny," she said, ignoring the cold air that rushed into her kitchen.

"Frances hasn't had any trouble with that car. Do you think it's gotten that cold out?"

"Yeah, I do. I think it's pretty cold."

She had turned the porch light on. His face was dimly lit. "I still have coffee."

"I'd like some."

She turned, hugging the kitten, and walked quickly toward the stove. As she prepared the cups with one hand she gauged his every move by sound. The door clicked shut. His coat slid off his shoulders and was draped over the back of a kitchen chair. His jacket followed. He took four steps across the linoleum and stood beside the counter.

She worked slowly, deliberately, because she dreaded facing him. She blinked and blinked, but the stinging tears wouldn't stay back, and she wasn't sure why. Was it because he'd left or because he'd come back?

She took a deep breath and tried her voice. "What do you think is wrong with the car?"

"I flooded it."

Laughter bubbled behind the tears, and she couldn't deal gracefully with either. She kissed the kitten and put her on the floor.

"Don't laugh. I feel dumber than hell."

"Dumber than hell," she marveled quietly, her back still to him as she fitted her fingers into the handles of the two mugs and braced herself to face him.

"And don't tell Frankie. I'll be able to hear the two of you laughing at me all the way to . . . Hope?" She was holding two cups of coffee in unsteady hands, and her face was pink and sweet with tears. "Honey, you're not crying, are you?"

"No." It was a raspy answer.

He took the cups, set them aside, and folded his arms around her. They sighed together as they clung to each other tightly, relieved by the stay in the execution of his plans. He could have been gone, but he wasn't. Not yet.

"Don't cry," he whispered. The tears were like silk bonds, making him hurt, making him hold her tighter. He was afraid of them, but he wanted them on his shirt, on his skin, in his soul. They gave him power and made him feel helpless all at once. "Please don't cry, honey."

"I'm really not," she insisted. She wasn't sure what this was. She never cried.

"Okay." He kissed the top of her hair and rubbed her back. "Tell me why you're not crying, then."

"Because you're not leaving yet."

"I can take another shot at it."

"No." Her arms tightened around his middle. "I mean, you're not leaving town yet. I mean, you don't *have* to go yet." She looked up at him. "You said you had to go, and you don't. Not tonight."

"I was trying to do the right thing, Hope." He took a tear from her cheek with a gentle thumb. "If I had anything to offer you, I'd give it to you in a minute, but I don't. Not for a woman like you. I'm just a—"

"Give me the time you have left, Luke." She said it quickly, because she knew how awful it sounded, but she wanted every minute. Every moment they had together was precious to her now that she knew how badly she would ache for him once he was gone.

"A couple of days, honey. That's all." If neither of them had wanted anything more than a good time, a couple of days would have been plenty. But she wasn't thinking that way—he could tell by the way she was looking at him now—and, God help him, he wasn't, either.

"I want as much of that time as you'll give me," she whispered. "I'm in love with you, Luke."

He closed his eyes and touched his forehead to hers. Her skin was warm, and his was cool. How could she love him? She was a princess and he was a tin soldier.

"We've only known each other—"

"Since Christmas," she whispered. "Since the beginning of time."

"I want to make love to you, Hope. I hurt with it."

"Then let's ease the hurt—" their lips met in a brief and tender kiss "—with love."

They went to her room, and she turned the key on the hurricane lamp beside her bed. The small light glowed inside the milk-glass base. Luke tugged at the knot in his tie as he watched her turn down the bed. There were pastel sheets under a white, ruffled spread on a bed big enough for two. A far cry from what he was used to. He wore the only drab green in the room, and he was about to shed it.

She sat on the bed and folded her hands over her skirt. Pausing as he pulled the tie through his collar, he reconsidered. This wasn't the season for shedding. He tossed the tie on a chair and took his place beside her on the bed. She lifted her chin toward him, then her eyes, bright with her faith in him. He moved her hair aside and touched the nape of her neck as he leaned closer. She laid her palm against his cool, starched shirt, and his heart thudded beneath her hand as banked coals burst into flame.

They came into each other's arms as though the lost had been found. The kisses they exchanged lit the dark corners of the night with flashing colors and filled their heads with bells and tambourines. They unwrapped each other, hearts beating wildly in anticipation of gifts that were pleasing even before they were unveiled.

This was Hope, who had braved the high horse in order to spend the day with him. She had opened her mind to customs that seemed different and her mouth for food that looked strange as she made a place for herself in Luke's heart. This was delicate, soft Hope, pale as moonlight. So touchable. So responsive. In her arms he could be more, do more, give more. She filled him with possibilities.

This was Luke, who had brought laughter and tears and kissed her on the heels of both. His body had been honed and shaped to muscular perfection by the job he did, but he took pains to touch her gently. It was his nature to guard and protect, and he was prepared to do that for her. It was his custom and his pleasure to give, and he was prepared to do that, too.

He gave her unexpected joy. She gave beauty he expected to experience this one time and never again. After the heat of their coupling there was still the warmth of their loving, the time of hazy satisfaction and shimmery wonder. Wrapped together in pastel sheets and soft shadows, they touched, nibbled, nuzzled, and sipped, admiring every marvelous aspect of the gifts they shared.

"You must exercise all the time." She watched her fingertips skate over the contours of his chest. "You're all muscle."

"Not all." He chuckled. "Not between the ears."

"You're beautiful there, too." She traced a circle around his nipple with the tip of her fingernail, and he sucked a quick breath through his teeth. "Does that tickle?" she asked.

He cupped her breast in his hand and imitated her teasing, until she groaned. "Does that?"

"Mmm, not exactly."

"Not exactly," he confirmed, and he kissed her eyebrow. "I've never been AWOL, but it's a tempting thought right about now."

She smiled against his cheek. "Why would you want to do a thing like that?"

"I'd like to take you places."

"You took me places tonight, Luke. Places I never even imagined."

He looked into her eyes and touched her face in a way that said he'd been with her all the way. "I want to take you other places, Hope. Places that are always pretty, always . . ."

"I've been other places," she said, "but never where we went tonight. I don't think anyone else can take me there. Just you."

Holding her in his arms, he rolled to his back, and she ended up on top of him. Her hair brushed over his shoulder, and he smiled wistfully. "The hell of it is, the only other place I could take you when I leave here is Fort Leonard Wood, Missouri."

"I've never been there, either." She offered a teasing smile. "Is that a place where it's always pretty?"

"It's an army post. In the last twelve years I've seen a lot of army posts."

With her thumb she explored the shape of his chin. "Some of them must have been pretty."

"You know what's pretty?" He moved his hand along the slope of her back. "Your face is pretty. Your eyes, your mouth . . ."

"I've never been to an army post," she told him. "I suppose they have guards at the gate."

"Mmm-hmm. Gotta have a pass to get in."

"What if I went down there and asked to see you?"

He chuckled. "They'd say, 'How could a sweet dream like you be interested in a coldhearted DI like Tracker?'"

"And I'd say, 'We can't be talking about the same man.'" She kissed his chin before she slid down to touch her lips to his chest. "The Sergeant Tracker I know has warm smooth skin all over his sleek . . . hard . . . beautiful body." Her foray led her to his abdomen.

"Sweet heaven . . ."

"And I can make every inch of him—"

"Feels too good to be . . ."

"—stand at attention."

SHE HAD LOVED him well. He had given her all he had, and it seemed worthless by comparison. He was still a visitor in her bed. He was in the habit of leaving what he loved behind, and he was leaving soon. The life he'd made for himself was fine for him. There were no ruffles or frills, but he told himself he didn't need those things. And he'd gotten over being homesick long ago. He had worked hard at it by stretching the bonds until they were slack. Now he was a visitor in the town where he'd grown up and a visitor in this woman's bed. Hell, he was a visitor in *any* woman's bed. After all, he belonged to the army. He was a soldier.

It wasn't that simple, and he knew it. The truth was that, after all, he was a man, and the woman who slept in his arms was not a ruffle or a frill. He had also loved her well. When he left her, he would carry a gaping hole in his chest.

HOPE REFUSED TO believe she had made a mistake when she woke up New Year's Day and found that Luke was gone. The note she found in the kitchen said that he'd left before daylight to avoid "embarrassment or complications," but he'd said nothing about seeing her again before he left. Neither had he said goodbye. She'd spent New Year's Day waiting for a call that never came.

Avoiding any mention of Luke to Frances on their first day back in school had left Hope in doubt all day. Was he still home? Had he mentioned any plans to see her before he left? Had he talked about her at all? Why hadn't Frances kidded her a little, or at least dropped a hint about his frame of mind? Why hadn't Hope just leveled with her friend early that morning and spared herself the rest of the day's anguish?

She was a coward, she told herself. That was why. As the doubts tumbled over and over in her mind, she straightened out her desk and gathered her homework into her canvas satchel. She decided that the need to know outweighed the fear of finding out that Luke had left without a word of goodbye. Her shoes followed the papers into her satchel, and she bent over to put her boot on.

A pair of spit-polished black shoes stepped into the doorway of the classroom. Hope lowered her boot to the floor as her eyes traveled up the path of army-green trousers to a brass belt buckle to a narrow tie, a square chin, and half-smiling lips. His dark eyes brought her visual travels to an abrupt, breath-stealing halt.

He stood there with his hands in his pockets, his jacket and his overcoat tucked behind his arms, waiting for some sign from her. She left the chair slowly, her heart racing ahead of her inefficient feet. Without taking his eyes from hers, he stepped across the threshold and pulled the door shut behind him.

"My bus leaves Mobridge at seven-thirty." He spoke quietly, but the words seemed to rebound off the high ceiling. It sounded as though he were announcing the scheduled end of the world.

"Tonight?"

He nodded. "I should be able to sleep most of the way. I've been saving up for it."

Her mouth went dry. She swallowed hard. "You came to say goodbye, then."

"I came to ask you to drive me to the station."

"Oh." She took one step closer. "How did you get here?"

"I had Frankie's car. I dropped her off this morning. She'll take me if you'd rather—"

"I'll take you," she said quickly.

"I thought we could have supper together."

"That would be nice. I'll get my—" Her hands fluttered as she thought coat, shoes—no, boots.

"Hope." She turned, and the pain in his eyes immobilized her. "I didn't want to leave you the other morning. I don't want to leave you now."

She went to him, put her arms around him and pressed her face against his neck. His overcoat nearly swallowed her as he wrapped her in his arms, and he had a wild vision of buttoning her up inside his coat and smuggling her past the gate.

"I didn't know what to think," she whispered. "After such an incredible night, to wake up and find you gone."

"I knew that if I woke you, I wouldn't be able to go. God, these last two days have been the longest of my life."

"Then we should have spent them together."

He pulled back from her and took her face in his hands. "I don't like goodbyes, Hope. I thought a clean, quick break would work out best, but . . . it didn't work at all. I couldn't just leave, and I can't stay. Hell, I don't know what to do. I love you."

The words made her eyes sparkle. "Then you could kiss me."

He slipped his fingers into her hair and slanted his mouth across hers. It felt like a homecoming. Before he let himself get lost in the feeling, he put his arm around her and nodded at the boots on the floor. "Get something on your feet and let's get out of here."

Luke said goodbye to Frances, transferred his duffel bag to Hope's car and got behind the wheel because he had "a couple of quick stops to make." The first was on a hill overlooking the frozen Missouri River. The sun stood low in the western sky, and the clouds were tinged with red. He parked the car near a monument that purported to mark the grave of Sitting Bull, the famous medicine man of the Hunkpapa Lakota.

"I was driving around earlier today," Luke told her, "and I wandered up here. You know, this rock is a hoax. This isn't Sitting Bull's grave."

Hope studied the marker. "It says it is."

"If it's carved in stone, it must be true, right?" He considered the inscription on the marker. "It's supposed to be a tourist attraction. Years ago a bunch of businessmen from Mobridge said they'd robbed the grave the army *claimed* to have put Sitting Bull in up at Fort Yates, which is where they took his body after he was killed. Alive, you can bet those same businessmen would have had no use for that foxy old man, but dead, they figured he might be worth something."

"People can't just go around digging up—"

"People can do anything," Luke argued. "And even if they don't succeed, they can claim it's true, and pretty soon they even believe it themselves. The army claimed that lime was poured into the casket before Sitting Bull was buried because they thought the Ghost Dancers might try to resurrect him somehow. So, according to them, there weren't any remains. But these guys said they stole some bones, and here's the monument to prove it." He raised a gloved index finger as if to scold the rock for its lie.

"Now the Lakota people say that Sitting Bull's family claimed his remains in secret, and that the army made up the lime story to save face for losing the body." Luke scanned the distant hills and the sky. "The people say that he rests near his home in Little Eagle, north of here."

"Which story do you think is true?"

"The truth is that Sitting Bull is home." He smiled as he shifted his gaze back to the river. "Even if they found some bones, those businessmen probably wouldn't have known the difference between a hand and a hoof, unless there was meat on it. And the lime wouldn't have changed anything, either." He looked at Hope. "Those ties are too strong for the army to break. There are times when a man has to be home."

Hope turned her face toward the window, but, with a gentle hand under her chin, Luke brought her back. "It must be true for a woman, too," he said.

"If she has one."

"If she doesn't, she needs to make one. That's what women do." He smiled. "What do you think of my family?"

Her eyes softened. "They made me feel welcome in their home. They gave me the nicest Christmas I've ever had. I love them for that."

"It would be easier to come back from time to time if I knew that, each time I left, I'd be taking you with me." He saw something like disbelief in her eyes, and it scared him. "We could make a home, Hope. You and me. We love each other. We could start with that." The look was still there, and he rushed on. "I know we haven't had much time to get to know each other, but we'll work on it. We'll—"

Suddenly she was in his arms, and she was up to her eyebrows in the sting of bittersweet joy. "I'll come and see you," she promised. "Easter break, summer—whenever you think—"

"I want to buy you a ring before I leave." He kissed her hair, her temple, her cheek. "I want you to wear my ring. Will you do that?"

"Yes, Luke. Oh, yes, yes."

"You're my road back home, honey. I need a home. I need family. I need you to root my seed and make my love grow."

"Where will our home be?" she asked.

"Here, for starters. We won't live here, but it'll always be home to me. I understand that now." He laughed. "Beyond this, it'll be wherever the army sends us." He thought about cots and lockers and army blankets, and decided it was time for something else, if what he was held enough promise for the woman he loved. "I'm a soldier, honey, and a good one. I believe I can be a good husband and a good father, but I'll always be a soldier."

"Then I'll always love a soldier. And wherever you do your soldiering, I can teach."

He kissed her, and the temperature that dropped with the setting sun had no effect on the warmth they shared. "It was stupid of me to waste these two last days brooding over all this. I want to give you Christmas every day. We can still make it to the jewelry store and ring in the new year."

She laughed and covered the back of his hand with hers. She ran her little finger along the callused edge of his hand and wondered at the contrast of this hardness with the gentle way he touched her. "I'll take one Christmas a year if I can spend it with you. Just love me, Luke, and make every season feel this beautiful."

"How extended are we going to make this engagement?" he asked. "Give me something to circle on the calendar."

"Circle the Twelfth Moon."

"Aw, Hope," he groaned. "That's a year away. How about July, the Cherry Ripening Moon? Or August, the Moon of the Ripe Plums?"

"Do you think I'll be ripe for the picking then, too?"

"I think you're ripe right now," he teased, touching her soft brown hair. "But I'll marry you whenever you're ready. The Twelfth Moon is a nice time for lovers."

"With all that frost inside the tipi . . ."

"And that cozy pile of buffalo robes," he added. "A perfect time for planting a seed in a warm, deep place . . ."

"It's always supposed to be warm inside at Christmas," she mused, loving the warmth in his eyes. "No matter how cold the weather gets."

"Then we'll keep Christmas inside you," he promised, his mouth hovering over hers, "all year long."

About Kathleen Eagle

Kathleen Eagle published her first book, a Romance Writers of America Golden Heart Award winner, in 1984. Since then she has published more than 40 books—historical and contemporary, series and single title—earning her nearly every award in the industry, including the RWA RITA. Her books have consistently appeared on regional and national bestseller lists, including the USA Today list and the New York Times extended bestseller list.

Kathleen lives in Minnesota with her husband, who is Lakota Sioux. They have three grown children and three lively grandchildren.

CPSIA information can be obtained
at www.ICGtesting.com
Printed in the USA
BVHW030024300920
589942BV00001B/306